A FAMILY ALBUM

A FAMILY ALBUM

a novel by DAVID GALLOWAY

HARCOURT BRACE JOVANOVICH

NEW YORK AND LONDON

Copyright © 1978 by David Galloway

Copyright © 1978 by Harcourt Brace Jovanovich, Inc.

Printed in the United States of America

Grateful acknowledgment is made for permission to quote from the Introduction to *Wisconsin Death Trip* by Michael Lesy, © 1973, Pantheon Books, a Division of Random House, Inc.

Library of Congress Cataloging in Publication Data

Galloway, David D
  A family album.

  I Title.
PZ4.G173Fam [PS3557.A4155] 813'.5'4 77-84387
ISBN 0-15-130153-0

First edition

B C D E

In the preparation of this book the following sources have been of particular significance: Helmut and Alison Gernsheim, *L.J.M: Daguerre: The History of the Diorama and the Daguerreotype* (New York: Dover Publications, 1968); Eaton S. Lothrop, Jr., *A Century of Cameras* (Dobbs Ferry, New York: Morgan and Morgan, Inc., 1973); La Maison de la Photographie, Châlon sur Saône.

for Gantt

THE IMAGES

PREFACE: 3

my dear son: a letter

25 *ONE*

THE CAMERA: *Lancaster Instantograph*   27

THE FIRST PHOTOGRAPHER: 29
   Elihu Zachariah Morton,
   Born May 30, 1871

THE PHOTOGRAPH: 41

57 *TWO*

THE CAMERA: *Bulls-Eye*   59

THE SECOND PHOTOGRAPHER: 61
   John Presley Jarvis,
   Born January 1, 1878

THE PHOTOGRAPH: 71

83 *THREE*

THE CAMERA: *Collapsible bellows-type camera by J. Valette*   85

THE THIRD PHOTOGRAPHER: 87
   Martha Mary Tupelo Pearl
   Independence Day McBryde,
   Born July 4, 1870

THE PHOTOGRAPH: 102

119 *FOUR*

THE CAMERA: *Argus "Model A"*   121

THE FOURTH PHOTOGRAPHER: 123

    Cyrus Lawrence MacDonald,

    Born June 6, 1901

THE PHOTOGRAPH: 133

145   *FIVE*

    THE CAMERA: *3A Autographic Kodak Special*   147

    THE FIFTH PHOTOGRAPHER: 150

    Juanita Rose Lowndes,

    Born January 2, 1910

    THE PHOTOGRAPH: 168

187   *SIX*

    THE CAMERA: *Minox*   189

    THE SIXTH PHOTOGRAPHER: 192

    David Bonner Dyer,

    Born May 5, 1937

    THE PHOTOGRAPH: 203

A FAMILY ALBUM

PREFACE

my dear son: a letter

Je vous propose donc, Monsieur, de coopérer avec moi au perfectionnement de mes procédés hélio-graphiques et de leurs différents modes d'application en vous associant aux avantages que ce perfection-nement donne lieu d'espérer....

Letter from Joseph Nicéphore Niépce to L.J.M. Daguerre, 23 October 1829

My dear son,
This letter began to form itself on that tragic day more
than four years ago when we learned that your uncle
Claude had died the week following my departure from
England. Even during his frustrating years on that chill island, we had maintained the closest communication about
our respective researches, and though the dropsy had tinc-
tured his imagination, his discussion of the perpetual motion
machine on which he was then at work often struck me as
remarkably lucid. If his success was delusory, his experiments had pointed him toward numerous avenues of future
research, any one of which might have produced results of
immense benefit to mankind. Nonetheless, despite the intensity of our relationship, I have been continuously haunted
by the sense that I scarcely knew this enthusiastic collaborator in all my youthful experiments. Even now, I remember him best as the magically capable older brother who
held me tightly against his chest with one arm as he can-
tered his horse through the woods and fields that then led
unbroken to the Saône. Here, to be sure, the details are
smudged and blurred, as in an imperfect lithograph pulled
from one of the early stones you assisted me in preparing;
and yet the emotional reality of that image is astonishingly
clear. You will perhaps have such images of me, but ones
that will be clearly fixed only after my death. I do not seek
now to improve or embellish them, but only to provide
you with certain facts with which you may, as time passes,
find it useful to compare your own images. As my devoted
assistant in all those later experiments that I have identified
under the typos of heliography, you have shared my joys
and frustrations in seeking to make permanent transcrip-

6 tions of scenes from nature. But is the reality you have witnessed in itself any more permanent than those early images we transcribed? Think only of the festive dinner we enjoyed on the day we first recorded, on paper sensitized with chloride of silver, the view from the workroom window at Gras, and the grimly silent breakfast we shared the following morning, after discovering that only the faintest ghost of our accomplishment remained. Are the images of the mind more stable, or do they not undergo similar permutations? It is with the presumption that the chemistry of perception shares something of the fickleness of those chemicals with which we have experimented, that I feel compelled to set forth this record of my researches—not merely for you, but for your children and for theirs. Above all, since I bequeath you a sadly diminished patrimony, it may prove useful to you to possess a precise record of my relationship with M. Daguerre, on whose judgment and skills you will someday rely for whatever commercial benefits may accrue from the heliographic process.

Had health permitted me to continue that military career I began with such boyish zeal during the Revolution, I might never have embarked upon the scientific experiments that became the ruling passion of my life after 1801. Whatever natural gifts for invention I may possess were, to be sure, strongly encouraged and shaped by Claude, together with whom I achieved the first noteworthy success of my career, the explosive motor designed to propel a river boat, and for which we obtained an imperial patent in the year 1807, under the designation of *pyreolophore*. Although you were then only twelve years of age, you will certainly remember the skeptical crowds that gathered on the banks of the Saône for our first official voyage. Your mother was too nervous (and too fearful of an explosion) to attend, and of those present, only the mayor seemed genuinely convinced of our success. At that time, we used vegetable powders as the basis of our fuel, and the motor functioned rather more erratically than it did later with essence of petroleum, but no witness could have doubted, then or during the later demonstrations in Paris and London, that a simple engine could accomplish work that once tormented the shoulders of man. (I am, by the way, still persuaded that a vegetable compound will eventually prove more satisfactory than petroleum products, which have the disadvantages of offensive odor and excessively high flammability.) In those idealistic years, Claude and I never once doubted that the world would greet our invention with anything but enthusiasm, as its applications both military and civilian seemed so obviously broad in scope. Certainly, neither of us dreamed that more than two decades later we would have encountered no serious interest in our invention, and that the alarming expenses of promoting it would necessitate the sale of the house in Châlon where both of us, as well as our sister Victoire, were born. When your uncle departed for Paris to arrange for commercial development of the *pyreolophore*, it seemed unlikely that he would be absent for more than a few months. Those few promising months stretched into years of frustrated promise that concluded in Claude's lonely exile in England. When your mother and I arrived at Kew in the autumn of 1827, we were far more dismayed by the erosion of his once fine, robust spirit than by his acute physical deterioration. He had learned too well, as I learned in submitting my description of heliography to King George IV and the Royal Society, that the English are constitutionally even more hostile to innovation than the French. Scarcely different in its essential conception from the principle of the windmill (though using the explosions of combustible substances to provide energy, rather than relying on the vagaries of nature), it might be argued that the *pyreolophore* seemed too fantastical a device to the stolid, bureaucratic minds whose

8　interest we sought to engage. The same could hardly be said of the *draisienne*, which I perfected in 1818, and which has seemed to provoke such universal amusement. That one should use the legs to propel a pair of wheels, and thereby extend the body's inherent capacity for locomotion, should be obvious to even the most wooden-headed peasant. That it is not might serve as one measure of my continuing lack of comprehension of that mysterious mechanism designated as human nature. Suffice it to say, that despite our most arduous efforts, neither Claude nor I was able to strike the faintest note of private or official interest in these locomotive devices. Indeed, on but a single occasion has the government of this nation seen fit to acknowledge our activities: in a contract for the development of sugar substitutes and artificial colorants to replace those natural products of which we were deprived at the time of the blockade.

I thus have no ground to encourage you in the expectation of material reward from the heliographic process that you have so ably assisted in developing, save for my faith in the clearly established commercial abilities of M. Daguerre. To judge from the camera chamber he produced for us, one can expect little from his technical skills, but he has an intuitive understanding of that great beast, the public. Had I not elected to spend my life in this rural village, believing that the familial roots so deeply planted here would assure the response my studies required, perhaps I should have developed some of M. Daguerre's facility for dealing with the world of affairs. Lacking that quality, and believing him to be more advanced in his own researches than circumstances have since revealed, I entered into a partnership whose fruits—bitter or sweet—will be your harvest. But I anticipate the record, which considerably predates the arrival of M. Daguerre's first blunt epistle.

Some years before Claude's departure for England (in 1813, to be exact), I first became interested in that process

termed lithography which reached us with such clamor of
enthusiasm from its Bavarian birthplace. Both Claude and
I at once recognized that it must be possible to transfer to
the printer's stone a pre-existent design, thus eliminating
the arduous and rather uncertain manual labor necessary
to the German process. We soon enjoyed modest success
by soaking engravings in wax and placing them on stones
coated with a light-sensitive varnish of my own composition, but the results lacked that clarity of detail that would
have made the process commercially viable. This and
subsequent experiments with light-sensitive materials (for
which I am indebted to the *Recherches Physico-Chimiques*
of Gay-Lussac and Thénard, as well as the advice of our
friend Vauquelin) prompted my interest in recording in
permanent form the images of the camera obscura. These
experiments began in April of 1816, after Claude's departure for Paris and London, but he continued to be, through
our steady correspondence, a most valuable critic of my
methods. In order to establish a comparative base for these
experiments, I mounted a locally made camera obscura in
the corner window of the attic workroom at Gras, where
it stands today, and following Claude's suggestion, pro-
jected the view onto paper sensitized with chloride of silver. As Claude had foreseen, lights and shadows were
reversed by the process, but a recognizable image was obtained, and was considerably sharpened by the addition of
a cardboard diaphragm in late May. The earliest of these
images could be viewed only in deep shade, as further
exposure to the light quickly blackened the sensitized paper.
Later images, bathed in nitric acid, could also be viewed
in daylight for a brief while. It should, I felt, be possible
to use this negative image as a device for printing successive positive images, but my attempts have thus far borne
no fruit.

It was, indeed, maddeningly difficult to advance beyond

10 the early success in seizing an image from nature. Above all, it was necessary to obtain a light-sensitive substance both more sensitive and more stable than chloride of silver. Despite the considerable assistance of M. Vauquelin, who supplied me with chemicals not available here, and communicated most generously about his own experiments with chromium, no substantial progress was made until July of 1822, when I was able to produce the first successful permanent heliographic copy of an engraving (of Pope Pius VII) on a glass plate coated with bitumen of Judea. Somehow, until 1820 I had entirely neglected this asphalt substance so familiar to engravers and lithographers, perhaps because it was associated with results so different from those I now intended. Once the riddle was solved, it possessed that alluring simplicity which always shines brightly at the end of the researcher's mazy path. Dissolving the bitumen in oil of lavender, I placed a thin layer of it on a glass plate, and over this laid an engraving made transparent by oiling it. Exposed to the light, the bitumen under the white parts of the engraving hardened, while the dark lines remained sufficiently soluble to be washed away with a solvent composed of petroleum and oil of lavender. This first successful image produced with bitumen of Judea no longer exists, as it was dropped and broken by an enthusiastic but thick-fingered admirer. Most of the images produced in the following years were rendered on zinc or pewter, with the idea of drawing prints from them; the most successful of these, a copy of an engraving of Cardinal d'Amboise, was produced in 1826, and printed by the Parisian engraver Augustin Francois Lemaître in 1827.

In the same year in which the Cardinal d'Amboise heliograph was made, I first succeeded in permanently fixing, to my own entire satisfaction, an image from nature. This, too, was executed on a pewter plate, and as you well know, since you were my patient companion on that day, it was

necessary to expose the bitumen of Judea for eight hours
within the camera obscura. While this inevitably creates
the somewhat comical effect of showing sunlight on both
sides of the courtyard, the image is nonetheless scientifically
exact and aesthetically pleasing. It has, as well, the advantage of giving a positive image when the bitumen not
hardened by the light has been washed away, and hence
is a considerable advance over the earlier (and more perish-
able) images produced on paper. While it was still necessary to isolate a substance more responsive to the light, at
this point it was clear that the heliographic process itself
was essentially a success, and I even dared to dream of re-
couping some of that fortune drained away by our unsuccessful efforts to promote the *pyreolophore*.

It is at this point that Louis Jacques Mandé Daguerre
enters the story, through a chain of coincidences I have
often found too extraordinary to ascribe to pure chance.
In January of 1826, when my cousin, Colonel Laurent
Niépce de Sennecey-le-Grand, visited Paris on business, I
charged him with calling on the firm of Vincent and
Charles Chevalier, to obtain for me a new camera with
meniscus prism. Seeking to impress the opticians with my
need for a lens of exceptional quality, he explained that I
was engaged in experiments to fix permanently the images
produced within the camera obscura, and showed them an
example of our work with heliographic copies of engravings to support what then seemed his fantastic claims.
M. Daguerre was also among Chevalier's clients, and as he
had already made extravagant claims for his own work in
this field (but without producing results for examination),
it was inevitable that M. Chevalier communicate with him
the substance of his discussion with Laurent. Within a few
weeks, I received the first letter from M. Daguerre, which
struck me then as a gross impertinence, coming as it did
without introduction of any sort. Today I recognize that

12 M. Daguerre's enthusiasm often overrides his modest sense of propriety and convention, though his perhaps is the tone of the new world in which you are destined to live, my son. Unfortunately, the letter was lost, together with several others, when my pocketbook sprang, as it seemed, from my coat, to disappear with the uncanny speed of a homing hare down a Parisian toilet in August of 1827. (The precise circumstances of this confounding loss I was unable then—and have been no more able since—to detail for your mother.) The tone of the letter was, on the whole, quite outspoken in its claims for the author's success in his own experiments, and yet the enthusiasm was qualified by such phrases as "for a long time I, too, have been seeking the impossible." It seemed likely that M. Daguerre, of whose splendid dioramas I had at the time heard nothing in my provincial retreat, was simply seeking to milk me of information, and my first instinct was to ignore him. Eventually, only a sense of the distinguished tradition of communication among men of science led me to send him a cautious reply. A year later, M. Daguerre addressed me in rather more pressing terms, and as I was then in regular communication with M. Lemaître, who was producing our Cardinal d'Amboise, I took the liberty of inquiring of him whether he was acquainted with M. Daguerre. Lemaître replied that he had met the gentleman at several evening parties, but first truly made his acquaintance when he visited him for the sake of showing a drawing he had made of a picture of Daguerre's, intended for publication in Paris. M. Lemaître complimented M. Daguerre's great talent for imitation and his exquisite taste in the composition of pictures, stressing above all his gift for everything that concerns mechanics. It was, apparently, well known that M. Daguerre had long been at work on improving the camera obscura, but there was no known evidence of his success in fixing its images.

Despite Lemaître's praise of the Parisian's mechanical
skills, it seemed improbable that my own researches could
be advanced by a lengthy correspondence, and on 3 February, 1827, I sent M. Daguerre a brief note to explain
that the winter months were not favorable to my process
of engraving on metal; that my researches were temporarily
at a standstill; and that I was consequently unable to send
him the sample of my work that he had requested. I wished
him luck in what he termed his search for perfection, but
revealed nothing of my own experiments with the camera
obscura. The following month, I received from M. Daguerre a prettily-framed sample of his graphic art, produced by the *dessin-fumée* process and much altered by the
brush, and I in turn sent him a comparably unrevealing
pewter plate lightly etched according to my technique—
but with all the bitumen coating carefully removed. My
request for a sample of M. Daguerre's experiments with the
camera obscura went, of course, unanswered, though my
correspondent was most prompt in criticizing the faults of
my heliographic representation of an engraving of the Holy
Family.

It seems to me now most improbable that such epistolary
jousting would ever have proceeded further, had not the
sad news reached us in August of 1827 that Claude was
dangerously ill in London. Your mother and I at once set
forth on the journey, but were obliged to spend some days
in Paris, awaiting our passports, and were delayed still
further by the advent of King Charles X in Calais, the
consequence of which was such a jamming of all roads to
the port with both public and private conveyances, that no
seat on a stage was obtainable. It was in consequence of
these delays that we first made the acquaintance of my
impetuous correspondent, whose understandable nervousness perhaps accounted for his exaggerated animation during that initial meeting. His bright eyes flashed, his full

lips continually broke into leering smiles at the most inappropriate moments, and when he wished to stress some point, he did so by seizing locks of his shaggy, rather unkempt hair in both hands and tugging vigorously. Yet he struck us then as a handsome man, despite the generous dusting of freckles on his broad face, with something of the firmly modelled good looks of a healthy peasant. M. Daguerre's visit to us, at our hotel, lasted nearly three hours, and we returned his call shortly before our departure, when he accompanied us on a tour of the Diorama and permitted us to study, quite at our ease, the magnificent pictures exhibited there. The interior view of St. Peter's executed by M. Bouton was an admirable work, and one which produced the most complete illusion with respect to depth and light. But nothing could have been better than the two views painted by M. Daguerre: one of Edinburgh taken by moonlight during a fire, and the other of a Swiss village showing a wide road, facing a prodigiously high mountain covered by eternal snows. These representations were so true, down to the smallest detail, that one believed he actually saw rural and wild nature, with all the fascination that the charm of color and the magic of chiaroscuro could produce. The illusion was indeed so great, that one was tempted to leave his box and go over the plain to climb the mountain. The story was much told at the time, and I can easily credit its authenticity, that a somewhat frail and elderly spinster, on seeing a representation of St. Peter's, leaned toward her escort and requested him to assist her in advancing along the aisle to the altar.

Despite my fascination with M. Daguerre's accomplishments in this new art form, I was, to be sure, more curious about his experiments with the camera obscura. He flattered me, whenever the subject arose, by asserting that I was clearly more advanced than he, and his remarks made it clear that our processes were, in fact, quite different. His

effects were capable of being produced with a speed com-
parable to that of the electric current, and also entailed
the fixing on a chemical ground of some of the prismatic
colors. Still, he was frank in admitting that the process was
capricious, and that the results could not be preserved for
prolonged periods. Therefore, he frankly pronounced my
method the superior one, but suggested that I might in the
future consider certain experiments with colored glasses.
Impressed as I was by M. Daguerre's work with luminous
substances, it seemed to me improbable that his researches
and mine could ever be regarded as complementary in
methods or intentions. Nonetheless, our meetings had in-
stilled in me a respect for the man, for his ingenuity, energy, and seriousness, which his correspondence alone
would never have achieved.

As soon as the weary struggles with bureaucracy had
produced our passports, and places could be booked on the
Calais stage, your mother and I departed for England,
where we lodged at the Coach and Horses Inn at Kew. Our
hosts were kindly people, but the meals were bad, the beds
worse, and it was all shockingly expensive. Yet such con-
ditions scarcely seemed to matter when compared with our
grievous concern for Claude. Not only were his body and
mind awesomely deteriorated, but it soon became clear that
the perpetual motion machine on which he had staked his
final energies and the last of his monies was not the perfect
work he imagined. Claude was most enthusiastic about the
new examples of heliography that I showed to him, and
despite his ill luck in finding English sponsors for the
pyreolophore, he encouraged me to seek official recognition
for the process in England. My first, somewhat naive, approach was directly to the king himself, through the good
offices of William Townsend Aiton, Director of the Royal
Botanical Gardens at Kew, and the Marquess of Conyng-
ham, Lord Steward of the Royal Household. All their

16 efforts proved to no avail, for heliography had not yet been examined and approved by one of the official bodies responsible for such matters. I consequently applied myself to obtaining the requisite attestation from the Royal Society. Despite the increasingly strained and unhappy circumstances in which the document was produced, that "Memoir on Heliography," which I wrote to accompany my specimens, still serves, I believe, as a reasonable description both of our successes and of the defects that required further experimentation. (Of the latter, optics must now take first place. Only by perfecting the apparatus of the lens, can a faithful image from nature be obtained and properly fixed, and these researches should thus take precedence over consideration of the materials on which the image might best be rendered.) I was, perhaps, rather too modest in my description of the advantages that this discovery promised in its various applications, laying the chief stress on its novelty. Had I underscored the numerous commercial advantages of my invention, both in the arts and the sciences, perhaps the Royal Society would have responded more positively, for I have since been compelled to recognize sadly that official bodies are characteristically loathe to respond with the disinterest, the philosophical and scientific objectivity, to which their charters dedicate them. Perhaps, too, because all but one of the heliographs were copies of engravings, the Society members who studied them believed them to be but an extension of that long-established technique. In any event, the proposal was never formally put before the general membership. In the hope of having planted some seed of interest through these efforts, and in order that it might yet bear fruit in my absence, I presented to Francis Bauer the manuscript of my communication to the Royal Society, together with three heliographs of engravings, two prints of Cardinal d'Amboise and a landscape after Claude Lorraine,

as well as the single view taken from the workroom at **17**
Gras.

I departed England in early February of 1828, and
shortly after my arrival in Paris was greeted by a new
overture from M. Daguerre, which I was more readily
prepared to entertain favorably due to the failure of all
the energies expended by Claude and myself in England.
My enthusiastic correspondent further assured me that
such discouragement could never be my lot in France, and
if my experiments succeeded in producing the results for
which I hoped, it would be a pleasure for him to be able
to indicate how I might derive profit from them. Following
the arrival of this letter, I met with M. Daguerre, and indeed saw him on several occasions during the following
week. Although he expressed some bewilderment that I
had left my sole successful study from nature with Francis
Bauer in England, and was perhaps suspicious of its authenticity, he nonetheless spoke warmly of the benefits that
might accrue from a joining of my experimental talents
with his demonstrably keener instincts for the world of
affairs, to say nothing of his justly celebrated mechanical
abilities. Such a partnership for the improvement of the
heliographic process seemed a not unreasonable solution
to my dilemma, but M. Daguerre understandably wanted
to see a camera picture first, having himself no interest (and
seeing but slight commercial advantage) in the copying of
engravings by superposition. Inasmuch as M. Lemaître
also encouraged me to concentrate on views from nature,
I determined to supply myself with more suitable lenses
before quitting Paris. To this end, I ordered from Chevalier
both an achromatic lens and one of Wollaston's periscopic
lenses, either of which seemed likely to give a greater
clarity of image than the bi-convex type customarily fitted
to the camera obscura. Permitting the use of a larger aperture, such lenses should also allow the image to be recorded

18 in a shorter span of time. Unfortunately, I was unable to resume my experiments until May, for Claude's death preoccupied me with unhappier and more pressing business. However, by late August I could report to M. Lemaître that the periscopic lens gave results far superior to those obtained with ordinary lenses, including the meniscus prism of V. Chevalier, and that the sole present object of my experiments was to copy nature with the greatest possible fidelity. That achieved, I could then seriously engage myself in the various fields of application of which my invention was capable, including the use of the exposed surface as a printing plate from which multiple images might be made. To this end, much of the work that followed was produced on silver-plated sheets, which gave the brightness necessary for a picture from nature to be exhibited in its own right, combined with the hardness requisite to engraving.

The perfections that followed this stage of my work are all refinements on the original concept of heliography as described to the Royal Society, but that you should be aware, and have this record in my own hand, of the particulars of my discoveries, I will briefly describe them here. First, I ascertained in 1829 that by exposing the bare parts of the silvered plate to vapor of iodine, the contrast of the picture could be greatly enhanced, and the bitumen could then be entirely removed. M. Daguerre greeted this advance with particular enthusiasm, but warned me against publication of my results (which I was then considering), lest I sacrifice both the profit and honor of my invention. Inasmuch as heliography seemed then sufficiently perfected, though not without unexplored refinements and implications, I once more communicated with M. Daguerre about the possibility of a partnership, the aim of which would be the attainment of complete success, stressing that above all we must seek a lens that would shorten the exposure

time while still giving a sharp and brilliant image. However,
M. Daguerre's announcement of technical improvements in the form of the camera itself also seemed to bode well for the realization of that objective. When it arrived, his camera proved novel only in being constructed of metal, and its subsequent improvement was entirely my own work. My most significant alteration consisted in the construction of a series of zinc discs, to be placed in front of the lens and adjusted to varying degrees of aperture in much the way that the pupil of the human eye can be seen to enlarge and contract with alteration in the light. M. Daguerre's work was considerably improved by this entirely novel invention, but because of the material used in his camera, it seemed impractical to alter the basic mechanism by which the focal length of its interior could be shortened or extended—i.e., by means of a handle on the outside of the camera, which shifts the wooden plate in which the lens is mounted. My own method I believe to be superior by virtue of its greater flexibility and compactness. It consists of a leather bellows, inspired by an early morning visit to our blacksmith to supervise his repair of a carriage spring; and while leather has the disadvantage of deterioration, it can also be easily replaced. Both the zinc diaphragm and the pliant chamber were invented after the signing of a partnership agreement between M. Daguerre and myself, but both are exclusively my own inventions.

In November of 1829, the year before those most regrettable circumstances compelled the sale of our family home in Châlon-sur-Saône, M. Daguerre journeyed there from Paris, and on the following morning I brought him by carriage to Gras, where he was given numerous demonstrations of the heliographic process. The immediate result of his enthusiasm was the contract signed in Châlon on 24 November, 1829, with some additions with respect to technicalities of procedure, which were made on 5 December, 1829. Therein I am expressly identified as the sole *inventor* of heliography, to whose further improvement and exploitation M. Daguerre was committed to the fullest exercise of his talents and energies, in exchange for one half of any and all profits deriving from the process. Since M. Daguerre's visit here, we have not met again, but I am continually impressed by the persistence with which he pursues his own experiments, and by the unflagging zeal with which his letters proclaim our imminent success. Whenever that long-awaited day arrives, it will assure the recognition for which Claude and I so vainly strove in the decades that followed the invention of the *pyreolophore*, for our family name stands first in the contract signed by M. Daguerre and myself, and hence Nièpce will forever be associated with the technique of preserving views from nature.

In the twenty months that have followed the establishment of this partnership, I have enjoyed little success in my researches into the fixing of images with iodine, by which M. Daguerre sets such great store, but I feel nonetheless encouraged by our progress. Whatever time remains to me on this earth is unlikely to encompass the full decade of my legal agreement with M. Daguerre, and hence you must continue to supply the fundamental talents of research of which our Parisian correspondent has only the most intuitive knowledge. You may, however, trust his good judgment in determining the most propitious means and moment for publishing these researches, and arranging for their commercial development. If, in my own name, I was reluctant to detail to the Royal Society the probable consequences of my invention, I hesitate not at all to do so in the name of my descendants. Even the most primitive peoples of whom we know seem to have been intrigued with the making of images. At the time of my birth, that passion

was most complexly realized through painting in oils—a
method calling for natural talent, extensive training, and a
fat purse. In my own lifetime, both engraving and the new
art of lithography have greatly extended man's ability
to produce such images, and the universal enthusiasm with
which they have been greeted testifies to the deep and
fundamental hunger they fulfill. Yet think, dear Isidore, of
that moment when even the unskilled laborer can, with the
simplest materials, himself strike such images. Think, too,
of the joy with which man will behold heliographic representations of the great pyramids, the Parthenon, the jungles
of Africa, and the wild forests of the New World! Such
records, created without the intrusion of the painter's or
engraver's hand, will be living history. Through their
naturalness of effect, their clarity of detail, future generations—your children, perhaps—will be able to contemplate
the world in which we lived, the conveyances in which we
rode, the quaint costumes that we wore, the streets that we
walked—and they will see these things as they were, rather
than as the spirit of art has interpreted and embellished
them. It is not that I find such embellishments in any sense
unworthy; indeed, they speak of the finest resources of the
human imagination, but the heliograph will give us another
kind of record as well, and one which will almost certainly
alter in the most fundamental manner both our perception
of the world in which we live, and of the past that has
produced us.

Above all, perhaps, the heliograph will appeal to the
sentimentalist who resides in even the most scientific heart,
and once the exposure time of our process has been reduced
from hours to minutes (which the proper lens will yet
achieve), the images of persons can also be rendered in this
manner. I consider now what joy I have known from the
miniature on ivory that was painted of my mother, and
with which she presented me when I left Gras to follow

the flag of the new liberty in 1792. Despite its crudeness of execution, it has often assisted me to achieve the needed perspective on my own life, by reminding me of the place it occupies in the stream that flows ever onward out of the past. And my mother's portrait has been a talisman for me on more than one difficult journey—a claim I freely make despite its overtly unscientific tone. Consider the implications if we could but possess such likenesses of our great-grandparents, and of theirs. What quaint narratives and fragments of narratives would they suggest? What moments of splendor or decline would they insinuate to our willing eyes? And yet, I wonder, will we in reality obtain a more reliable sense of persons and places and events, or only a different one? I think again of the treasured miniature of my mother, and it compels my return to those ruminations with which this letter began, for no doubt I contemplate this picture with very different eyes from those with which I beheld it as a young soldier. Its meanings shifted radically on the day of my mother's death, and yet again on that ill-fated day when Claude, her first-born son, departed for Paris, and no doubt there will be other changes, though perhaps not so radical in effect, in the remaining years of my life. When this miniature becomes your own, it must have yet another meaning than it has for me, or than it has for you now. Hence, though we succeed in permanently fixing views from nature, we cannot hope to fix the mind that observes them. Nor can I expect to fix the images of myself which will have been laid down within the sensitive chamber of your mind, though I would venture to suggest at least this much correction to one of them. I have often seemed, no doubt, to be lacking in that enthusiasm with which the inventor is traditionally endowed, and to approach my researches rather too methodically, too coldly. You must, in this regard, recall the bitter frustration of my earlier expectations, and those of Claude, all of it brought most painfully near once more in the auction of our home in Châlon. The reduction of worldly fortunes has been the common lot of many of my youthful comrades, and I grieve not for these things in themselves, but as unhappy symbols of the world's indifference to accomplishments that would have bettered the lot of men in all stations of life.

I would not, however, bequeath you such bitter thoughts, and it gladdens my heart to think that, if only because of its novelty, the heliographic process seems destined to be far more enthusiastically received. Hence, I dare to set forth in this letter some of the dreams I have been loath to express aloud. The speculations into which I have occasionally strayed in this description of my researches want the application of a more fundamentally philosophical mind than my own, but their greater import will, I believe, be entirely legible to you. We have succeeded in the near-perfection of a process destined someday to make an immeasurable impact on the mind of man. Like any tool, it will be capable of abuse, and its eventual applications are too numerous for either of us to imagine. You, at least, will live to see some of the dreams of your father's twilight years translated into reality, and nothing would please me more than to think that together with the inevitable consequences of my errors, I can bequeath to you something of my passionate faith in the ultimate justification of our labors. I wish you all the joy, the honor, the fortune that this will one day bring to you, dear Isidore—my loyal friend, my worthy collaborator, my most beloved son.

Nicéphore Niépce
(Written and signed by his own hand.)

24 *When Nicéphore Niépce died of a stroke on July fifth, 1833, debts compelled the sale of all that remained of the family properties. Despite the pension awarded him by the French government in 1839, on the occasion of official publication of the Daguerrotype process, Isidore Niépce led a life of extreme penury in the tiny village of Lux, situated midway between Châlon and St.-Loup-de-Varennes. Shy and retiring by nature, he was nonetheless energetic in voicing his father's prior claims to the invention of photography.*—Author's note.

ONE

Light is that silent artist
Which without the aid of man
Designs on silver bright
Daguerre's immortal plan.

J. P. Simon, *A Practical Description of that Process Called the* Daguerrotype

The wish to capture evanescent reflections is not only impossible, as has been shown through German investigation, but the mere desire alone, the will to do so, is blasphemy. God created man in His own image, and no man-made machine may fix the image of God. Is it possible that God should have abandoned His principles, and allowed a Frenchman in Paris to give to the world an invention of the Devil?

Leipziger Stadtanzeiger

THE CAMERA

SIZE: *1 ¾ x 4¾ x 6 inches, collapsed.*
LENS: *Achromatic meniscus.*
FOCAL LENGTH: *5 inches, f/11.*
SHUTTER: *Lancaster's Patent, rotary, in front of lens; T and instantaneous, variable speeds (by varying spring tensions); cocking lever on front, release at lower front.*
FINDER: *Ground-glass viewing.*
BODY: *Finished wood, brass fittings; leatherized fabric bellows; body detaches from camera bed; bed fits on special tripod head and extends by means of a worm gear; horizontal sides on camera front, rear section tilts.*
LIST PRICE: *£22/–.*

This example of a Lancaster Instantograph camera was manufactured in 1886 by J. Lancaster and Son, Birmingham, England. It is a collapsible, bellows-type stand camera for single exposures, 3¼ x 4¼ inches, on standard dry plates.

The Instantograph was a relatively compact and portable stand camera, first introduced in the early 1880s. During the period of its production, its design underwent numerous modifications. Between 1886 and 1888, the basic design was altered to make it a folding camera. The bed was hinged to the main body at its rear, and swung down so that the front standard could move forward. It also had rack-and-pinion forward movement. The back on this later model had, to a limited extent, both swings and tilts.

In 1888 the camera was offered in the following sizes:

3 ¼ x 4 ¼; 4 ¼ x 6 ½; 6 ½ x 8 ½; and 10 x 12 inches. By 1889 the model name was added to the camera's name plate, and 4 x 5, 5 x 7 ½, and 12 x 15 inch sizes were available. Later, in the 1890s, the Imperial Instantograph, the Folding Instantograph, the Aluminium Mounted Instantograph, the Cyclo Instantograph, the Pocket Instantograph and a Special Brass Bound Instantograph were added to the line. By 1907 the line had dwindled to the triple-extension Excelsior Instantograph and B.B. (Brass Bound) Instantograph. The camera was discontinued soon after that time.

The Instantograph cameras were well-made and compact, enjoying considerable popularity during their lifetime. A large number were manufactured; a 1907 Lancaster advertisement claimed that more than 150,000 had been sold, many of them for export to the United States.

THE PHOTOGRAPHER

Elihu Zachariah Morton, Caucasian male,
born May 30, 1871, in Paducah, Kentucky,
to Bertha Louise (née Fitzwilliam)
  and Zachariah James Morton;
died July 2, 1931, in Kansas City, Missouri.

The third of three children and the first to survive infancy, Elihu is lovingly indulged by his mother—a point of some contention with his harness-maker father, who maintains that the child will become nothing better than a "mama's boy." His fears are justified, as Elihu will always be heavily dependent on the ministrations (financial as well as emotional) of women, and a quarter-century after his birth will be clearly identified as a "sissy" by the brilliantined side-part in his hair and the habit of smoking cigarettes. Cigars, he maintains, are too coarse for his lungs, and pipes altogether too bulky and complex. Elihu excels, but without the stigma of genius, in reading and writing as well as arithmetic, in the one-room schoolhouse he attends for six years. His moment of glory arrives when he recites William Wordsworth's "Daffodils" without error, and with contagious, foot-stomping rhythm on the occasion of the Central School Class Day exercises in 1883. It is the last noteworthy success of his life.

In 1884 the Mortons move to Kansas City, Missouri, where Mrs. Morton has inherited a modest dry-goods store from her father. Elihu's schooling is forever interrupted, for his skills in reading, writing, and arithmetic are now in daily demand behind the counter. Mr. Morton has never before reckoned, save in the inches of harness leather, and Mrs. Morton only in the number of pages remaining in a Dickens novel. Furthermore, though he is precociously, clumsily tall, and his hair springs out in disorderly tufts from his head, Elihu looks quite competent behind the counter, and seems to have a natural talent for selling a lady a yard more of dotted Swiss than she had intended to buy. And so, Elihu and his mother dominate the small store, fluttering over customers and banishing imaginary flecks of dust with turkey-feather dusters, while Mr. Morton seeks the unfluttered quiet of the combination stockroom and office, where he drinks steam beer and stares at the spines of tightly bound ledgers that he never removes from the shelf. Perhaps he daydreams of the grained suppleness of deeply tanned harness leather, the manly sturdiness of brass rivets and buckles; if so, it is a closely kept secret.

Where the father wilts, the mother flourishes, enjoying from the depths of distantly aristrocratic Fitzwilliam blood the socializing atmosphere of the small shop. The old man grows gaunt, his eyes cavernous, while the woman waxes from plump to stout to obese, and Elihu discovers brilliantine as a way of taming the brittle straw of his hair. At fifteen, tending the shop alone, Elihu also discovers the fringe benefits of good grooming. Beguiled by a strip of ostrich-feather trim she cannot afford, his customer suggests some other form of payment might be negotiated. Puzzled by her innuendo, Elihu nonetheless allows himself to be led into the dusty cubicle of an office, where her mittened hands guide him expertly, and the ancient transaction is completed with brisk efficiency. Five minutes later, fumbling with fly buttons that seem mysteriously enlarged, Elihu can only remember the squeaking of the table against which she braced her hips, and the sharpness of her whalebone corset as it cut into his abdomen. Al-

though he doubles the applications of brilliantine after this,
the lady returns only as the versatile star of his wet dreams.

None of this was particularly memorable for Elihu, who had early developed the habit of allowing life to take care of itself. It did so in the death of his father, which the son observed from afar—as though from the third balcony of a dimly-lighted music hall. Mrs. Morton grew more corpulent, so that she bustled less behind the counter and tended to sit in radiant attendance, a talcumed Buddha gossiping with customers and diligently overseeing her son's work. She was, of course, always more than delighted to advise on color coordination, and the difficult matter of suiting button to fabric. There was something smugly approving about her mountainous presence, and sufficiently ample in spirit to embrace even the bony saloon-keeper's daughter to whom her son became engaged. Perhaps it was the prosperity of the girl's father that so democratized Mrs. Morton's social vision. When the young woman died, her blue-lipped, stillborn baby clutched to her scrawny chest, Mrs. Morton briefly wondered if the proud Fitzwilliam blood was not avenging itself. But chiefly she mourned that Elihu would now realize no benefit from his father-in-law's snug little fortune. After all, he had been a model husband to his unpretty bride, and had done so much to improve her grammar. To take her son's mind off his loss, Mrs. Morton set about redecorating the store for the first time since they had occupied it ten years before. That is, she oversaw the redecoration—including a large, plate-glass store window which lured the passerby with bountiful flourishes of silk and cambric, with garlands of feathers and satin ribbons. Then, having set her son's house so superbly in order, and although she had never had so much as a sniffle, his mother put on a new cambric nightgown trimmed with Belgian lace, arranged her hair in a single sausagelike coil, took to her feather bed, and died.

32   Perhaps as compensation for his loneliness, Elihu began to smoke cigarettes. They marked him as rather fast and wild, perhaps a little sissified, certainly a good deal citified. Each morning he descended from his room overhead and opened the shop doors promptly at 8:00; he closed them just as promptly at 7:00 in the evening. His grooming was refined now by the use of cologne, and his bookkeeping was monkishly immaculate; visually if not arithmetically, the intricate columns were wonderfully balanced. It was no doubt such neatness that first recommended him to a neighborhood widow, an exceptionally tidy woman more than ten years his senior. After their marriage, the bride transferred from her furnished rooms to the small flat over the shop a canary in a wire cage inspired by the Crystal Palace, two domed horsehair trunks, and her dead husband's photographic equipment. A clumsy mechanism of oak and glittering brass, the camera seemed to fit into no available corner of the tiny flat, and so was installed as a curiosity in the shop below. Photography was yet something of a novelty in this Western town, and there was no photographer's studio in the neighborhood. Ladies amused themselves by disappearing beneath the black drape that shrouded the camera and wondering at a silvery world turned upside down. On slack, rainy mornings, Elihu himself began to experiment with the camera, and after numerous failures produced a quite agreeable portrait of his new wife. The portrait still exists. It shows a matronly woman with ample bosom, tidily encased in a simple dress which leaves only her face and hands exposed. The high collar seems to force her chin up, and her short, white hands sprout like anaemic fruit from the tight circles of her sleeves. These details, taken together with her rigidly cinched waist, suggest a miraculous underworld network of buttons, snaps, gussets, bands, straps, hooks, cinches, stays, and ties—and yet the effect is quite simple. The photograph was much admired as a likeness, and universally deemed natural in its effects.

The genesis of the Morton Photographic Parlours, though modest and casual, was nonetheless propitiously well-timed. The large mail-order houses, with their budget-priced finery, had already begun to pare away the profits of the small, independent dry-goods store, and there seemed less and less interest in either fashion or quality. But even before the last of his customers had embraced the heresies of the mass-produced and the ready-made, Elihu produced his first portraits of neighborhood ladies and their children. He did so somewhat protestingly, hating the stink of acid in the cramped office-storeroom, which now served as a darkroom as well. And the acid marked his well-manicured hands with angry amber splotches. But as the dry-goods business dwindled, the photographic trade burgeoned, and in time it was necessary to make appointments to accommodate all the wedding and christening studies. Photographs joined the fabric in the window, crowded it, defeated it; and one day the letters of "Morton's Photographic Parlours" appeared in golden, Gothic fanfare across the window. Elihu never complained, and yet he found something lacking in this new career. First of all, his sitters were nervous, fluttering into the shop with agitated concern for stray hairs and wrinkled bodices. They sat like granite statuary before the midnight-blue velvet drapery, and bustled away as soon as the lens had clicked, as though to say they were used to this tiresome ordeal of photography and could not give it another precious moment. He missed the casual chatter of the dry-goods store, the sibilant apostrophizing of various weights of muslin, though he may not have known it. His wife, on the other hand, took obvious pleasure in arranging the hems of christening dresses and deciding whether or not to include a potted palm or a spray of dried asparagus fern for background

34 effect. Thus, the new enterprise went well enough until dyspepsia isolated Mrs. Morton in the flat upstairs, confining her for weeks at a time to her bed, where she muffled gassy rumblings with pillows and eiderdown comforters, even on the hottest summer days.

The gilt lettering on the window began to flake, and the photographs of brides and babies achieved a delicate patina of fly-specks and dust. Elihu's camera was old-fashioned, and he continued to use the original glass plates; while his customers would not have understood such technical distinctions, they knew that the photographs made downtown were a good deal smarter, with their backdrops of classical columns and rose-covered arbors. In time appointments ceased to be necessary, though the trade was still brisk enough for the proprietor to afford his brilliantine and cigarettes, and there was always his wife's small inheritance from her first husband to tide them over. Then the neighborhood took a much-lamented turn for the worse, as the Irish invaded its outer precincts and slowly but sturdily pressed toward the center. One by one, the accustomed faces disappeared, and the Morton Photographic Parlours became the neighborhood's sole remnant of White Anglo-Saxon Protestant culture. If the invasion was bad for property values, it was not entirely bad for business. The Irish hardly ever drifted downtown, and their hunger for wedding and christening and confirmation photographs seemed insatiable. Elihu installed a row of straight-backed chairs to accommodate those waiting to sit for him, and for a few years enjoyed something like prosperity. His wife fretted in gassy isolation at the frequent sound of infants screaming in outrage and fear, but she suffered it all with a dignified, matronly stoicism.

When the first strains of gray began to appear in Elihu's hair, he touched them daintily with black boot dye—a good deal cheaper and also easier to apply than conven-

tional hair dye. When the wooden shell of his camera split
slightly with the dryness of age, he mended it with adhesive
tape. Though the Irish still came bearing platoons of babies
in outrageously expensive christening dresses, his profits
dwindled. As the cost of materials rose, his prices remained
fixed, and the sure slide from modest prosperity to modest
subsistence began. In his entire lifetime, Elihu Morton had
but a single idea for arranging his own destiny; only once
was he possessed of a scheme not engineered by the women
in his life. The scheme was original, bold to the point of
outrageousness, and the sole instance of his thinking about
his profession. He quite literally trembled when he con-
sidered the heroic dimensions of his conception, and was
awed by the fathomless depths from which it must have
sprung. The new venture was to photograph young ladies
in swimming suits or underwear, to produce these photographs in multiple copies, and to sell them at immense
profit to traveling salesmen. Mentally, he invented many
poses for the young ladies, holding baskets of flowers,
beachballs, feather fans, or gardening tools. In preparation
he transferred the midnight-blue drapery from the rear
wall to the front window, where he pinned onto it the
best and least discolored of his older photographs. This
would guarantee the discreet privacy he required. Naturally, it also left him with the problem of the blank wall, discolored both by water stains and by the horizontal stripes
where shelves had formerly stood sandwiched tightly with
rainbow bolts of cloth. It was a problem never to be con-
quered. He imagined various painted backdrops, but that
which suited the beachball was all wrong for the garden
tableaux, and the cost of more than one such painted
canvas scene was more than he could afford. He pondered
the problem by the hour, but a solution evaded him. With
the window blacked out, the shop was now cavernously
dark, but he found this restful for his eyes, and purchased

36   two new spotlights with portrait filters to compensate for the gloom. Having failed to solve the problem of the backdrop, however, he could at least avoid the yet greater dilemma of how and where he would find the young ladies who would strike those coy and fair poses he had mentally prepared for them. And so the drapery remained on the window for several years, and the wall before which his sitters posed was eventually painted olive green. It looked quite smart, even though the old water stains stared like ghostly spectators through the surface.

There is little more of note to be recorded. After two years of swaddled invalidism, Mrs. Morton emitted a final gassy sigh and died, whereas twenty years later Elihu was to go "just like that," as the neighbors said, from a stroke. The Morton Photographic Parlours were unoccupied for two years after his death, served briefly as a shoe-repair shop, and were torn down along with the entire block of buildings to make way for a Kroger supermarket and parking lot. Elihu's camera can be traced to a Salvation Army thrift store and no further. The grained oak cube of the camera (without its tripod, of course) may well survive as a smart table lamp, crowned by a pleated, brown patent-leather shade, in the Westchester cottage of a successful New York publisher. None of this, however, is relevant, and is still in the future. What particularly concerns us now is that on a summer afternoon in 1912 or 1913, a young newspaper boy entered the shop with his dog.

He enters the shop with his dog, a tough, stumpy, well-fed mutt. The dog is white with a black patch over one eye, looking rather like the dog in the R.C.A. Victor ads, except that he is shorter and even more bulldoggishly muscular. Elihu is suspicious at first, thinking the boy wishes to sell him a newspaper. But before advancing all the way into the Morton Photographic Parlours, the boy drops his weathered canvas bag of newspapers just inside the door, making it clear that the present business has **37** nothing whatever to do with newspapers. Elihu is sitting in a bottom-sprung easy chair, and the boy walks up to him with his left hand extended, holding a bright new quarter in his open palm. He wants his picture taken with the dog. Not unaccustomed to children having pictures made for their parents, yet not entirely accustomed to their looking so raggedly pieced together as this child does, Elihu takes the quarter with a business-like sigh and struggles up out of his chair. The child might at least have put on better clothes—if he has any. Poverty is no cause for shame, of course, but even poverty can be softened by good grooming. The boy's hair is a mess. Never mind. A quarter is a quarter.

Taking the photograph presents no problem—or, rather, only a single one, easily solved. The problem is how to include the dog in the photograph. The boy could sit with the dog on his lap, but the boy is slightly too small and the dog rather too large for such a pose. So Elihu simply removes his ashtray and a copy of *Deadwood Dick's Revenge* from the table that sits beside his easy chair, and drags it to the rear wall. He motions for the boy to lift the dog onto the table. With a quick eye, he estimates that they are well within the camera's present range, which was set that morning for the golden anniversary portrait of a withered railway conductor and his wife. Of course, it will not show the boy's legs, but then he has not specified a full-length photograph, and the closer range will show the dog to greater advantage. Besides, it is easier not to move the clumsy, splay-legged tripod with its heavy oak cube of a camera. Elihu backs up, tilts his head to the side to squint at his subjects, nods, and disappears beneath the dusty black cloth. Were such matters of interest to him, he might observe that the boy and the dog compose well together. Not at all inclined to notice such details, he simply

38 utters the automatic commands: Look at the birdie. Smile. Hold it.

In a quick etching of light, the photograph is finished, laid down in invisible silvery negative on the coated glass plate. The boy, however, has not looked at the birdie. He has looked away, over the photographer's right shoulder— out of the photograph, out of Morton's Photographic Parlours. He also has not smiled, being somewhat sensitive about the large gap between his front teeth, which he has been variously told indicates a miser, a generous person, and a thief. His right arm is locked round his dog, the right hand pointed at an uncomfortable angle against the dog's neck, so that the entire back of the hand is visible in the photograph. Elihu notes none of this. The image recorded, he tells the boy to come back in an hour. In that time, he develops the plate, prints the image onto thick, velvety paper, and virgorously stamps his name onto the reverse side. Then he slips it into a rough grey cardboard mounting with "Morton Photographic Parlours" embossed in gold across the bottom. As the years pass, the gold lettering fades to a dull green, and slowly the indelible stamp on the back eats its way through the paper, to imprint its pale oval on the photographic image itself. This oval runs just under the collar of the boy's sweater, across the dog's nose, down over the dog's collar, and back onto the front of the sweater. It does not really deface the photograph or diminish its nostalgic value, but it has a rather disturbing effect if studied too closely, for it then resembles a cancellation stamp. You must, of course, look at the photograph very closely to grasp these subtleties, and few of us are accustomed to studying such images in exacting detail.

Your first response, when you see this photograph, will almost certainly be to call it charming, and then rather quickly to dismiss it as an object of sentimental worth, if any. There are, of course, junk shops and attics almost

without number filled with completed and uncompleted
albums of such photographs, and boxes and bales of such
photographs, and individual ones that fall to the floor when
you reach for something else, and get trod under foot. For
each of these, someone put on a new hat, waxed a moustache, spit-polished a boot, and arranged the flow of his day
to pass for a moment in front of the camera. It is touchingly
vain, this gesture, in its bid for immortality. Most of these
documents rest in junk shops or cellars or multi-purpose
bureau drawers. Even if you have some in an album, you
almost certainly cannot identify them all. (It is different,
perhaps, with more recent photographs. No one having
bought and paid for and put on at its most becoming angle
a new hat, it seems less worth the while of even bothering
to remember; and the taking of snapshots is, in any case,
a far less ceremonial matter.) And so a face stares up and
out at us—a face with good cheekbones and superb handle-
bar moustaches—and we can give the face no name; we
are even less likely to know whether the sitter died of
cancer or tuberculosis, or suffocated in a hotel fire in
Barstow, California. The matter of his death would be of
greater historical interest than his name, really, but if we
wonder at all, we wonder about his name, and then, perhaps, how he made his living. Isn't that Grandmother's
second cousin who went to Hollywood and did something
in silent pictures? Now who *could* that be with those
funny waxed moustaches?

Inasmuch as naming tends to dominate this matter of
recognition to such a degree, I will tell you that the name
of the newspaper boy who enters with his dog and requests
a photograph is James. As for the matter of his death, you
can make a note that he lived to be nearly eighty, when he
died of nothing in particular, but the general and simul-
taneous cessation of all vital bodily functions. The less
easily measured other functions—hope, love, lust, ambition

40 —had all died several decades before. If you look at this photograph closely, you will see many of these things. Or, if you prefer, you can merely flip to the next section, where a very different image awaits you.

THE PHOTOGRAPH

To the left, a dog sits on a table. To the right, his arm around the dog, stands a boy in a checked cap. It is necessary to understand that the designations left and right are for the convenience of the observer. For either the boy or the dog, the terms would be meaningless. The dog is actually to the boy's right, hugged against his shoulder, and the boy's arm embraces the dog in such a way that his entire right hand is visible at the side of the dog's neck. The position is clearly awkward to maintain, placing great stress on the muscles of forearm and wrist. Two possibilities exist to account for such stiltedness. Either the photographer has bent boy and dog into this essence of boy-with-dog pose, or the boy himself has adopted it for reasons of his own. Such evidence as we have would point to the latter as the more probable explanation. The boy's hand, held in stiff right angle to the neck of the dog, bears on the second finger a squarish ring whose glint suggests at least an approximation of silver.

Thus, the hand would seem so awkwardly stiffened by vanity. As the boy cannot be more than ten or eleven years of age, there is something tender, even touching, in this small detail. At any rate, it is unlikely that the photographer himself placed the hand in such a position. Had he enjoyed the vanities of art, he would almost certainly have placed the hand in a gentle, downward-sloping arc, along the dog's meaty shoulder. No, there is something too bare and utilitarian here to suggest the maverick photographer striving to pleasure the muse of photography. We know him already as a simple tradesman, given to neither pretension nor success, and even if we did not know him already, we would see him in the crude, homemade table on which the dog sits. The half-visible drawer, the squarely utilitarian thrust of the leg, the coarse grain and dense varnish of the

42 table scarcely suggest a striving for the aesthetic. Only the softly feminine rounding of the corners of the table top suggests an eye for either comfort or effect.

Thus, the hand is clearly extended in vanity—to show to advantage the worn, squarish silver ring as token of the boy's movement toward manhood. For it is not a boy's ring but a man's ring—bought from a pawnshop, found on the street, or given him by his father. Least likely is that it was given him by his father, who had given so little in the past, and never gave him anything in the years to come but an insurance policy inadequate to pay for a pauperish burial. Since the boy made his own way now, hustling papers in one of the poorer neighborhoods of Kansas City, it is hardly improbable that he found the ring. Had he bought it, he might have sought a better fit; and that he could have saved enough money to buy even a cheap ring, heavily alloyed with zinc or steel, seems almost as unlikely as his father's having given it to him. Besides, the father is now wandering the twisting road that will take him finally to a square, one-room wooden house braced in hard right angles in the center of fields of sweet white Indiana corn.

Since I have already made such a great deal of this rigid hand, and will shortly make yet more, it is only fair to confess that this complexly revealing detail has just now caught my attention. My omission would not in itself be so astonishing, since the hand is only a small fragment in the total mosaic of the photograph, except for the fact that I have known this particular photograph for more than a quarter-century. I could easily have drawn it forth from a jumble of photographs of the same age and size and cloudy coloring. Indeed, had you papered an entire wall with similar boy-with-dog poses, I could instantly have separated this one from the mass. My immediate recognition, to be sure, would have had less to do with details of hands and buttons than with compositional masses and curves, with

abstract arrangements of light and dark. Still, my earlier
omission of this single pregnant detail might in itself lead
us to labyrinthine speculation on the contrast between
looking and seeing. Yet I had studied this photograph in the
minutest, most exacting detail on a score of occasions,
seeking some whisper of myself in this pinch-mouthed
boy. Perhaps I concentrated too exclusively on the face, or
on the cocky, playful brightness in the eye of the dog. Only
one other explanation remains to account for my oversight
—that the photograph itself has altered with time. We
know that alterations occur in these old photographs, that
entire colonies of restless molecules shift and rearrange
themselves, not so rigidly cribbed and cabined as they are
by the more authoritarian chemistries of modern photography. Thus, we are called upon to explain that Aunt Flo
did not have a moustache, that Grandfather's chin did not
really protrude at such a threatening angle, but that their
photographs have altered with age. Some of these molecular changes are so extreme, some of the chemical emigra-
tions so vast, that we must call upon the professional re-
storer, feathery camel-hair brush in hand, to approximate
the original approximation. Discounting the intervention
of magic, it is improbable, to be sure, that even in their
myriad permutations, the contentious molecular families of
this photograph rearranged themselves into an awkwardly
stiffened hand accented by the dull, base-metal glow of a
squarish ring. They have been known in other cases, however, to conspire to create double chins, birthmarks, pim-
ples, moles, and scars. For now, I am prepared to accept
my earlier ignorance of this vainly extended hand as a
complex oversight.

At any rate, the ring we are observing is not a boy's but
a man's, so large that it extends almost from knuckle to
knuckle, and has to be worn on the second finger. In another two or three years, the hands will have grown

enough to bear it on the ring finger, and by then the boy will have fathered his own first child, a daughter whom he will never see. This will happen when he is thirteen; at fifteen he will marry. More than two decades lie ahead, however, before he marries my mother for the first time. But before we assess this awkwardly mannish ring as simple vanity, we should search for other clues. The photograph offers two. First, the checked cap, obviously wool, is tilted at a jaunty angle over one ear. The ears are large and low-set, making the head look small and vulnerable, though it is surely not small for his age. The jaw is wide and full, the features strongly defined. Yet there is something wistful and unguarded about it, despite the strength of jaw, and it is clear that the cap is consciously arranged at this tilted angle, allowing a fringe of hair to fall across the forehead. Perhaps there is, as well, some sign of vanity in the closely buttoned sweater he wears. It would, in any event, be interesting to see something more than poverty here, though this coarse, waffle-knit sweater with its small, bluntly pointed collar has tongues enough to tell of poverty. Resembling more some remnant of winter underwear than a sweater, it has seen long service. The shoulders are a neat fit, and so the sweater's ragged wear must have come from other owners. The left sleeve, pushed back to show a firm round of wrist, ends not in a cuff but in a blunt fringe from which the cuff has been worn or torn or cut away. Most of the jagged edge has been tucked under, as though to hide it. This is perhaps more vanity, though it may, to be sure, be the corrosive shame bred by poverty. None of this is so important to the eye, however, as the snug buttoning of the sweater-front. Here neatness does sturdy battle with decay.

The six buttons of the sweater all match. Rather, five of them can be seen to match, and the button at the top, partially covered by the small, square collar, may very well match too. The buttons are tightly sewn, and it seems

improbable that they have consistently remained so through **45**
the stresses, washings, stretchings, and assaults that the
fabric has survived. They have, of course, been sewn by
the mother, sitting solitarily among the shrinking collection
of cut-glass which, together with diamonds, she had always
regarded as the most secure way to save her money. The
original source of these purchases is not clear, but the saga
of their ruthless diminishment is told with relentless fre-
quency. With each reinstatement of each vagrant button,
there is perhaps one less diamond to glint on her fingers,
one sparklingly jigsawed vase fewer standing in mutely
crystal audience.

The ring, the angle of the cap, the neatly stitched buttons, the partially hidden fray of cuff, however, all support our sense of a tender, boyish vanity. Other qualities
are more difficult to determine. We might read a great deal
or very little into the slight tilt of the head, the upward-
glancing eyes that seem to search into depths far beyond
the grimy rectangle of the photographer's shop, with its
window crammed with dusty and fly-specked commemora-
tions of infancy, baptism, virginity, and marriage. The eyes
are so dark that they must, in reality, be nearly black, and
there is clearly a yearning in them. We cannot, however,
know for what. The dog stares straight into the camera,
as though seeking the man who has just disappeared beneath the black drape. The boy looks up and to his left—
away from the dog, the camera, the photographer, the
Morton Photographic Parlours, and Kansas City.

If there is something dreamily inattentive about the look
on the boy's face, his dog is all attention. The eyes take in
every detail, the ears are slightly cocked in listening, and
the jowls seem puffed, as though he is growling, or about
to bark. It is, all in all, the tough readiness of the street
fighter which characterizes this animal. He is a mutt, bulldoggishly broad in the chest, short-necked, long-nosed, and

46 with sturdy legs. A twist of tail is half-visible between his legs, curled on the table top. He has stiff white hair, greyish mottlings on his stomach, and a large piratical spot over his right eye. Although he is more stocky, he resembles the dog in the old Victor ad, one ear raised to the melody of His Master's Voice. Indeed, he is so perfectly tailored for such boy-with-dog shots, one could almost imagine him a stuffed photographer's prop, except for that springiness of his body and the sizing-up brightness of his eye. The boy treats him well. He is no rangy street dog, but an almost plump, clearly well-fed dog, and he sports a leather collar with brightly faceted metal studs. It seems hardly possible that such a dog would be walked on a leash, and so the collar is ornamental. Even as an old man, the boy will find it easier to extend his clumsy, gruff affection to a dog than to another human being. But as a measure of affection for his dog, the collar is important evidence. One would have needed to sell a great many newspapers to be able to afford such a handsomely crafted collar of cowhide and steel. And it suits the dog—a crisp black band that theatrically accents the sporty patch on his eye.

The dog seems, in fact, a good deal better cared for than the boy. Not only is his sweater raveling toward eternity, but the brim of his checked cap dips and curls like an improbable flower, its cardboard lining softened and swollen and disintegrating with seasons of sweat and rain. The trousers are hardly better, hanging in shapeless, baggy folds. If they are trousers. The photograph stops just below the boy's knees, but something about the drooping crotch and looseness in the thighs suggests they may be knickerbockers. As the year of the photograph is 1912 or 1913, it would seem reasonable to guess that the boy is wearing knickerbockers rather than trousers. They are made of a coarse twill or corduroy, its ridges clearly visible in the photograph, looking almost like careless fingerprints

laid onto the surface. So voluminous is this garment that
we must presume it held up with the aid of suspenders,
invisible to us beneath the sweater. Also invisible—or
nearly so—is some white undergarment whose neck peeks
over the collar of the sweater. It appears clean.

The boy's left hand is thrust into the pocket of the
trousers. It is not thrust all the way in, as we still see the
range of his sturdy but childishly rounded wrist between
sweater-cuff and pocket, but just far enough to protect
what he carries there. What you cannot know is that this
pocket does not contain the assorted nails and string and
broken penknife that you might expect. Such articles are
perhaps in the other pocket. Indeed, there is a faint bulge
that suggests the right pocket may well contain such a
horde, together with the nickels and pennies of newspaper
sales. But the pocket into which the hand is thrust contains
a quarter. Fifteen minutes before this photograph is taken,
Bud Fisher gives the boy the princely tip of fifty cents, in
the form of two shiny and unimpeachably new quarters.
Fisher is a cartoonist whose saga of "Mutt and Jeff" appears
in the very papers the boy sells, so that for him the cartoonist is a hero and famous man, which seems more important than the more obvious fact that he is an alcoholic.
Each evening he buys a paper from the boy, even though
he could no doubt simply stop by the newspaper office and
collect a free one. Perhaps he could not walk so far, or
could not decipher the numbers on the streetcars. In any
case, he always buys a paper from the boy, and is thus one
of the regulars. Sometimes, when very drunk, Fisher gives
the boy a nickel tip. Today, though it is not Christmas and
Fisher seems no drunker than ever, he gives the boy two
quarters. "Don't spend it all in one place!" he cautions. The
boy promptly advances on the Morton Photographic Parlours, deposits his unsold newspapers within the door where
he can watch them, hands the proprietor a single quarter,

48   and asks to have his photograph made. He insists that the dog be with him in the picture, and a sturdy, thoroughly pragmatic table is dragged into service so that the dog can be raised up to camera level. The boy stands beside the table, his right arm round the dog and his right hand pointed at a right angle into the dog's neck, so that the camera will record his ring and his dog, his two most cherished possessions. The glint of the ring matches the glint of the studs and buckle of the dog's collar. The boy's left hand is thrust into his left pocket in order to protect his remaining quarter. This hand and pocket naturally appear on the right-hand side of the photograph as we look at it.

There is much of interest that is not visible in the photograph itself. One of these things is the quarter, which we know about already. Another may be the boy's shoes, which we cannot know about but can guess would have been merely serviceable. More interesting would be to know the places to which the boy has walked in these shoes, how many months or years he has worn them, who bought them, how much they cost, and whether they will be discarded or passed on to someone else. It is no longer possible to know these things, though a photograph that included the shoes would be a valuable research source. For the shoes may *not* have been of a serviceable, broguish sort at all; they may have been the most impractical tan leather with ornamental stitching on the toes and round the laces. What we also cannot see is the boy's body, wrapped as it is in rather shapeless clothes, and yet we still have the vague sense that it is straight and strong and healthy. This is true, although it would certainly surprise many if they could see the scar tissue, like a coating of molten wax, across the upper left arm, under the arm, and puckering across the left breast. Later, this scar tissue will resemble aged tallow in color, but now, even though several **49** years old, it has a tender, pinkish cast.

This severe scarring resulted from the boy's dress catching fire from a candle, and although a photograph of the boy in this very dress, with his hair smartly parted in the center, is also in existence, it is not under examination here. The cotton dress with its puffed sleeves and eyelet skirt, a bouffant cloud of whiteness enveloping the child, became a robe of fire, and even rapid hands could not remove the fragment of flaming sleeve that stuck to the left arm. This much of the story will not seem hard to believe if you consider the classic construction of such dresses—a tight band at shoulder and elbow (the latter frequently lace-edged) to give the sleeve a fashionable puff. The rest of the flaming dress was torn away, but this sleeve stuck fast, flamed, and left its charred fibers imbedded in the open wound. The child nearly died, and after advising amputation in sternly professional tones, the family doctor walked briskly away down the brick walk, thinking once more about the criminal carelessness of parents. Here, however, the familiar horseman comes riding, riding to save the arm that bears the hand that is now thrust into the pocket to protect the quarter that Bud Fisher gave. The horseman is a country doctor of somewhat unclear credentials who has invented a wonder ointment, and this wonder ointment, repeatedly applied according to Dr. Vaseline's careful instructions, softens the crust of the burn, permits the skin to breathe, and saves the child's arm. None of this is visible in the photograph, though it is of course essential to what we see there, as well as suggesting a curious chapter in the history of American folk medicine.

Other than this single, violent scar, the boy's body is unblemished. Though his mouth is closed in the photograph, his teeth are even and straight, and distinguished

50   only by a large gap between the upper two center ones. His back and arms and legs are straight, and his general physical development accords in every way with the textbook standards for a boy of ten or twelve. If anything, his development—especially of the sexual organs—is slightly advanced for his age. He will eventually require the substitution of a tiny dacron sleeve for one section of his aorta, but this is in no way apparent in the study before us.

When we consider the problem, the number of things not visible in this photograph bulks overwhelmingly large. Neither dreams nor fears are indicated here, though some are perhaps suggested. Nor are date, time, and place of death visible, though surely these are matters of considerable importance. We see neither the women this man will love, nor the ones he will cease to love, nor those to whom he will simply make love. We see only one of the dogs he will own, and do not know if the brightly studded collar will wear out and be replaced, or if it will long outlive this dog and eventually be worn by one, two, or even three other dogs. Some of these are rather abstract matters of speculation; others are matters of fact. Among the facts that we cannot know is why the boy has had the photograph taken. Is it intended as a gift for the mother who so patiently sews buttons in cut-crystal solitude? Is it a whim? Is it merely the same vanity that inspires him to extend so awkwardly the hand that wears the ring? Is it the belief that he will one day be a great man, and that such a record may prove of use to his biographer? Perhaps it is all of these things. Perhaps it is none of these things. Perhaps even the boy does not know. He does not, however, become a famous man.

Further facts and speculations will appear in brief glimpses of other photographs. The other photographs, however, have not all been sorted, and are in any event less revealing than this one. That is because the others are

largely snapshots belonging to a later age, when the matter
of making photographs no longer entails tightly buttoning
your sweater and handing over half your fortune to a
photographic parlor to be recorded there in the name of
immortality. This photograph of a boy with his arm round
the shoulder of his dog is not merely a photograph; it is a
document, an event, an artifact, a unique moment in time,
an investment, an occasion, and the sole but intricate collaboration among cartoonist, photographer, boy, and dog.
It is therefore deserving of the closest scrutiny, and furthermore, requires it if we are to realize fully its nuances. This
would be true in any case, but is the more so now since
the photograph itself has faded slightly, acquiring a silvery
patina that heightens its charms but rather obscures its
details. Hence, it is seen to greatest advantage when held
directly under a light.

Even so, the photograph yields its secrets slowly, re-
luctantly, and perhaps not at all. The face, which should
tell us most, tells us least. It is not alone that distant, searching look in the eyes which is so puzzling. It is a face of
contradictions. The ears, awkward and coarse, seem not to
fit the gentle curve of the face. There is something almost
feminine in its softness, but that is contradicted as well by
a tired, pinched look under the eyes and at the corners of
the mouth. The oval symmetry of the face is contradicted,
too, by the fact that the right eye seems slightly cocked.
This is something I have never before noticed—either in the
photograph or in the man himself—and I am therefore
unable to judge if this is reality or some trick of the photographer's lens. If studied too closely, that slight cock to the
eye is decidedly unnerving.

Still, taken as a whole the face inspires trust. It is vaguely
pretty without being cherubic, softly rounded but not
effeminate, and although the eyes stare into some imaginary
distance, it is clear that they could also quickly and ac-

curately size up a house. They do so when he works as a stage hand at the Pantages Theater, and even more calculatingly when he stands before an audience there equipped with his fine, clear tenor voice. For the moment he is only a boy, but clearly the kind of boy you can trust. You can send him with a dollar to fetch you a pail of beer, and he will return without spilling a drop, and with all ninety cents in change. He will mail your letters and not be cheated of a penny, and he will fold your paper crisply with a single hand, even as he is drawing it out of his bag. And it is a widely acknowledged cliché that any boy that kind to his dog must be a good boy. As a man, he will still be kind to his dog, though the kindness will grow rough at the edges, and he will pay his bills on time, even during the grim depths of the Depression, so long as they are bills that can be paid with money.

Yes, even if some details are obscure or ambiguous, we certainly feel that this is a boy we can trust. The street boy here is not too far from the frontier, and so to be untrustworthy would be to show oneself unmanly. In another year, he will demonstrate this dramatically, though he will also demonstrate that such integrity does not exclude its own kind of ruthlessness. He does not remember how the female cousin came to be there, but she arrived. He has also forgotten whether or not this was related or unrelated to the vacation of his mother and newly acquired stepfather. He does, however, remember that he and his stepbrother and his female cousin attend the vaudeville show together, and that the female cousin sits between himself and his stepbrother. Anecdote demands that the cousin be pretty; she is, at any rate, a female cousin. The boy, made bold perhaps by her fragrant daintiness, places his left arm onto the back of the seat in which she sits—not close enough to touch her shoulders, but close enough to tingle from such proximity. No sooner is this arm strate-

gically settled on the back of the chair than the stepbrother
reaches round, knocks it off, and puts his own in its place.
As the stepbrother is two years older, this is perhaps the
simple right of seniority, but his greater age might have
led him to think of the idea first. In any case, there would
seem no reasonable grounds for asserting his claim by vio-
lence. For now, honor demands that the boy appear to
ignore this affront, which he does by concentrating with
puckered brows on the quartet soaring with ragged vigor
into the final chorus of "Sweet Adeline."

Given the seniority of his stepbrother and the fact that
this is, after all, the stepbrother's own female cousin, he is
even inclined to forget the matter. And so the three stroll
home through the summer streets. The boy walks near the
curb, having heard once that this is the place of a gentleman
accompanying a lady. The sidewalk is narrow, and as they
walk three abreast, the boy's steps are teeteringly balanced
on the edge. The female cousin is beside him, and his stepbrother to her left. He enjoys the coordinated swing of
their bodies as they walk, but their rhythm is destroyed
forever when his stepbrother reaches behind the cousin and
gives him a push that sends him sprawling into the gutter.
This, of course, cannot be forgiven, and though he continues home quietly enough, his eyes fastened on his stepbrother's arm now draped lightly round the waist of the
daintily female cousin, he is all the while demanding revenge. He names the terms on the following morning, the
stepbrother agrees, and they use a chisel to pry open the
gun-case. Then, having gone so far, they gain courage to
force the lock of the small cabinet containing cherry
brandy. Thus fortified, and with loose shells jingling in
their pockets, they choose their positions—the stepbrother
behind the woodpile, the boy behind a large, lightning-
split oak. And then they begin to fire, plucking violent
clouds of wood into the air, while the female cousin shrieks

54   and shrills from a bedroom window. Then it is still—the duel seemingly finished, the two boys unhurt. Slowly they step from behind their fortresses, and the stepbrother grins with relief. The boy's face, however, is concentrated and grim, and he slowly raises the barrel of the rifle. "I'm littler but I'm smarter," he says. "I got one shot left, and you can take it standin' still or you can run for the house." The stepbrother spins, runs, and jerks to the ground with a bullet embedded in his calf.

That is not what I meant by a frontier mixture of ruthlessness and honor, however. To understand this, you must know that a few minutes later the boy is digging the misshapen lead from his stepbrother's leg with a penknife. The knife has been sterilized in a candle flame, and the wound is later cleaned with alcohol and poured full of iodine. The stepbrother never cries out and the boy never flinches, and afterward the two swear never to mention the episode to their parents. Neither ever does, and the female cousin is perhaps too frightened by this carnival of frontier justice ever to mention it herself.

None of this is visible in the photograph under consideration, or in any of the other photographs which will eventually be presented. Its potential is there, however, if we could but read this document closely enough. The rest is no doubt there, too—the women loved and unloved and the children legitimate and illegitimate, and the blending of coarseness and prudishness. The failures are foretold in the pinched lines at the corners of the mouth, and the bitterness of unfulfilled desire in the longing look of the eyes. It would be more difficult to foretell careers, but not hard to see that they will be many: singer, poolhall hustler, politician, policeman, insurance adjuster. His mind delights in numbers, and he will for a time pick up winning bets by racing an adding machine in calculating sums, but adding machines were slower then. Each career will leave

something unsatisfied in the searching eyes. So will each
wife, each child, each dog, each quarter. This will become
clearer when you see the other photographs, but it is all
there now. It is there, perhaps, even in the sweater. Its tight
waffle-knit is clearly machine-made, but the buttons seem
to be bone, so tightly stitched that the fabric puckers when
they are fastened. A placket approximately two inches
wide runs along the side that contains the button holes.
Only this side is visible, although there is surely an identical
placket on the side to which the buttons are so firmly
attached. The color of this sweater cannot be determined,
but is likely to be cream, pale grey, or powder blue. The
fact that such a sweater is worn tightly buttoned from
bottom to top may suggest that the photograph is taken in
winter, except that the knit itself seems not to be a very
heavy one. Also, the boy's face appears tanned. The appearance of a tan does not necessarily guarantee the actuality of a tan, for this may well result from a simple
discoloration of the photograph. It is, to be sure, not impossible that the boy is tanned, so that the photograph could
date from the summer of 1912 or 1913—or, perhaps, to the
autumn, which would better account for this sweater being
buttoned as it is, unless the sweater is buttoned at all only
to conceal a yet more decayed garment beneath. It would
be interesting to know the season. We can estimate the
time of day, because we know the boy sold an evening
newspaper. But it would be reassuring to know the year,
the month and day, the precise hour. These, however, are
among the things we cannot know. It is unlikely that the
Morton Photographic Parlours, even if they still existed,
would have an exact record of the date and time when this
photograph was taken.

We must therefore make do with what we have. What we
have is a photograph, approximately five by seven inches, of
a most alert-looking dog, with a young boy of perhaps eleven

56   or twelve years of age standing beside him. The boy wears a
checked cap, knickers, a tightly-buttoned sweater, and
suspenders which are not visible in the photograph. The
dog wears a handsome collar made of top-quality cowhide
and steel. Considering its age, the photograph is in excellent
condition, despite the faint, oval-shaped blot that resembles
the cancellation stamp on a discolored, undelivered letter.

TWO

By simply isolating a group of forms and textures within the arbitrary rectangular frame provided by the edges of its glass plate or film, a snap-shot forces us to see, and thereby teaches us to see, differently than we could have seen through our own unaided eyes, and also differently than people had been taught to see by pre-photographic pictorial conventions.

John A. Kouwenhoven, "Living in a Snapshot World"

THE CAMERA

SIZE: *4½ x 4¾ x 5¾ inches.*

LENS: *Achromatic meniscus.*

FOCAL LENGTH: *5 inches, f/18.*

SHUTTER: *Oscillating sector; self-cocking; instantaneous exposure only, fixed speed; release lever on right front of top of camera; arrow on shutter indicates direction to move lever.*

FINDER: *Waist-level, reflector; circular window; in upper front of camera body.*

BODY: *Wood, covered with simulated leather paper; inner box lifts out of outer box; black enamelled brass fittings, aluminium shutter blade; D-shaped "red window."*

LIST PRICE: *$7.00; with leather covering, $8.00.*

First introduced in 1892, the Bulls-Eye camera was the earliest simple, durable, and inexpensive roll-film box camera manufactured in the United States. It provided twelve exposures, 3½ x 3½ inches or 3½ inches in diameter, on roll film. The shutter was designed by Abner G. Tisdell, Brooklyn, New York (U.S. Patent No. 464,260, December 1, 1891). The camera was produced by the Boston Camera Manufacturing Company, Boston, Massachusetts.

The Bulls-Eye camera relied on, and introduced, transparent roll film backed with black paper numbered as to exposure position. These numbers could be read through a small window made of red celluloid, which prevented the film from being fogged. The earliest models of these cameras appear to have had the window in the shape of a D. Sometime around 1894, the window was changed to a circular one, and a lever to provide for time exposures was added. A variant model with detachable back and hinged sides appears to have been manufactured around that time. It also had a D-shaped red window. An "Ebonite" model Bulls-Eye (apparently made of thermoplastic) was produced as an alternate form in the years 1893–1894.

The red window and numbered film were such desirable features that the Eastman Kodak Company employed them under license in their Pocket Kodak of 1895. The popularity of this type of film was so great, that ultimately Kodak purchased outright the Boston Camera Manufacturing Company and all its patent rights as a preferable alternative to continuing to pay royalties. The Eastman Kodak Company subsequently introduced its own model of the Bulls-Eye, eventually labeling the 3½ x 3½ inch size the No. 2.

The Boston Camera Company had first produced the Hawkeye cameras, but their rights to these were sold to the Blair Camera Company of Boston, Massachusetts, early in 1890. Apparently, the right to use the name Boston Camera Company was also sold, because in 1892 production was resumed under the name Boston Camera Manufacturing Company. There is considerable evidence to support the claim that the Boston Camera Manufacturing Company never actually manufactured cameras. Some maintain that it was merely a marketing concern, and that all manufacturing was done by either the Blair Company of Boston or by the American Camera Manufacturing Company of Northboro, Massachusetts, Thomas H. Blair, Proprietor.

THE PHOTOGRAPHER

John Presley Jarvis, Caucasian male,
born January 1, 1878, in Tupelo, Mississippi,
to Bernetta Louise (née Williams)
  and William Presley Jarvis;
died July 8, 1970 in Clearwater, Arkansas.

It is simpler if we call him Uncle John, a name he earned
at an early age and carried throughout his life. His brothers, sisters, nephews, nieces, parishioners, barbers, distant
kin, next-of-kin, neighbors, insurance agent, and both his
wives called him Uncle John, so the precedent is ample.
As the youngest of sixteen children, all of whom lived to
adulthood, he was born an uncle to more than twenty
nephews and nieces, and so had the honorarium, as it were,
as his birthright. Throughout his childhood, the title was
used somewhat mockingly—though never without affection. At the age of nineteen, when his black hair turned
silver almost overnight, he seemed to look the part of uncle
with particular distinction. Of course, he had looked it
even as an infant—with his puckered old-man's face and
the sweet, all-forgiving light that shone in his eyes until
the last moments of his long life. He seemed a natural
peacemaker for the six other children who remained at
home, and in time even adults came to defer to his intuitive
fairness, and to a sense of justice far greater than his years
would indicate.

He learned quickly and without apparent effort, and was
the kind of boy praised for never giving anyone a moment's

62   trouble. His sturdy maturity as a child seems the more remarkable when we consider that his mother breast fed him until he was almost six years old, and gave it up only because he had to go to school then. The boy's father grumbled a good deal that the boy was not weaned earlier, and grumbled rather more loudly the first time he noticed that John's feet now touched the floor when he nursed. But he doted on this son of his middle years almost as outrageously as the mother doted on him, and no one had the heart to speak sternly to a woman of more than fifty who sought the last morsel of pleasure from her last, unexpected child. They all doted on him—the brothers and sisters and the ever-increasing ranks of nephews and nieces, as well as the aunts and uncles and cousins, but all their attentions failed to spoil his sweet, quiet ways. His favored position as last-born in the family ultimately had more advantages than candy and more clothes than he could wear and a new bicycle every year and a wonderfully varied assortment of playmates. John's father, about whom we otherwise know little, had a great respect for learning. He was a druggist who supplemented his modest income with a vegetable patch and a noisy coop of chickens, largely tended by his wife and children. The children ate well, and their bodies grew strong. They went to Sunday School at the First Methodist Church every Sunday, and eleven o'clock church when they were older, and Wednesday night prayer meeting, and Vacation Bible School every summer, and occasional revival meetings, and so their souls grew strong, too. To ensure the strength of their minds, they all attended school until at least the sixth grade, and if they showed real aptitude for book learning, they went on to high school. John, however, was the first to go to college. Born at the most choice position among the children, he not only found himself blessed with generous and attentive parents, but with brothers and sisters just as keen as his parents were to see to it that he had nothing but the best. And he fulfilled all their expectations. He graduated from the Tupelo High School as class salutatarian, and would have been valedictorian, as everyone knew, had he not missed sixth months of school in his senior year as a result of influenza, which turned to galloping pneumonia and almost killed him. It was the first, last, and only time he would ever be ill.

And so Uncle John went on to excel at the University of Mississippi in Oxford, and gave thorough satisfaction when he chose to continue his studies at the Methodist Seminary in Memphis, Tennessee. This all added up to something far larger than just being educated—something for which no one exactly had a name, but which nonetheless inspired awe. A distant relative on John's mother's side was rumored to be a college professor at Sophie Newcomb in New Orleans, but John's accomplishments came to outshine his, largely because they were nearer home. It would be interesting to have photographs of John's homecomings, especially of those first Christmas festivities when he came back from Oxford as an undergraduate. There would have been nothing Faulknerian in this, no buried guilt, incestuous longings, or historical impotence. The photograph would show a large group clustered before the mantel-piece—the men standing, the women sitting, children clustered on the floor, and an occasional infant held in an awkward, half-sitting position on its mother's lap. There might be a glimpse of a tinsel-edged Christmas tree in the right-hand corner of the photograph. We could recognize John at once, of course, because he would be tall and clear-eyed and grey-haired, and one of the few men wearing a celluloid collar and a four-in-hand tie. No doubt he would not be standing in the center of the photograph, as he was too modest to take up such a position, but he would still seem to be the center—partly because a number of heads would be turned to glance in his direction.

There may well be such a photograph in existence, though I have not seen it, and of course there would be more, for accomplishments such as John's are triumphantly photogenic. There would be one taken by the local photographer just before his graduation from high school—perhaps on that very morning, of John looking self-consciously smart in his first man's suit. He will, of course, be uncomfortably warm in it, for it is wool, with a tendency to feel like damp sandpaper in the crotch. Still, a winter suit recommends itself, because the university is in session in the winter, and a suit will occasionally be called for there. You must understand that while the young man is indulged, the family has too long struggled to keep body and soul together to give way to the gross impracticalities of a cream-colored linen suit and a panama hat. In this photograph, John stands very erect, and we should not make fun of the way his too-large collar stands away from his prominent Adam's apple. Note, instead, the light that seems to play about his eyes even in this dim old photograph. Other photographs must exist as well—of his graduation from Ole Miss and from the Seminary, and of course a particularly interesting one of his ordination, when he stands flanked by his mother and father, and with a black leather Bible in his hand. This one is also rather heartbreaking, for the mother's back is by now so bent by curvature of the spine that her head is scarcely higher than John's waist, and she has to distort both her neck and her face in the most painful way in order to look into the camera. Nonetheless, she is smiling. There is another photograph of John on his wedding day, standing with surprising solemnity beside a petite, brown-haired girl who looks no more than a child. In fact, she is over twenty, and already a schoolteacher. They will live together with improbable

happiness—their only sorrow the fact that they have no
children. Soon after she dies, at seventy, John remarries, but that is long into the future.

With a good map, a dependable car, and sufficient strength of purpose, we could locate a great many photographs of this man, for he was universally loved by his parishoners, and must often have been asked to pose with brides, with the aged, with newly-christened babies in dozens of small towns in Tennessee and Mississippi and Arkansas. The marvelous thing about these photographs is that even though we have not seen them, we can be perfectly at our ease in assuming that they exist. Indeed, we can focus a representative few in the mind's eye. There is one, for example, taken at a church picnic in Hernando, Mississippi, in 1917. It shows Uncle John sitting on a picnic table, the sort that has its own benches attached—a kind of clumsy but highly serviceable wooden pyramid. To his right, but lower down, sitting on the bench itself, is a girl wearing a large straw hat and a dress ornamented with a symphony of ruffles and furbelows. Her face is largely shadowed by the broad straw arc of her hat, and yet her eyes have a crossed look. Perhaps the dress is an attempt to distract us. Also on the bench, but to Uncle John's left, is a boy in uniform. The uniform looks silly now, as though the war being fought must have been some kind of game, and hardly a real war at all. From the photograph, we cannot know whether the boy was killed in action during the Battle of Verdun, taken prisoner at Amiens, or returned home without so much as a scratch. Indeed, we cannot even know if he went to Europe at all, or was one of those many soldiers to whom the news of victory came in a training camp near Fort Worth, Texas. Perhaps he and the girl have just announced their engagement—the boy eager to tether his childhood sweetheart before marching off to the man's work of war; perhaps they are total strangers. In the front of this photograph, and rather spoiling the symmetry of the three sitting on the picnic table, is the slightly blurred face of a small boy—blurred both by motion and by a streak of what appears to be chocolate on his face.

We would no doubt learn a good deal by scouting up these photographs and browsing through them. Of course, none of them exist so far as we know, and yet any of them might, and some of them surely do. They are, in any event, peripheral, since we are not interested in Uncle John as the subject of photographs, but as a photographer in his own right, although we welcome all information that focuses our vision of the photographer himself; understanding the photographer better, we have a stronger grasp of his handiwork. The matter can be particularly elusive when one is dealing with the amateur photographer, and it is certainly the amateur who is responsible for the discolored snapshot that follows. In fairness, it should be pointed out that Uncle John became rather more expert in his old age. There are two superb studies of dried thistles in satiny, cream-colored mounts, professionally framed, that hang now in his widow's lavender-scented bedroom. So finely etched is the detail and so lacy the shadows they cast, that they really should have been submitted to some photographic contest. The judges of the contest could not know, of course, that they are almost unique among Uncle John's photographs, in that they are not of people.

This is the kind of tantalizing question that presents itself in amateur photography. Why does the photographer concentrate on people, or on dogs, or on nature studies? An entire cycle of complex choices, preferences, passions, and prejudices must go into such decisions. Of course, there are rather indiscriminate photographers, often known as shutterbugs, who press the button simply because the camera is there and loaded, or to "finish off the roll." Uncle John, respecting thrift both as a necessity and a holy ob-

ligation, would hardly be a shutterbug, and so would be
one of those who choose. He chose people, and he chose
them as his subjects for the same reason that he elected the
ministry as his calling, because it was a way of expressing
the love and concern he felt for his fellow creatures. He
was neither noble nor particularly self-sacrificing, as those
terms are commonly understood, but he possessed a quality
of patient stillness often described as wisdom, which encouraged the afflicted to seek comfort in him; and he re-
warded them by hearing them patiently out. He was a good
listener, and photography for some is a listening with the
eye. Uncle John rarely made photographs for himself. He
made them of grandchildren in order to send them to distant grandparents; he made them of brides and grooms
to surprise them on some future anniversary; he made them
of his own family's gravestones in Tupelo and New Albany
as a record for future generations; and he sometimes made
them because the sheer making gave pleasure to subjects
who had too little pleasure in their lives. The photograph
we will soon consider is of the last sort.

Do we judge a photograph by the photographer's intention or by the technical perfection of his results? If we
judge by intent, then Uncle John's photographs are all
perfectly accomplished; if by result, we have to conclude
that the early work is badly flawed. Still, the apparatus he
used was a cheap one, even though lovingly given by his
parents on the occasion of his graduation from Ole Miss.
He took with it many photographs of his fellow seminar-
ians in Memphis—almost all of which he mailed to their
parents with Christmas greetings written on the back. He
and his new bride carried the already scuffed leatherette
case all the way to Fort Lauderdale on their honeymoon,
and he took many seaside snapshots of Ellen; she took
a few of him asleep in a striped canvas deck chair on the
hotel veranda, but most of them were overexposed. And

68   in the coming years, whenever they were assigned to a
new parish, the camera was packed up together with the
clothing and books and the bisque figurines of a shepherd
and shepherdess and the brass andirons with claw feet. Thus
it was transported from Holly Springs in Mississippi to
Cotter, Arkansas, to Whitehaven, Tennessee, and was still
packed up and moved long after Ellen had bought John a
new camera from Sears, complete with a light meter, which
he never troubled to use, and a glittering concave of flash
attachment that held bulbs fat as plums.

But it is with the older, more primitive camera that we
are concerned now, the one that made a wedding journey
to Fort Lauderdale. The year is 1914, and Uncle John and
Ellen have been in Tupelo, where John has christened his
youngest sister's twins, the same two who will eventually
be so popular on radio. It has, of course, been a grand
occasion, with Jarvis kin from three counties on hand, and
only Ellen, who keeps names and birthdates of all the
nephews and nieces and great-nephews and great-nieces in
a special little leather-bound book, can get all the names
right. It has been a time of high ceremony and the church
crammed full of vases containing more flowers than anyone
can remember, and also a time of anecdotes and back-
slapping, watermelon, great wedges of golden pound cake,
platters mountained with fried chicken, much wiping of
noses, much tying of sashes and shoelaces, and, naturally,
much taking of photographs. Uncle John alone shoots more
than six rolls, for this is a family reunion as well as a christening, and they don't all come together so often now that
the old ones have died. It is not, however, any of these
photographs which interest us, but the final photograph
which Uncle John took on the sixth roll. Only this one
oblong of film remained unexposed when he arrived at the
farm near New Albany, Mississippi, and his taking it rather

startled the little girl who was his subject, as she had never been photographed before.

The taking of this particular photograph came about in this way. One of Uncle John's older brothers seemed doomed to ill luck. Indeed, he was the only one of all the Jarvis sons who had not made a comfortable life for himself and his family. Slow in school, shy of strangers, he seemed to have a talent for not quite getting by, and yet he was too proud to accept the aid his family would gladly have offered. You will understand more about him when you see the photograph of his daughter, the little girl startled by Uncle John's camera. Hugh Jarvis went to the christening without his wife, who lay ill in the two-room shot-gun house that for months now had reeked with her festering illness. He also didn't bring "the little cusses," as he called his four children, suggesting by his tone that it would not have been manly to take charge of them on such a journey. Everyone recognized this as bluff, for Hugh Jarvis loved these children with an almost insane devotion, and with his wife ill they were, after all, always in his charge. No, he had not brought them because he had had to hitchhike to Tupelo, and perhaps, too, because he would have been ashamed for them to be seen without shoes. Uncle John and Ellen understood this very well, and when the christening and reunioning and eating festivities were all over, they offered to drive Hugh home, seeking to blunt his pride by telling him he could walk for all they cared but they were going to see Cora after all, and he could come along for the ride unless he objected to the company. But sometime that night, while the others slept, Hugh Jarvis slipped away, hitched a ride on the highway, and was working in his own parched fields by the first light of dawn. And so Uncle John and Ellen drove alone to the farm a mile outside New Albany, and fifteen minutes later

70 Uncle John took this snapshot of the little girl, just before she turned to run across the fields shouting "Papa! Papa! Boyce! Frank!" The following Christmas he sent it to Hugh and his wife in a Christmas card imported from Japan, with snow glittering on the rooftops of a Bavarian village. The card was far more highly prized than the photograph, except by the little girl. The faded, dog-eared snapshot was found among her papers when she died.

THE PHOTOGRAPH

A realist would no doubt have disposed of this particular photograph years ago, along with the solitary cuff link, out-of-date business cards, laundry receipts, postcards from shipboard friends, expired passports, cancelled checks, and furled sheets of Christmas seals that nest together in the back of the second bureau drawer. It has, indeed, only the faintest, most tenuous voice with which to plead for clemency. Despite its mellow sepia tones, it lacks the obvious charm of the picturesque, and its sociological value is, at best, marginal. The photograph forms a square three and one-half by three and one-half inches, so that even its size is insignificant. There is no place for it, smartly cased in an antique, cut-velvet frame, on the walnut Parsons table that holds the spray of coral, the imitation Fabergé eggs, and the paperweights brought back from Venice last summer. Yet even the realist might agree to preserve this chip of glazed paper if it were the only photograph of this particular subject in existence. It is not. Others exist in a score of albums, in the dusty storage bins of newspaper morgues, in photographer's files, in magazines, for the subject was once much sought-after as a photographer's model. With so many cleverly side-lighted, expertly coiffed, expensively tailored poses to choose from, a decayed snapshot of such poor quality seems trivial. Only the sentimentalist would have preserved it.

The photograph shows a small girl, perhaps four years of age, standing on a dusty, barren strip of earth that fills the foreground of the picture. Behind her one sees cultivated fields, and beyond them a wood. In the distance, on the border between the field and the trees, stands a simple, square, wooden house. The picture thus composes itself into four bands. Reading from the top, there is a cloudless sky, then a ragged line of trees, the planted fields, and the dusty earth. It is the last of these that tells us most, and not merely because it forms the foreground. The earth is pale, as though stripped of all nurture, and its surface is powdered into a fine, choking dust. When children work their bare toes into it, it sifts between them in warm, quick caress, and when they run, it springs into the air as though they splash through shallow water. The dust coats the plants in the field, dulls the trees in the distance, sifts through invisible cracks in doorjambs, window frames, planking and floorboards, and discreetly powders every corner, every object in the house. It leaks through dampened cloths to garnish the side-meat, film the milk, and clog the saltshaker. It commingles with flour and baking soda, dulls the surface of the blackstrap molasses, nestles in the corn-shuck mattresses, sheathes the black cast-iron stove. The father, in his wry wisdom, tells his family, "Man must eat a peck of dirt before he dies."

From this barren strip of earth at the bottom of the photograph, a few weeds spring in an irregular line that suggests water may collect here when it rains. Standing perhaps six feet away from this ragged, tentative patch of green, her hands clasped before her, is a small girl, wearing a shapeless dress that reaches to below her shins. Its slack, graceless lines suggest it was sewn from flour-sacking, and it appears to have no buttons or other fastenings. There may, to be sure, be buttons on the back of the dress, invisible in this photograph. There are three of them, all in silvery mother-of-pearl, the last survivors of the crisp regiment that once marched in orderly file down the front of the wedding dress worn by the girl's mother more than a decade before. Or the dress may simply be pulled on and off over the head, without benefit of button, snap, or hook. In fact, something about the tentlike drape of the dress suggests that kind of expediency. The sleeves extend almost to the wrist, and a glimpse of the child's arms suggests the

dress was made the previous year, and she has since grown
slightly taller. But obviously the ample folds of material
would accommodate more years of growing, except that
long before that time its coarse fabric will have frayed and
torn, and will serve better for applying lamp-black to the
stove.

The girl's hair seems theatrically pale in color, the delicate white-gold known in the South as "cotton-top." It will
darken with time, of course, but as she becomes a young
woman it will, in combination with blue eyes that shade
toward violet, memorably dramatize her classic beauty.
Later still, chemistry will restore some of this pale luster,
and her hair will remain her pride. Indeed, when her head
is shaved for surgery, she clutches the two dense blonde
braids in her hands, seizes them so rigidly that even the
anaesthesia will not loosen her grip. This, of course, is not
visible in the present photograph, where the hair, cut bluntly
into the shape of a mixing-bowl, forms a bright corona.
Otherwise, we get little physical impression of the child.
Her face and neck are shadowed; only the nose and cheeks
are really visible, brushed by stripes of sunlight. Hands and
wrists, bare feet, ankles, the lower part of the legs tell us
only that despite the impression of dirt-grubbing poverty
that the photograph conveys, the child seems well-fed and
healthily plump. There will, of course, be inevitable bouts
of ringworm, an attack of pellagra, a rage of impetigo, and
the more common cycles of measles and chicken pox,
mumps and whooping cough, but no serious illness will
trouble her for a full half-century. Coughs and colds are
treated with brimming tablespoons of kerosene and sugar;
merthiolate bronzes cuts and scratches and raw mosquito
bites; tic salve eases skin infections; and warm mustard
packs on the chest remedy a vast spectrum of physical and
spiritual ailments. There is, in short, nothing exceptional
about the child who stands in the foreground of the photo-

graph. She is a reasonably healthy, well-fed, ill-clad, normally developed female Caucasian of four or five years of age. From what we can see of hands and arms, feet and legs, her skin seems deeply tanned by the sun, though this may be an effect of the faded sepia tint of the paper. Something about the way the child's hands are clasped before her suggests shyness and hesitation, but perhaps she feels awkward about being photographed for the first time. Indeed, despite her brief but intensive career as a photographer's model, she will never entirely lose this awkwardness.

She is also, of course, rather astonished by the newcomer, for though she vaguely remembers having seen him before, visitors to the isolated dirt farm are few, and always, for her, a fresh astonishment. She cannot remember his name, and later has to be prompted to greet him as "Uncle John," but there is something familiar about this tall, lean man. Perhaps it is the thick shock of gleaming silver hair, which he habitually but unsuccessfully flattens with gliding palms into correct ministerial tidiness. She is struggling to carry a metal basin filled with food across the dusty yard when his Model T comes champing and clanging along the rutted farm road from the highway. Every muscle tautens and bows against the weight of the metal pan. Her body reaches back for the tug of gravity to balance her against the fierce downward pull of the load she carries, and her feet shuffle drunkenly in the dust as she seeks to aim herself in a straight line across the farmyard and into the field. And then, behind her, she hears the complaining engine, and tries to look over her shoulder, but turning disturbs the harmonies of parabola, of weight and counterweight, so that she stumbles. For a moment, the pan threatens to pitch from her hands, but she finds a teetering balance, leans forward, and sets the pan in the dust. Then she turns and sees the car stop in the rectangle of shadow beside the house. A tall man steps—or, rather, seems to unfold himself—from behind the steering wheel. He waves to her and shouts, "Hi, Kay!" She feels she knows him, though the woman who steps from the car to join him is a stranger. Clutching his arm, leaning against him in a dress of flowing blue panels, the woman seems like a flower. The girl takes a few steps forward and stops. The man raises a camera slung around his neck on a leatherette strap, focuses, and clicks the shutter. A dark red rooster, which saunters by just as the shutter opens, appears in the lower right-hand corner of the photograph. Perhaps the girl has not understood the man's actions at all. She has almost certainly never seen a camera, though she is well acquainted with photographs. There are two pinned to the wall beside her mother's mirror. One shows her parents on their wedding day. The father's Adam's apple protrudes dangerously over a high, knife-edged celluloid collar, and the mother looks like a doll in her lacy dress. One can see here the high, strong cheekbones the girl will inherit, together with the long, finely-modeled nose that completes her Indian heritage. Also pinned beside the mirror is a photograph of the girl's two older brothers, both wearing brittlely starched cotton dresses. The dresses, edged with fine eyelet ruffles, are beautifully sewn, and were later worn by the two sisters. They date, of course, from the time when the father was employed as supervisor in the broom factory in New Albany and purchases were made in cash, not as debit entries against the next year's failing cotton crop.

No sooner is the photograph made than the girl turns and runs through the field shouting, "Papa! Papa! Boyce! Frank!" The dishpan filled with boiled greens, cornbread, and chunks of fatty side-meat is forgotten for the moment. The rooster will peck his way toward it, nibble at the bread, and then be shooed away by the mother, who has come down the three sloped steps of the house, alternately smoothing her sleep-wrinkled dress and apologetically fingering the loosened coils of her hair. The girl shouts in excitement and perhaps, too, in fear. The men must, in any case, be informed of these newcomers. The girl holds her father's hand as he strides across the parched cotton rows. The two boys race ahead.

Everything about the photograph suggests it was taken in midsummer. The weeds in the foreground might signal spring, when there is enough water to coax weeds out of the packed dirt of the farmyard, but the margin of trees on the horizon, like the fields that lie between, suggest midsummer growth. The cotton plants are nearly waist-high, and occasional white flecks signal that some of the bolls have cracked into bloom—in which case the photograph must date from late summer, from August or even September. But the white dots may simply be flaws in the surface of the photograph itself. The fields begin a few yards behind the girl and extend to the woods. With a single exception, they seem to be uniformly planted with cotton. The exception is a rectangular area of green on the near side of this field. Here the plants are considerably taller, and the foliage more dense. These are certainly bean plants, set together in tight, orderly rows, and supported by warped, weather-silvered poles, round which they have braided themselves. The height and thickness of these plants also suggest that the photograph was taken in mid or in late summer. It therefore seems possible to agree that the photograph was made shortly before noon on the 25th of August, 1919, three weeks after the little girl's fifth birthday. Midday is clearly enough established. First, the shadow of her basin-shaped hair falls directly onto the child's face and neck, while the crown is brightly haloed by the sun. Shadow from her flour-sack dress falls over her legs and stains a perfect circle on the dust.

If further evidence of time were required, the vessel on the ground to the left of the girl and a few feet behind her would provide it. This is, to be more precise, a dishpan, **77** a round metal vessel that might, however, also be used for washing small quantities of clothes, for carrying chicken feed, or for catching water that leaks through the roof. It has a grey and white enameled surface in a mottled or tortoise-shell pattern, and is available in several sizes from Sears, Roebuck, and Company. Each day, shortly before noon, the little girl carries it to the field, filled with turnip or collard greens and chunks of freshly-baked cornbread. Sometimes there are chunks of beef or pork mixed in with the greens, to flavor them. It requires a unique concentration to transport the pan down the uneven stairs of the house, across the dusty yard, and over the corrugated field to the brothers and the father who wait there for their midday meal. And then she makes a second trip, with two Knox fruit jars filled with cool well water. When they have finished their meal, the girl places the fruit jars and tin spoons in the pan and returns to the house. Now, of course, the journey is easier. Within a few years, the girl's younger sister will help her in this task of feeding the men, and they even devise from an old orange crate a kind of transport train that can be drawn with a rope, but it tends to lodge against clods of earth and capsize on the furrows. Ultimately, only Margaret will be concerned with these deliveries, for Kay will tend to the cooking, will struggle to keep a spark of flame alive within the sooty carcass of the wood-burning stove, while her mother calls faint phrases of encouragement through the doorway of the adjoining room. And during those long days, the odor of rotting flesh will do steady battle with the acrid stench of boiling greens.

These are, to be sure, later developments, which no one could have foretold simply by looking at this particular photograph. Indeed, when the family received the photograph, together with a Christmas card, the following December, they promptly pinned it up beside the photographs of the bride and groom and Frank and Boyce. They would never have done so had they thought that coiled within its dense chemistries there lay such tales of decay and death, or of deprivation, unfulfilled yearning, shorn braids, lungs that flooded with the body's own waters, sex that was a loathed ritual submission, and millionaire courtiers who disappeared on the wings of private planes into the empires of society and wealth. No, they scarcely even saw it as a photograph of a particular person—for, indeed, little of the girl was visible there—but as a souvenir of Uncle John's surprise visit with his young bride.

Several details of the photograph could use further clarification. In the middle distance, silhouetted by the trees, stands a wooden structure of some kind. It can hardly be the house of a neighbor, because the cotton fields seem to border it so tightly, and any such house must have its unplanted yard where children and chickens can scratch in the earth, and clothes can be boiled in a cast-iron pot over an open fire. The building may, of course, simply be abandoned, and serve now only as a hideaway for the children, particularly mysterious and exciting on dark, rainy afternoons. In this case, the windows have been removed, as well as occasional planking from the walls needed by neighbors for repairs to their own houses. Or it is perhaps a cotton-house, located within the field as a convenient, central place for emptying out the long, snake-like cotton sacks that men, women, and children drag between the rows at harvest time. The fingers pluck deep into the bolls to bring away the entire mass of seed and silken fiber, but when they reach to the curved depth of the dried, burst blossom, the pointed edges of the boll score the hand, drawing fine incisions along the fingers. Yet the fingertips are not sufficiently sensitive to the elusive fibers if one wears gloves. Hence, hands soon look as though they have

been mauled by kittens, but the smarting is less painful than
the deep wrenching at the shoulder as the long sack slowly
fills with cotton and drags against the earth. The weight
is far greater if there has been a recent rain or a heavy dew
(an advantage only when one is picking for someone else
and is paid by weight). The full sacks are emptied into the
cotton-house, from there to be hauled by wagon to the
cotton gin in New Albany, where the fibers are trussed
and bagged, pressed and banded into symmetry.

The second somewhat obscure detail in the photograph
is a board that seems almost to float in air behind the girl's
right shoulder. This is, of course, only an illusion, aggravated by the deceptively flat plane of the photograph itself.
Though distances and perspectives are difficult to judge,
the board would appear to be more than six feet in length;
one end must rest on the earth, though weeds rather obscure this fact, and it leans to the left at a mathematically
precise angle of forty-five degrees. The apparent levitation
of this board is not the only thing that lends it mystery.
It is a straight, sizable, entire length of lumber, and surely
it would not be wasted. Perhaps it is there for some necessary repair to the porch of the house, or to the roof of the
cotton-house. But in that case, why is it propped or suspended at this absurd angle in front of the bean field?
Given this single detail, the average viewer of the photograph would no doubt be beggared for narrative. Is this
some primitive soothsaying, water-divining, devil-deterring
device? Is it an act of homage, and if so, to whom? Is it
a trick devised by Frank and Boyce? Is it the beginning
of a playhouse for the girls, a chicken coop, a rabbit hutch,
a unique species of lightning rod? It might be any or all
of these things, but only when read out of context. The
function of the board is revealed when we consider the
other unexplained detail in the photograph—a square of
fabric visible, or partly visible, on the right-hand margin

of the photograph. The exact construction and function of this object is not at all clear. It is at least four feet in length, but it has possibly been doubled over, so it could be much larger. In the photograph one can see a width of only two or three feet, but obviously the object extends beyond the edge of the photograph. It could be a tablecloth, a bedspread, a braided cotton rug, or a panel of drapery. This object, too, seems to float in space, without obvious support, but unlike the board, whose foot is concealed by weeds, we see the entire, unobscured, unsupported bottom edge of the fabric. It hangs suspended from a clothesline—a strand of baling wire that is fastened, on the left, to the mysterious board. To the right, perhaps, it is attached to a tree or a post that has been fixed into the ground, whereas the board on the left is held in place by tension, friction, counterbalance; indeed, the principle is not so different from that used by the little girl to carry the heavy pan laden with dinner for the men.

It is reassuring that some of the mysteries can be solved so neatly. Others yield less gracefully to analysis—if they can be said to yield at all. Are there, for example, shadows on the earth near the bottom border of the photograph, or does one merely see a certain mottling of the surface here? If these are shadows, then obviously a tree stands just out of range of the camera. It would be the tree in which Kay and Margaret built a makeshift playhouse and where Kay so often read when she was not cooking, scrubbing, mending, and nursing the fire in the stove. So far as I know, no photograph of this tree exists. And what of the rooster in the foreground, the upper half of his body visible, his head turned away to look toward the bean patch? Is this the pet rooster the little girl was given for Easter? Did he die a respectable death from revered old age, or did he find an early grave in the family soup pot? Is there an article of some kind lying on the ground beneath the clothes-

line, perhaps an apron blown off by the wind, or is this
only a scratch on the surface of the photograph? And
perhaps the little girl's hands are not clutched before her
out of shyness, but because she is concealing something. In
that case, what would this be? The mysteries proliferate.
Why was she given the name Dorothy Kathlyn? What was
the first word she pronounced? What was the first word
she read without assistance? What did she think when the
bed-frame trembled with the older brothers' vigorous
nightly masturbating? Did she later envy her younger
sister's sudden wealth? How many men did she love in her
fifty-seven years? Was she a virgin when she married
James?

Even if the photograph under consideration was larger,
sharper in focus, more suggestive in details, most of these
questions would remain unanswered. The sentimentalist
can treasure this small, tattered scrap of paper, but he cannot hope to decipher all its complex hieroglyphs. Even
when it was new, the picture would have been undistinguished. Its composition is acceptable, though the dark blot
of the rooster in the foreground slightly spoils the symmetry. But the picture is indifferently focused, and the photographer should have stood nearer his subject, who is
ruthlessly diminished by parched earth, sky, fields, and
woods. The effect is to stress a helpless, waif-like quality,
which may not have been her character at all. Yet this
prompts the viewer's protective instincts. As in newsphotos
of refugee children, there is something winsome and vulnerable about this small figure. Draped as she is in a baggy
flour-sack dress or smock, it is not even easy to determine
the child's sex. There is no trace here of the graceful femininity she will later display, or of her gently mothering
instincts. Those instincts would, of course, be amply expressed when, at the age of twelve, she took over the care
of the family, but there should be some trace of them

82   even now. Perhaps if we could see her move, could see the look of total concentration as she balances the pan containing the men's noonday meal, this would all be more clear. But we are left only with this tattered shadow of that reality. The photograph is clouded and discolored. The corners are all damaged, and indeed, the lower left-hand corner has been torn away. In another half-century, the image itself will almost certainly have become unreadable. Even now one makes out only the broadest details—a wood, a field, the dusty earth, beans spiraling around silvered poles, a flowered tablecloth hanging out to dry, an Easter chick now grown to strutting cockhood, an enameled pan, a clump of weeds, a little girl with golden hair who wears a dress made from flour-sacking and stands with her hands clasped before her. Sunlight gleams in her hair, and as the camera is raised and pointed toward her, her breath catches in wonder.

THREE

From today, painting is dead!

Paul Delaroche

℮   ℮

While we give it credit only for depicting the merest surface, the photograph actually brings out the secret character with a truth that no painter could venture upon, even if he could detect it.

Nathaniel Hawthorne, *The House of the Seven Gables*

THE CAMERA

SIZE: *6½ x 8¾ x 9½ inches.*
LENS: *Lachenal Opticien, Paris, France; length 60 mm.,*
f/3.5.
SHUTTER: *Flap-type, in front of lens; T only; front section*
of camera box hinges upward to uncover lens.
FINDER: *Viewing on ground-glass focusing screen.*
BODY: *Finished wood; brass fittings; upper and lower sec-*
tions joined by rack and pinion; upper section divided
into 4 segments, lower section consists of 3 compart-
ments.

This collapsible bellows-type camera with attached developing section was manufactured by J. Valette, Paris, in
1873. It is designed for single exposures, 13 x 18 cm., on
wet-collodion plates. This camera, which received honor-
able mention at the Paris Exposition of 1872, is a self-
contained photographic unit, with developing materials
contained within the camera.

The upper portion of the camera is divided into four
sections. The first serves to cover and protect the lens, to
cover the front compartment of the lower section, and,
in addition, could also serve as a shutter. It was hinged at
the top and swung upward. The second section housed the
lens-board and acted as a point of attachment for the front
of the bellows and front cover. It employed a rack and
pinion for the focusing process and was coupled to the
third section during the process of development. The third
section served for the rear attachment of the bellows, had

86 rack-and-pinion motion, and moved the plate-holding section, which was attached to it.

The rear section held the focusing screen and contained the plate during exposure; the latter was housed in a metal frame suspended by a string. When a sliding panel in the bottom of the rear section was opened, the frame and plate could be lowered into the rear compartment of the bottom half of the camera. Within this compartment were four hard-rubber "baths," narrow, deep trays which contained the solutions for the process. Labels on the outside of the lower box indicated the contents of the baths: *Argent* (silver nitrate), *Pyrogallique* (pyrogallic acid), *Eau* (water), and *Cyanide* (potassium cyanide). The labels also served as a register for positioning the upper section holding the plate. The lower center section had grooves for holding six clear-glass plates, and the front section served for storage during transportation of the necessary chemicals in bottles.

The camera was first mounted on a stand or tripod, and the image brought into focus. Collodion was poured on glass plates from the storage compartment which were then placed in the plate rack. The plate, now light-proof in its housing, was lowered into the light-sensitive silver nitrate, raised into position again, and exposed. Racking the camera forward allowed the plate to be successively immersed in pyrogallic acid (the developer), water (the wash) and cyanide (the fixative). It could then be air-dried and set aside for printing at some later time.

THE PHOTOGRAPHER

Martha Mary Tupelo Pearl Independence Day
* McBryde Jackson,*
Negro female, born July 4, 1870, near Natchez, Mississippi,
to Sally and Sam Jackson;
died August 29, 1947, in Detroit, Michigan.

Her mother took to bed at six o'clock in the afternoon to
recover from Fourth of July feasting, from a happy over-
dose of hog maw, barbecued ribs, sweet corn roasted in the
shucks, and massive slabs of seed-speckled watermelon.
When the cramps grew worse, she prayed aloud in a rhythmic dirge whose only intelligible words were "Oh, Lawd.
Oh Lawd. Olawdolawdolawd—" Pressing the leathery
palms of work-worn hands against her belly seemed to help.
Sweat washed her body, stung her eyes, and she thought
she saw Death perched on the rocking chair beside the
cast-iron cook stove. He hunched his shoulders and glared
at her, ran his tongue over meaty lips, then sprang on bat
wings to rest on the kindling piled by the stove. "Ah'm
dyin'," she cried. "Ah' is daid!" Her husband bolted from
the room, overturning the straw-bottomed chair he had been
dozing in, and all the way to the kitchen door of the big
house he cried out, "Miz Henrietta! Miz Henrietta!" The
woman felt something ease, a sudden slackening of pressure
like a knotted fist unclenching, and she pressed her hands
harder against her stomach, raised her knees to ease the
cramps in her legs, and felt water flow out of her to soak
into the corn-shuck mattress. When Sam returned with

Henrietta McBryde, the woman was sitting up in bed, staring at the tiny infant that writhed in contortionist ballet against the flour-sack covering of the mattress.

The plantation records, though otherwise meticulously detailed, showed only that Sally and Sam had been purchased in 1838, in New Orleans, and that they were then teenagers. Thus, at the time their first and only child was born, both would have been over fifty, and long resigned to childlessness. There were always so many children to care for, both black and white, that it hardly mattered, and if Sally had ever yearned for a child of her own to press against her immense black bosom, it was a well-kept secret. Both Sam and Sally had long since settled into the comfortable roles of honorary aunt and uncle, honorary grandparents, guardians and custodians of all small children, black and white, with a hunger for molasses candy, or the desire to learn how to sit perfectly still at the edge of the pond watching a wooden twig looped to a fishing line. Sally, furthermore, had rocked, diapered, fed, walked, dressed, amused, chided, and praised two generations of McBryde children, yet she could scarcely hold her own child in her arms, so great was her fear that she would drop it. Often she sat up throughout the night, watching the baby sleep in the same padded wicker crib in which her white charges had slept, always fearful that the baby would stop breathing. Once or twice a week, she stood in the darkened kitchen of the big house, shouting for Henrietta in terror, urging her mistress with trembling hands down the steep wooden steps of the house and along the smooth dirt path to the cabin where the baby lay deeply sleeping, no longer grimacing from the pains of gas.

It was thus partly in order to guarantee herself an uninterrupted night's sleep that Henrietta took Pearl to the big house when she was only a few months old. Sally came to care for her daughter by day, as she had for the white

children, and occasionally she took her home, holding the **89**
child awkwardly on her lap while she rocked on the front
stoop of the cabin and nodded distracted greetings to the
neighbors. Later, of course, she could easily have taken
the child away from the big house and brought her to
sleep in the bed that Sam had built for her near the stove.
But Henrietta McBryde, her husband dead and her sons
all grown to manhood, had clearly become dependent on
the child's presence. Perhaps, out of some well-tutored,
well-tempered desire to please her white employers, and
perhaps because she sensed there were advantages for the
child, Sally never saw fit to alter the arrangement. In time
Henrietta McBryde taught the girl to read and write,
recited for her the great stories of the Bible, and told her
the Latin names of all the flowers in the garden. Pearl
visited her parents every day, and she showed them the
same clinging affection that other small children showed
them, but for her as for the others, they were Aunt Sally
and Uncle Sam. She would never think of the two simple
old people as parents. When Sally died, Pearl was fifteen,
and an aging Henrietta was totally dependent on her for
shopping, cooking, and general housekeeping. Her eldest
son had married one of the Heiskell girls in Natchez, and
the wife insisted they settle in town. The next son had
joined his uncle's bank in Greenwood, and was now vice-
president. The third remained at home, more than capable
of running the farm, but lacking a wife, he of course left
the house to his mother's charge, and her fingers were
already knobbed and swollen with arthritis. Her still quick
mind made the decisions, but Pearl's hands translated them
into action.

In order to keep the record clear and accurate, we should
note that Pearl's father died in the winter of 1901, and
Henrietta McBryde the following spring. Henrietta's
youngest son, Robert, presumed that Pearl would continue

to manage the household, and no doubt she assumed the same. She had known no other life, even in dreams, and would no more have thought of leaving the plantation to seek employment elsewhere than her parents had thought of leaving their two-room shotgun house when President Lincoln set them free. Nor did the situation change when Robert, now past forty, courted, became engaged to, and married (all in the course of three months) an art teacher at the Seminary for Women in Jackson. Accustomed to servants, Victoria McBryde had no desire to assume more household responsibility than necessary, though she re-decorated the larger parlor (once used only for weddings, anniversaries, and laying-outs) with yellow silk curtains, aquatints of Roman antiquities, gilded wall sconces, and a new velours love seat and chairs.

In the small room adjoining her bedroom, which Hen-rietta McBryde had used for sewing, Victoria installed her atelier, where she painted wonderfully lifelike violets and narcissuses and sprays of crepe-myrtle on bone-china plates and made dainty watercolors of pastoral scenes with pic-turesque ruins in them. Although it eventually became Victoria's favorite toy, it was actually Robert who bought the camera, from a cousin who had brought it back from New York and quickly tired of it. Robert photographed all the cousins, uncles and aunts, nephews and nieces, and all the black servants, but then his interest waned for lack of sitters. When he was at work, Victoria fluttered help-lessly, her mouth curved into a dainty bow of incompre-hension and wonder at his mysterious masculine compe-tence. But she learned from him, and when the camera had sat idle for some months on its wooden tower, she began her own first experiments. In all of them, Pearl was her able assistant, for she too had watched, and like so many of her race had learned the skills of her white employers even while maintaining the useful image of naive, unquestioning

simplicity. It was, for example, Pearl who held the pink
silk parasol, somewhat tattered but still an adequate filter
for the light, when Victoria made her remarkable studies
of dead crickets and grasshoppers, as it was Pearl who collected the insects and stoppered them into vials and later
laid their brittle bodies out on the velvet cushion. One
loses, of course, much detail in these studies, so that a
casual observer might think the cushion itself the photographer's real subject, but the studies of cut and withered
flowers are another matter entirely—wonderfully composed and artfully focused. Nor did Victoria ever falter
for lack of subjects. She photographed all the shoes on the
plantation, and then sent Pearl to collect more from the
neighboring farms. She also photographed moulding biscuits, decaying apples, baskets of pecans and persimmons,
spilled milk, litters of kittens, interesting stones, neatly
ordered ranks of hoe and axe and hammer handles, buttons,
false hairpieces, the chewed stubs of cigars, snuff tins, and
fried eggs. The total oeuvre constitutes a remarkable folk
art collection, the more remarkable when we contemplate
the daintily refined, china-painting woman responsible for
these bold compositions. If the proper judicious selection
were made, one might indeed arrange the works into a
superb exhibition. Unfortunately, few of the original
photographs have survived, and most of these are too badly
mildewed for one to appreciate their more subtle details.
When Victoria died in childbirth in 1912 and Robert
decided to sell the plantation, the original plates were sold
at auction, in a lot that contained old trunks, a miscellany
of unmatched glasses, a slightly mildewed edition of the
works of Sir Walter Scott, a few kitchen utensils, and a
half-dozen worn patchwork quilts. The photographic plates
had been packed into one of the trunks by the auctioneer's
assistant, and the buyer of the trunk did not suspect they
were there. Nor, when he opened the trunk, did he know

what they were, but thinking they might eventually have some value, he stored them away in his attic. Since the attic is marvelously dry, they are perhaps still in good enough condition to recreate Victoria's handiwork.

In the days preceding the auction, Pearl was as helpful as ever. She stacked, arranged, sorted, bundled, boxed, crated, threw away, mended and tied and organized, and generally made herself useful to Robert. He never doubted that usefulness would continue through his widower days in Jackson: Pearl would keep house for him as she had for his mother and his wife, and perhaps Pearl thought so too during these hectic days of dismantling. But her vague plan must have been forming even then, for certainly she was prompt in bidding ten dollars and then fifteen dollars for the camera and its unexposed glass plates. The bidding stopped at seventeen dollars and fifty cents and the camera was hers; it had taken a substantial part of the savings accumulated from carefully horded, handkerchief-tied nickels and dimes—all, that is, that she had not spent on candy, imitation pearls (because of her name), and other country-store treats. Touched by what he took to be a sentimental attachment to his wife's favorite toy, Robert returned the seventeen dollars and fifty cents to her when the auction was over. Furthermore, he was pleased, even relieved, when she asked him for the goat-cart, restored and brightly lacquered for the dead infant who would never be carried with whoops of laughter round the plantation. He couldn't have put it up for auction, yet he could not imagine taking it to Jackson to rust unused in the cellar, or giving it to his brother for children not his own to play with. The goat, General Lee, was already Pearl's by right of patient feeding and protecting when the mother stubbornly refused to recognize the kid as her own. Yet even when Robert saw her hitching the goat to the cart, he must have thought she only intended to entertain the local children. The servants would all remain, or could remain if they chose: this much was assured them by the new owner. But Robert never imagined that Pearl would do anything but dutifully follow him to Jackson, continuing to weave the invariable pattern of her life in baking and cleaning and washing and ironing. At what point, I wonder, did he realize her new plan? He sat on the sloping steps that led to the kitchen and watched her, a few hundred feet away, as she loaded cans of peaches and sardines, fruit jars filled with molasses and others with water into the goat-cart. She moved slowly, determining the best niche for each new addition, studying the load to be certain it balanced properly. Then she brought out the camera, hoisting it carefully into the front of the little carriage, the box of unexposed plates, the black velvet drape snugly fitted in beside it. Across them she laid the collapsed legs of the tripod, then turned and entered the cabin again. When she reappeared a few minutes later, she was wearing her best Sunday dress and a pair of high-topped kid shoes that had once belonged to Henrietta. Snugged tightly onto her head was a broadbrimmed straw hat of the kind her own mother had once worn when working in the fields. She set down a small cardboard suitcase and turned to close the door, giving an extra tug so that the latch clicked solidly into place. Her suitcase stowed on top of the load, she led General Lee to the porch steps, pausing there to look into Robert's eyes as she might have looked into those of a beloved but somewhat feeble-minded, and hence irresponsible, child of her own. "Don't forget to take you tonic," she said.

Thus her adventure began. She called it "seeing the world," though in the first two years she covered scarcely more than a hundred miles. Sometimes she would linger for a month or two in a small town or in a cluster of share-croppers' cottages. In exchange for her keep, she read wonderfully from the Bible, and she made photographs for ten cents or twenty cents or whatever a Negro family could spare—at least until she realized the cost of her materials and raised the prices to twenty-five ("for them as hasn't") and fifty cents ("for them as has"). She shared her clear, strong voice with the congregations of a score of country churches, she bought tough man's brogans for walking and a tarpaulin to cover the cart, and a smaller version of her own straw hat for General Lee, with holes cut in it for his ears. She helped deliver babies and nurse the sick, cooked cornbread and wonderfully light, flaky biscuits, learned the names of hundreds of children in the area, and tirelessly explained that she was not looking for a runaway husband but had set out to see the world before she grew roots from standing still too long. When she departed, she always thanked her hosts for their Christian charity. For most of the winter of 1914–1915 she was in Jackson, staying with a Pentecostal minister and his wife, but it never occurred to her to visit Robert. For the following five years, she wandered through northern Mississippi, and even spent a few months in Alabama. In 1920 she arrived in Memphis, where she became such a fixture on Beale Street that the *Commercial Appeal* ran a two-page feature on her in the Sunday supplement. Even shy Southern white women in immaculate gloves brought their children to be photographed sitting in the cart behind a stoically patient General Lee. Partly in deference to his age, partly because the fat she carried in increasing rolls and mounds and hummocks made walking so tiring, Pearl was most often found at a semi-permanent station on Beale Street, the goat-cart "parked" by the curb across from what is now W.C. Handy Park. But occasionally the old wanderlust nudged her, and she would be on her way again, exploring the northern and eastern reaches of the city, or even crossing the bridge to West Memphis in Arkansas. She was on such an expedition in the summer of 1922,

approximately three miles from her usual Beale Street post,
when the following photograph was taken.

North Manassas Street cuts through a neighborhood
that has begun the slow but inevitable tilt toward poverty.
Handsome turn-of-the-century houses, squat and stout as
Dutch burghers, are separated from the sidewalks by the
briefest hint of front lawn, to leave space in the rear for
kitchen gardens, an apple tree, a makeshift tool or coal-
shed. Most of the front lawns are now trampled into dusty
anonymity by children's feet, though an occasional hardy
strand of Bermuda grass fissures the baked earth. Here and
there, a house still echoes its earlier days of modest glory—
in a glistening coat of paint, a sprucely trimmed hedge, a
generously watered, velvety green lawn. But the signs of
decay already dominate. Boys play tag and cork-ball in
the street, escaping overcrowded rooms. Little girls skip
rope, roller skate, or push whining doll carriages along the
sidewalks. Here and there, an unidentifiable fragment of
dissected machinery rusts in an overgrown flower bed.
Despite the respectable fronts of the houses, there is a sense
that an excess of life has been densely assembled here—too
much quarreling and lovemaking, too many children, too
many unpaid bills.

It is the kind of neighborhood Pearl knows well, and
which she can size up as shrewdly as an Amsterdam jewel
merchant appraising uncut diamonds. Such neighborhoods
are the first stop and sometimes the last for families that
migrate from the farms, trading hard labor under the sun
for hard labor in the glare of fluorescent lights. They come,
most of them, from land fit to raise only weeds and children, and they bring the children with them. Intimidated
by the glittering shopfronts, they scarcely venture downtown, but subsist from the small neighborhood stores that
give easy credit and yoke them with niggling but inces-
sant debt as surely as the country cross-roads store had

done, feeding and clothing them for a year on credit against an expected crop that was always too meager to balance the account. Such families, as Pearl knows, are almost obsessively devoted to their children, at least until they reach the age of twelve or thirteen, when, on a farm, they would have assumed adult roles. Therefore, they are good customers, eagerly paying a dollar or two that they can't afford to have the children's pictures taken.

Pearl moves slowly, with a curious rolling, heaving, settling motion, and the great coils of fat which swathe her tremble as her feet make contact with the pavement. She wears a cotton dress cut in the shape of a tent, obviously hand sewn to her measurements, yet stretched to fragile tautness across her stomach and breasts. Despite the heat, she wears coarse cotton stockings, rolled over and knotted just below the knee, and high-topped men's work shoes. On her head, is a frayed straw hat, bleached by the sun, stained by rain, and fraying at the edge like a brittle, sun-dried flower. Around her neck are dozens of strings of pearls—a choker of plastic ones from Woolworth's, short strands of seed pearls, a double strand of cultured pearls and a great rope of baroque ones that drag against her stomach. Fastened flat against the crown of the hat with a knotted string is a cardboard sign reading "Fotos $1.oo." In the waves of heat that rise from the pavement, she seems to proceed in slow motion. It deepens the dimension of unreality that surrounds her, as though she has accidentally wandered away from a movie set, and is now ploddingly seeking the way back. She doesn't lead the goat, but allows him to follow along behind her, obedient as a good hunting dog, and content with the lingering pace she sets. They have not proceeded more than a block after turning onto North Manassas from Chester when the children begin to gather, to troop along beside the cart as though she were the spearhead of a Fourth-of-July parade. When she finds

a suitable break in the curb, she guides General Lee up
onto the sidewalk and rewards him with lumps of sugar.
She sets up the tripod at the edge of the street, locks it in
position, and heaves the camera clumsily into place. She
is breathing hard now. Sweat streams down her face to
soak the front of her dress, and dark, wet blossomings
decorate her stockings. She sits down on the curb, lowering
herself in careful sections, as she might once have set down
baskets of fragile eggs, and waits for the first customer. A
small boy appears, tugging his mother by the arm. A gaunt
woman with lank, thinning brown hair, she wears a faded
blue dress and a stained apron. Her left hand is thrust in a
fist into the apron pocket, and Pearl knows that the pocket
contains a crumpled, soiled dollar bill. The accumulated
wisdom of Pearl's years of wandering also tells her that the
mother would have refused her son new shoes that cost her
this same dollar, or the unimaginable horde of a dollar's
worth of jawbreakers, or four barbershop haircuts, and yet
with the primitive superstitiousness of the peasant, cannot
deny him this split-second alchemy which will preserve
an instant of his kneeskinned, bicycle-craving, bottomlessly
hungry youth. So the boy scrambles into the cart, beams at
the camera to dramatize the stunning new gap where his
front baby teeth have disappeared, and surrenders himself
entirely to Pearl and General Lee. Others come then, including a young mother, scarcely more than sixteen, who
climbs shakily into the cart and balances one infant twin on
each knee. An elderly woman brings five grandchildren with
rawly scrubbed faces and identical threadbare coveralls,
piling them into the cart like peaches in a market basket,
and sternly demanding that they all smile. A father comes
with a daintily beautiful girl, her hair dressed in elaborate
corkscrew curls. There are lean children and fat, shy ones
who drop their eyes away from the camera, small ones who
bellow in fear when left alone in the goat-cart, aggressive

98   boys who make spastic clown faces at the lens. Pearl tucks wrinkled bills and palm-smoothed coins into a Roi Tan cigar box, and carefully notes names and addresses in a wide-ruled composition book.

The last picture she makes on this summer afternoon is of two sisters. They are late because their father has just arrived home (he is working the swing shift for Southern Railways), and he gives them the dollar bill which the older one carries safely wadded into a small ball in the palm of her hand. Pearl knows they will make a pretty picture together, one of them so fair and the other so dark, and both of them easily as pretty as any of the McBryde girls. Therefore, she takes extra care in arranging them together, with the taller, blonde girl sitting to the rear, her arm around her sister's shoulder, their heads tilted toward the camera. Still, the younger one ducks her head slightly— not merely out of shyness, but as though to contain the laughter that threatens to bubble up out of her. The older sister, however, is perfectly poised, her radiant face offered as a frank, feminine gift to those who look on. Their bodies lean slightly together, and with the taller girl's arm encircling her sister's shoulder, they suggest the deepest dependencies of blood, love, trust, and deprivation.

Pearl does not often remember individual sittings, registering somewhat abstractly only the waves of faces that pass before her camera, but as she slowly plods back to her Beale Street boarding house, the faces of these two sisters are firmly fixed in her mind, as they are on the photographic plate. She is pleased that the photograph turns out so well, and it would be nice to think that the image endured in her mind as it does now on slightly yellowed photographic paper. Realistically, she could not have retained any one particular image for long, and had she done so it would have blurred, rearranged itself, been transformed into a composite image of all little white girls.

Too many other faces were to pass before the camera for
her to linger on these as I have done over the years.

Pearl remained a popular Beale Street character, a living
tourist attraction, until 1942, when street-corner talk ac-
claimed with new vigor the job opportunities and miraculous
liberties available in Chicago and Detroit. She was then over
seventy, and had long since ceased to keep regular street-
side hours. With a second General Lee now nearly as
decrepit as the first had been when he died, she was to be
found at her curbside station only on weekends. Her
wanderlust was awakened again not by the talk of high
wages and unheard-of freedom, but by the prod such talk
of northern cities inevitably gave to her fear of "puttin'
down roots." If she still needed a psychic nudge to move
on after so many years of semi-permanence, she got it
when General Lee died, and she proceeded then with the
same ready efficiency that had marked her last hours on the
McBryde Plantation. At Sol's Pawn Shop she struck a
bantering bargain whereby he acquired her camera and
she departed the shop with a small trunk, into which she
speedily packed dresses, Sunday shoes, a black hat for
funerals, and a Bible bound in red moroccan leather. She
withdrew her savings from the First National Bank,
bought a one-way bus ticket to Detroit, and was northward
bound less than eight hours after General Lee's death. It
might as well be noted at this point that the amount of her
savings was just over $10,000, and not a half-million, as
local rumor had it. An ancient, stuttering amputee, who
for two generations had peddled pencils and bubble gum
at the entrance of the Sterrick Building, had died the previous winter, and in his one-room shack the police found
over $200,000 in soiled and wrinkled bills stuffed into the
sausage-plump women's stockings that padded his mattress
and in silver dollars buried under the dirt floor in Prince
Albert tobacco cans. Naturally enough, the horde vigor-

ously stimulated the faith that all such sidewalk entrepreneurs had miserly fortunes tucked away. While Pearl's savings were modest in comparison to their rumored magnificence, they were sufficient to support her for the five remaining years of her life. In Detroit she was active in the Sublime Pentecostal Church of Christ Risen, and was particularly popular with the neighborhood children, who called her Aunty Pearl and trooped along behind her on the rare occasions when she left her one-room apartment. She always carried a large patent-leather purse filled with cellophane-wrapped candies, and generously distributed them among the flock. When she died in 1952, the church inherited what remained of her savings, providing her in turn with a bountiful wake and a song-filled graveside funeral.

After the Memphis years, Pearl made no other photographs, and certainly thought little about the fate of the ones she had taken—whether they were cherished or trodden underfoot, framed in leather or brass or silver or wood, restored and reproduced as mementos for another generation, or left behind in the empty house, stuck into the warped frame of a mirror. And yet, even decades after her death, she still plays a dominant role in these photographs, the central and pivotal figure in the collaboration that includes the subject and the viewer. In the case of the photograph before us now, we have a multiple subject and multiple viewers, as well as a host of minor assistants, grips, legmen, prop men, retailers, inventors, and bystanders who must be reckoned with. There is, as well, the shadowy figure of Robert's cousin, who first bought the camera in New York, and who would never have gone there at all except that, through yet another cousin, he had met a pretty Long Island debutante at a dance in New Orleans. Victoria McBryde must also be taken into account, together with the lesbian headmistress who gave her a position at the Jackson Seminary for Young Women less because of her artistic gifts than for the pretty sway of her hips when she walked. Obviously, then, the present photograph represents a massive, densely interconnected, if unconscious collective labor. Still, however wide we draw the circle of participants, Pearl remains central to the historic moment that produced the following photograph. Furthermore, we could never trace all the destinies, rules, caprices, coincidences, loves, and lusts that converged to make this moment possible. And so, in order to simplify, we reduce the experience to its rudest essentials: photographer, photograph, viewer. Of these three elements, the photograph is the most stable, though it fades and otherwise alters with age. Far more capricious are its multiple viewers. One may see it as "nice," "a good likeness," or "not worth the money." The next may think the dresses look horribly out of date, while a succession of viewers may find them charming. When I first looked at this photograph, lying on my stomach against a pleasantly scratchy wool carpet and turning with some effort the oversized pages of the album, I thought only how splendid it would be to own a goat-cart, and how lucky my mother had been to live in a time when people rode about in such wonderful private carriages.

THE PHOTOGRAPH

Even if you have not seen this particular photograph before, you will know others sufficiently like it in mood and general composition to experience a kind of *déjà vu* when you first encounter it. Perhaps your own attic would yield a similar one—of your grandmother and her favorite cousin in a pony-cart, of Uncle Henry and his sister (the one who died of tuberculosis) on a tandem bicycle, of your father standing with one foot on the broad running board of his first automobile, wearing a long white duster and with goggles pushed back with rakish nonchalance into his silken, curly hair. Certain old studio photographs provoke similar feelings of nostalgia for a past we never experienced, and it may be only the trivial detail which plays so seductively on our imagination—the particular angle of a coral brooch against a lace bodice, the curl at the tip of a moustache, the glossy center-parting in the hair. Such photographs are distillations of the past, and hence far less likely than most of those we own to be relegated to shoe boxes, musty cupboards, or the drawers of the linen-covered steamer trunk that sits mildewing in the basement. These are more apt to be displayed—some of them in brittlely filigreed imitation-gold frames bought at Woolworth's (with gaudy color-studies of Troy Donahue, Elizabeth Taylor, or Joan Crawford in them), in hand-tooled leather ones brought back from Florence last summer, in massively lustrous Edwardian silver, or frozen behind sleekly modern slabs of Lucite. Less, perhaps, because of the persons they commemorate than as symbolic heirlooms, pictorial antiques, they maintain their place on our visual/decorative horizon, and in so doing they also suggest that the past (which was, after all, only a preparation for our own existence) was a thing of grace, originality, and superior composition. With the public display of such intimate mementos, we bolster our own identities as surely as the fading movie star who heaps the vanilla-colored grand piano with inscribed studio portraits of more successful colleagues, or the ambassador who orders his autographed presidents and secretaries of state in silver-bordered and precisely protocoled ranks on the antique mahogany table that dominates the foyer of his official residence.

This photograph, of course, relates not to any official image, but to one's aesthetic view of oneself, for aesthetics more than family piety provokes the decision to display a particular old photograph. In this respect, family photographs differ markedly from family portraits of the hand-painted variety; the latter may well be hung despite their grotesque imperfections, on the presumption that paint-soaked canvas—of whatever quality or skill of execution—automatically appreciates in value with the darkening passage of time. By making portraiture universally accessible, photography eroded the aesthetic exclusivity of the *ancien régime*, but rather too abruptly, perhaps. Monsieur Daguerre's historic announcement may have sent all Paris scurrying to the rooftops to sample the new alchemy, but what he had given the bourgeoisie was, after all, only the newest of their shiny industrial toys. Others would come. And because of its ever-increasing accessibility, the photograph often tended to wane in value with the passage of time, while that of paint-streaked Belgian linen waxed. It thus requires a peculiar convergence of aesthetic energy, nostalgia, decorative flair, historical vision, and an available frame of the proper proportions to rescue even a single one of these photographic mementos from the mothballed recesses of the guest-room closet or the album with its bruised corners and discoloring pages.

With the passage of time, however, certain photographs seem to become particularly ripe for such display. Oddly enough, they may not have seemed so at the time they were made. Then, perhaps, one was deplored because Helga seemed to have faint traces of a beard, because a certain favorite waistcoat appeared unbecomingly outmoded, or the event commemorated (a seaside stroll, a picnic) seemed too trivial to warrant the price of a frame, or rearrangement of the handcolored Godey prints in the sitting room. Left long enough in the darkness of a bureau drawer, such studies can be radically transformed by generous patinas of sentimentality and nostalgia, and thus fittingly robed for resurrection.

The photograph before us now was almost certainly not treasured in its early years as it is now, though probably the event commemorated was cherished by the two girls who experienced it—at least for a matter of days. But either no one thought highly of this particular photograph at the time it was made, or the cost of a proper frame was judged a needless extravagance. It should, however, be made clear at the outset that what we have here is only a copy of the original (a photograph of a photograph), but the earlier careless treatment of the original is abundantly evident. In each of the four corners there are the traces of holes— bull's-eyes within faint circles—made by thumbtacks, and perhaps the picture was first displayed in this fashion, pinned next to the Mutual of Omaha calendar, with its bright color studies of American national parks. There are also two white streaks—one a simple line on the left-hand edge of the photograph, the other a jagged, reversed "7" near the center—that suggest the stiff paper of the photograph was creased or broken, perhaps when shoved carelessly into a suitcase on the day the family moved from their crowded two-room apartment to the shabby but roomy clapboard house on Dunlop. Furthermore, there seem to be two names written in ink in the lower right-hand corner. Only one of these is entirely visible, but we assume there are two—not only because a fragment of the second **105** one is visible, but also because there are two girls in the photograph. If this were a treasured portrait study, surely no one would write on it in ink unless he was dedicating it or presenting it to an intimate friend or loved one. On the other hand, this is no dedication, but simply two names: "Margaret and. . . ." Though little enough of the second name is visible, it might well be "Kathlyn." Obviously, after the names were written here, the photograph was trimmed round the edges. This would suggest it was in rather frayed and tattered condition when it was reproduced for a later generation—by which time, presumably, it had begun to acquire the requisite heirloomed patina. But at what point were the names added? It seems unlikely that they were placed there as soon as the photograph was received, for it is so intimately and incontrovertibly a family photograph that surely everyone concerned would have known the identity of the two girls. Of course, if it had been sent to the mother's absent brother, who had gone to California and begun to farm in the San Joaquin valley nearly twenty years before, such identification might have been necessary. On the other hand, there are certain details about the photograph that argue against this notion, as we will see when we examine it in greater particular. Surely for such momentous, trans-continental communication, a more formal, more conventional study of the two girls would have been in order. If we assume the mother of these two girls was almost excessively meticulous in her habits, that she had, furthermore, a family of eight children of her own (in addition to two nearly grown sons by her husband's first marriage) to nurture and discipline, she may almost routinely have recorded this information on the photograph, as though acknowledging the difficulties anyone outside the family might reasonably have in keeping the names and ages of the children straight. Certainly the names

106 appear to have been written by a feminine hand, while the photograph was in possession of its fullest borders. But the mother did not write the names. Had she done so, she would certainly have written the full names—Margaret Elaine and Dorothy Kathlyn—as well as the date. The date, certainly, would have been more useful than the names, for there are few details to date the scene: it might have been made at any time in the twentieth century. No doubt this vagueness as to time springs in part from the fact that we are concerned, in fact, with a relatively modern photograph of an old photograph. The original, with its sepiaed shadows, would be more revealing of its actual age. Surely any mother sufficiently concerned to mark a photograph at all for purposes of future identification would have indicated a date. We cannot entirely rule out the possibility that beneath the second name, which has been partially cut away, the numerals "1922" once appeared. There would have been little enough room for the date, as the names are written somewhat floridly, and estimating the original borders from the thumbtack holes, there would have been but scant space remaining. In fact, it is difficult to imagine that there would have been any space whatever for the date, though this could have been inked onto the back of the original photograph. Nonetheless, it seems improbable that the writing in the lower right-hand corner is even vaguely contemporaneous with the photograph. The probability is greater that the names were added at a later date, when the owner of the photograph first began to realize its significance as a family document. By that time, the mother had been dead for many years, and her handwriting, in any case, would have had some trace of Victorian ornamentation, whereas this handwriting is modernistically simple. The sense of ornamentation (which suggests the names have been added for more than simple identification) comes from the arrangement of the names

themselves. The name "Margaret" slopes upward from
left to right. The single word "and" is tilted downward at
a right angle to "Margaret," and the name not entirely
visible to us is nearly parallel with the bottom of the picture. Whoever added these names has thus sought in a
manner to decorate the picture, to enhance its total effect:
it would have been necessary to turn the photograph
sharply in order to produce the word "and" at such an
acute angle. The word "Margaret" may appear first because Margaret is the older of the two girls in the picture,
and sits with her arm protectively about her sister's
shoulder, or because she sits more in the foreground; but in
that case it would be the name of the younger sister (as it
indeed is). The names are almost certainly added by Margaret. Even though we cannot entirely see the name
"Kathlyn," the single word "Margaret" looks remarkably
like a signature rather than simply a name. All the visible
letters are formed with the most modest simplicity save
the "M" in "Margaret," and the concluding "t." The "M"
begins with a long, downward sweep. The "t" concludes
firmly and abruptly, without the final curl to complete
the letter, whereas the "d" in "and" demonstrates no such
peculiarity. It therefore seems reasonable to assume that
this photograph, made in the summer of 1922, was not
particularly treasured until it was discovered by Margaret
in a box of unsorted letters and photographs in 1940, the
year she added to it her name and that of her sister. Some
years later (in 1956, to be exact), copies were made for
other members of the family, and the carefully trimmed
original eventually came into the possession of David
Franklin Jarvis shortly before his own death in 1975, and
was then acquired by one of his children, none of whom
understand its real value.

In its present form, the photograph measures four by
six inches. It could, of course, have been either enlarged or

reduced from its original size, but probably was not, as the handwriting in the lower right-hand corner seems to be of entirely average proportions. Therefore, all that is missing is the white outer border and approximately one-quarter inch of the original surface of the photograph. The Norman Rockwell air of happy bygone days that hangs over the picture is not difficult to describe: it shows two young girls sitting, with obvious glee, in a small two-wheeled cart, one of them holding the reins of a goat that might well be stuffed, for he stands with such plumply lazy self-contentment between the traces of the cart. Both girls are barefoot and wear short, simple cotton dresses. Their straight hair is cropped tomboyishly short. The larger of the two girls has fair hair and a fresh, openly photogenic face. She sits to the left of the smaller, dark-haired girl, and her right arm is held round her sister's shoulder, so that her right hand is clearly visible in the foreground of the photograph. The total composition is entirely conventional, but that fact only contributes to its nostalgic charm. The goat-cart stands on a sidewalk which slopes slightly downhill to the right. Thus, from right to left (and in profile as it were), we have the horned goat, the glossy cart, and the two girls, silhouetted against a dark hedge of boxwood or holly with a brick wall behind it. The two girls are thus to the left of the photograph, but turned slightly in the cart to face the camera directly, as though they have been posed in this way by the photographer. Since Kathlyn sits to her sister's left, the younger, shorter girl is in the foreground. This could, of course, be chance, but more likely the photographer has placed the taller girl behind the shorter with full consciousness of the portrait effect. And yet, if this is the work of a professional, one wonders why the two girls are not dressed in their Sunday best. Surely for such a special occasion they would have worn their prettiest ruffled dresses and patent-leather shoes. Instead, both

wear simple, shapeless cotton dresses, and are barefoot. (Of
course, if this is the standard holiday dress of the summers
they spend on their grandfather's farm, it is understandable
that the gruffly indulgent old man would have wanted them
—despite their mother's protests—photographed in just
this way.) Kathlyn's dress somewhat resembles a collarless,
cut-down man's shirt, whereas Margaret's seems a trifle
more feminine, with a Peter Pan collar and slightly puffed
sleeves with a ruffled trim. Nonetheless, even Margaret's is
clearly not a Sunday-best dress. The sole hint of dressing-
up is in the tiny dark scarf each girl has tied loosely at her
neck.

These much-washed play dresses, ornamented with the
blue silk scarves their mother had brought from Greenwood the day before, were in fact what they were wearing
when the grandfather called them from the teepee (two
bean poles and a precariously draped blanket) in the or-
chard to see the surprise he had for them. General Lee they
already knew, for the goat was almost as domesticated as
grandfather's favorite coon hound, but the cart was a complete surprise. It had been in a loft in the big barn ever
since grandfather himself had outgrown it; he had carted
it to Byhalia in the pickup truck to have it repainted in the
automobile body-shop there, and to outfit it with new
bicycle tires. General Lee stands calmly within the traces,
as though he has found his calling at last, and while he
will never move faster than a dignified saunter, he carts
the girls tirelessly round the farm for the brief remainder
of their summer holidays. Shortly before these come to an
end and the two girls are packed aboard the sleeper for
Chicago with their mother, their striped suitcases, a box
containing a dozen jars of blackberry jam, and a wire cage
with three frogs in it, grandfather has this picture taken.
The local photographer is there to take a picture of him
as the new president of the County Agricultural Associa-

tion, and he asks that this one be made as well. He pins it with thumbtacks to the wall of the small, windowless room which he calls his office, and where women and children enter only when summoned. There it becomes a dusty square in the mosaic of cotton quotations clipped from the *Memphis Commercial Appeal,* postcards from Florida and Arizona, snapshots of prize-winning hogs, and the girlie calendar from Hank's Texaco Station. After he dies, his daughter finds it in the carton of letters, faded greeting cards, bank statements, and advertisements for rheumatism salves sent on to her by her brother. She writes the names Margaret and Kathlyn on it, in the lower right-hand corner, but hesitates before adding a date, for she cannot remember if the year in question was 1922 or 1923. At any rate, it hardly seems to matter.

But there are, without doubt, other narratives which would account equally well for the subject, condition, and age of the photograph, and certainly there are flaws in this account of grandfatherly generosity. First, the goat-cart stands on a sidewalk, so it is most improbable that we are dealing with a farm environment. Furthermore, the dark brick wall visible behind the hedge is almost certainly that of an apartment house and not of a farmhouse. The space between hedge and wall seems confiningly narrow, but the hedge is here as definition of a front garden, and as tenuous leafy shield to privacy and respectability. Perhaps it is a rear garden or side garden, after all, for in the left half of the photograph, too dark to identify clearly, is the outline of what might well be a doorway, and as there is no opening in the hedge, this would not be the front of a house. The rectangular shadow one can just discern here might, however, be a window rather than a doorway. Still, the red brick, the cramped ribbon of garden, the sidewalk all suggest an urban rather than a rural setting.

It might well be argued that a goat-cart is an unlikely

conveyance for two little girls living in a big-city apartment house; their bare feet would also seem to argue for some more pastoral setting. The anomalies are accounted for if we situate the house in which they live on the magnoliaed fringe of Jackson, Mississippi, where their father has recently been promoted to vice-president of the Merchants and Planters Bank. After graduation from Tupelo High School, Carter Peden had attended Tulane University in New Orleans. There he met Alma Cox, a student at Sophie Newcomb, whose father had founded the Merchants and Planters Bank, and though she clearly belonged (despite her half-breed's blood) to a social plateau higher than his own, Carter consistently impressed the Coxes as a young man likely to make his mark in the world, and hence a fitting match for their only child. Carter and Alma were married in September, 1908, only a few months after their graduation, and there is in existence (indeed, in my possession) a superb portrait of them, taken shortly after they returned from their honeymoon. Carter would seem to be standing behind the low-backed chair or stool on which Alma sits. One sees her head and shoulders, while he seems to tower above his dark-haired bride. Since we know there was not such an exaggerated difference in their heights, we can only suppose that she is sitting down. At any rate, the effect is to frame her oval face and white lace blouse against the smartly-cut double-breasted jacket he wears. There is an almost theatrically dramatic contrast between these faces. Hers is described in softened ovals, but his runs to points. The ears, standing slightly out from his head, are Pan-like, his nose long and sharp despite its fine modeling. But for the plump, boyish fullness of his jaw, this might be the face of a much older man. Certainly there is something prematurely old about the eyes, the downward pinched mouth, as though they seek to reassure both father-in-law and future mortgage seekers of his precocious maturity. He wears not only a white shirt but a white four-in-hand tie, which might have seemed rather dandified in 1908, though still elegantly correct; it relieves somewhat the somberness of his suit. Alma's face is unsettlingly beautiful. Her thick black hair, a legacy from her Chickasaw mother, is parted in the center with near-mathematical precision. Her eyes, beneath softly rounded brows, are fringed with heavy lashes, so that they create a languid, sultry effect, and her nose is so perfectly formed as to seem almost sculptural. The total impression, however, would be one of an almost vapidly pretty small-town girl were it not for the sensuously full mouth, the lips slightly parted as though about to ask a provocative question or to whisper some perversely erotic suggestion. Furthermore, while hair and eyes and nose possess a matchless symmetry, the mouth is irregular, fuller on the right side than the left, and the jaw-line, too, is uneven, as though in the final seconds of creation the perverse sculptor had seized the still-damp clay, cupped the jaw in his hands, and wrenched it slightly out of line. Perhaps he feared, otherwise, the storied vengeance of jealous gods. Alma wears her hair pulled back in a bun, and it seems to be ornamented with a scarf or ribbon, a corner of which is just visible to the left of the photograph. She is dressed in a round-collared white lace blouse (or perhaps even in a white dress with lace trim; we cannot be sure) and wears a double strand of pearls. Alma and Carter might be said to "compose" well together, and this photograph would seem to augur well for the future. We can note briefly that Carter's career is a success, in a modest, small-town, banker's-son-in-law way, at least until 1929, when the Merchants and Planters Bank is washed away on a bright fall morning by a wave of anxious depositors. For the remainder of his active life, Carter Peden is employed by the post office, and Alma helps to pay for the children's college expenses by working as a substitute teacher of English, vocal music, and Confederate history. There are four children—two boys and two girls—who, growing up in the stolidly respectable red-brick Victorian house on what was then described as the "outskirts" of Jackson, know both town pastimes and country ones. Their pet goat, General Lee, can normally be found browsing in a farmer's field less than half a mile from the house. But from time to time the brothers go there to put a halter on him and lead him to the house, to be fastened to the goat-cart that belonged to Alma when she was a child, and General Lee with plodding patience draws the two sisters round and round the block on which they live. The broad expanse of sidewalk that proclaims this town rather than country is, for him, the only acceptable course. On a bright summer morning in 1922, just as the girls are about to begin another ramble with General Lee, an itinerant photographer arrives, with the tripod-mounted camera hoisted over his shoulder as a farmer might hoist shovel and hoe. Stuck into the broad band of his straw hat is a card reading "PHOTOS: 50¢ and $1.00," and the mother readily enough agrees for the girls to be photographed as a birthday surprise for their father. The brothers find the idea unmanly, and content themselves with making demonically unphotogenic faces just outside the camera's range. Thus, Kathlyn and Margaret climb into the goat-cart, General Lee stands at self-conscious attention, and the photographer squeezes the fat rubber bulb that triggers the lens of the camera, recording an entirely conventional, everyday moment, which to later generations will seem ornamented with delicious layers of sentiment and occasion.

The straw hat the photographer wears is, at least, genuine. So, too, are the worn, broken work shoes in which he plods along the streets of Memphis in the summer of 1922. The ruined high-top shoes are like a relief map of his life, each bulge and furrow, cracked ravine, bald hummock, and leather gully a testimony to hard field work, drenching rains and blistering summer heat, stinking cabins and murderously volatile kerosene stoves, and the fat, jetty-black, childless wife who seemed to rock perpetually in the wicker-bottomed rocking chair that made a recognizable home of a dozen or perhaps a dozen dozen identical sharecroppers' cabins. She died in the rocking chair as well, and because the land now seemed poisoned by loneliness the old man went to Byhalia, where he found work sweeping out the photographer's shop, and then doing the foul-smelling darkroom work, and finally in photographing Negro customers in a tiny, airless, draped-off cubicle at the rear of the store. When his employer died, the old man (he didn't in fact know how old he was, but knew that he was already long a man when news finally filtered through to the remote plantation that the slaves were free) loaded the second-best camera and a scrap of velvet drapery onto a child's red wagon, and set off to see the world. Somewhere en route to Memphis, he bought the goat and cart, and with his equipment loaded into the cart he now walked the streets of the city soliciting business. He soon found that the poorer neighborhoods were the best, for parents there were less likely to seek the professional services of the smarter Main Street photographic parlors.

The unmistakable pleasure we see in the two sisters' faces is thus not only the result of sitting, for all to see, in this wonderfully lacquered carriage, but also of having their photograph made. Kathlyn seems more composed, if only because she is older, but Margaret is not simply smiling: her mouth is open in what is almost surely a melody of laughter. It is, for both sisters, a rare moment of pleasure, and made possible by the rarer moment of their father having an extra dollar to pay for it. The anonymous, shadow-frescoed wall visible as a one-inch stripe across the

top of the photograph is that of a still-respectable apart- **115**
ment house, but one already islanded by the brackisk waters
of poverty. A brisk summer breeze swiftly funnels into its
stuccoed entranceway the smells of decaying garbage and
rancid cooking oil and human sweat. For now, it is the
best Hugh Jarvis can afford, and perhaps rather more than
life had ever encouraged him to expect. Broken twice—
once by the unyielding clenched fist of hard-packed red-
clay farmland, and then again by his wife's slow, grotesque
dying—he expects little enough, and if he murmurs against
that pinched, shabby destiny, it is only occasionally, and
then in the name of "the kids." In his wedding portrait,
there is already a glazed, bewildered look in his eyes, as
though he has been dealt cards for a game whose rules he
does not know, and wonders if they are good, bad, or only
predictably indifferent. Three years before, as though to
mark him as an eternal loser, the plow had snagged against
a stone, caught him off balance, and sent him plunging
face-first against a hand-smoothed plow handle. The
broken nose spoils now that vague hint of refined symmetry
in his wedding picture. (By chance his second son is kicked
in the face by a mule only a year later, and now seems more
than ever his father's duplicate; the resemblance will in-
crease uncannily as Boyce grows older, the very sag of his
shoulders counterfeiting his father's.)

He works now, when he works at all, as assistant brakeman for Southern Railways. Kathlyn cares for the family
as she had done even as a girl of nine and ten and eleven
on the dirt-poor Mississippi farm, and his mutely wondering
gratitude toward her slowly evolves into such caustic guilt
that he can never look directly into her luminous blue
eyes. Margaret, meanwhile, is a silent, brooding child,
moved out of her protective cocoon only by sudden fits
of hilarious pleasure. And yet, to look at the two penny-
bright faces in the photograph, one would scarcely imagine

that these were any but the daughters of some prosperous, indulgent burgher. There are freshness, openness, and contagious exhilaration here which have survived disease and dust and poverty, bad food, pellagra and tropic heat. The photographer, in his spit-shined yellow shoes, his pin-striped trousers, crisp white shirt and straw boater hat, has spent the day touring the neighborhood, and has already made more than a dozen photographs of children—of individual children posed with petrified seriousness before the camera, of graceful pairs and giggling threesomes, and of a plump young mother, sitting in the cart with one squirming twin precariously balanced on each knee. This one of the two sisters is the last picture he makes today, and he takes some care in setting up the shot. First of all, the blonde is stunningly pretty, softly and unconsciously blossoming toward womanhood, and there is a haunted, bewildered, pixie quality about her younger sister. With carefully manicured hands he gently twists and arranges their shoulders, tugs the little one's shabby dress down and smooths out the worst wrinkles, and puts the traces in the older girl's hands. Then, murmuring with satisfaction as he gazes at the silvered, upside-down image, he clicks the lens open-shut.

He is right to be pleased, for this is as quintessentially and provocatively a portrait of two sisters as our first picture was boy-with-dog. Despite the fact that one is dark and timid, the other fair and gregarious (or perhaps even because of these dramatic contrasts) one body laps against the other in a way that suggests the deepest mutual dependence and a depth of affection that will lead them decades from now to buy adjoining cemetery plots (higher up the hill than that of their father, where the view is better). Something in the tilt of their heads, the crossing of plumply girlish legs, compels us to see them as sisters. Whether they are the daughters of banker or tinker, sailor

or assistant brakeman is, of course, less readily visible.
Here we can let play the force field of imagination as once we moved a magnet behind a paper covered with lead filings to make up new patterns and counter-patterns, but the sisterlyness we will not rearrange. And their moments of joy are so few and so brief that we are right to pause over this rare document. For all its nostalgia, its obvious aesthetic charm, it is no less a testament to the tragic ordinariness of their lives. Perhaps even Pearl sensed that, as she spun them into focus.

FOUR

... things are because we see them, and what we see, and how we see it, depends on the arts that have influenced us.

Oscar Wilde, *Intentions*

ɞ   ɞ

Look at the birdie!

Folk saying

ɞ   ɞ

Say 'cheese'!

Folk saying

THE CAMERA

SIZE: *1⅛ x 2⅞ x 5⅛ inches (plus lens, ⅜ inches collapsed, 1¼ inches extended).*
LENS: *I.R.C. Anastigmat.*
FOCAL LENGTH: *2 inches. Variable stops (f/4.5. to f/11), iris diaphragm.*
SHUTTER: *"Rapid" self-cocking, between lens elements; T, B, and instantaneous, variable speeds (½₅ to ½₀₀ sec.); cock and release lever on right side of shutter.*
FINDER: *Eye-level, direct optical; rear and front lenses; mounted on top of camera body.*
BODY: *Bakelite with aluminium and chrome-plated fittings; removable back; frame counter coupled to film advance gears.*
LIST PRICE: *$12.50.*

The Argus "Model A" camera was manufactured by the International Research Corporation, Ann Arbor, Michigan, in 1937. It is a rigid-bodied miniature camera for 36 exposures, 24 x 36 mm., on standard, perforated 35mm. film.

This particular Argus model was introduced in 1936, as the first mass-produced, American-made camera to use 35mm. film in the full-frame format. Although the camera was proclaimed as "The first All-American, precision-made, 35mm. miniature camera," it was in fact preceded by the half-frame Tourist Multiple (1914) and Ansco Memo (1927), and by the full-frame Simplex (1914), all of which were produced in the United States.

When first introduced, the camera was simply designated

122   as the "Argus Miniature Camera." When subsequent models were produced, the camera was named "Model A." Argus produced a large number of cameras, including the very popular C-3, which was used by innumerable amateur photographers. Among those models of Argus cameras that employed the same basic design as the Model A were the Model AF (1937–1938), with full focusing lens mount; Model B (1937 only), with Prontor II shutter; Model AS (1939–1950), with fixed-focus lens and extinction meter as part of the body, located on the top left of the viewfinder; Model A2f (1939–1941), with full focusing lens mount and extinction meter; Model AA (1940–1942), with fixed-focus lens and built-in contacts for flash attachment; and Model FA (1950–1951), with full focusing lens mount and built-in flash contacts.

The Model A Argus featured a fixed-focus lens in a collapsible mount throughout its years of production (1936–1941). From the beginning, an enlarger was offered, which employed the backless camera as an integral part.

THE PHOTOGRAPHER

Cyrus Lawrence MacDonald, Caucasian male,
born June 6, 1901, in Cincinnati, Ohio,
to Sarah Lee (née Lawrence)
*   and Augustus Cicero MacDonald;*
died September 2, 1950, in Cincinnati, Ohio

Cyrus MacDonald is the least interesting of the six photographers presented here, having been pressed into service more or less at random, and therefore playing no really dramatic role in this collection. With each of the other photographs, we sense some act of devotion, curiosity, or need that transforms the mechanical-chemical process, so that the moment at which the shutter is clicked becomes historical—that is, filled with the raw materials of storytelling. Cyrus—or "Cy," as he always insists on being called—is merely a bystander; the camera is set and focused for him, and this single photograph is the only one he makes in his entire life. Despite that fact, he forgets it almost immediately, although he remembers the woman who posed with her husband for rather a longer time.

As a child, Cy combines a sunny good nature with a bullying streak, and as a man he refers to his cronies as sons of bitches, but redeems any possible insult with the buck-toothed smile that creases his florid face. As boy and man, he is stout and sturdy, with fat, bowed legs, and his smiling aggressiveness rather puzzles the many women with whom he comes in contact. His mother, oblivious to her pregnancy until well into the sixth month, is thus first startled by the boy before his birth, and remains startled by him until her death, not quite believing that her frail, middle-aged body could have produced this fire-haired, obstreperous, ever-smiling offspring. Her husband seems less puzzled, but as a railway conductor he is not often at home, and accepts Cy's presence much as he would accept another addition to the family menagerie of cats, dogs, rabbits, and chickens. The menagerie is expanded again a few years later with the addition of a daughter, a fair, doll-faced girl who does much to revive Mrs. MacDonald's faith in her own femininity. Increasingly, Cy is left to his own devices, which come at a precocious age to include sexual games with the neighborhood girls, a taste for rye whiskey, the smoking of grapevines, and the idea of bluffing younger children into yielding him the tastier morsels from their lunch boxes. Thus, Cyrus Lawrence MacDonald bullies, grunts, and smiles his way into adulthood. When his sister marries shortly after the death of their father and goes with her sailor husband to live in San Diego, Cyrus shows a tenderness and concern for his mother that surprises both of them, and he never neglects to bring a little something for the old lady when he returns from his travels.

Those travels almost always take him south—into Kentucky, Tennessee, Arkansas, and Mississippi, where his face becomes well known before he is twenty-one as a salesman of ladies undergarments. It is known not only to the small-town merchants to whom he provides everything from heavy-duty serviceables to naughty Parisian novelties, but to the madams of half-a-hundred whore-houses where the overnight fee is, after all, not much more than that of a first-class hotel. Cy prospers, assembles an entire rainbow of silk shirts and ties, and always has at least one fifty-cent cigar protruding from the breast pocket of a spiffy custom-made suit. He prospers, and yet he frets that, after all, he

does the real work, lays down the miles, lives out of a
suitcase, eats in joints that could give you ptomaine, but has
to split his profits with some Jew in Brooklyn who sews
the fancy labels into the underwear.

In short, Cy has ambitions, and with his head for business
and his connections, all he needs is the right little product
(as he assures madams and waitresses, fellow salesmen and
merchants, desk-clerks and filling-station attendants) to
make a nice bundle all for himself. Cut out the middle man.
When Cy takes the following photograph, he is thirty-four
years old, and no longer works for a Brooklyn Jew but for
"yours truly," selling a range of patent medicines manufactured in his mother's basement in Cincinnati. The brand
is called Cyrus Says, and the trademark is the face of a
benevolent, Ben Franklinish country doctor, with one finger raised before his face as though giving stern but sage
advice. Cyrus Says advises a tablespoon of nerve tonic
morning and night; the nerve tonic consists of 80 percent
homemade cherry brandy and 20 percent tap-water, with
a few grains of codeine. Cyrus Says advises one teaspoon of
pain killer every two hours for toothache, rheumatism, and
inflamed joints; Cyrus Says Pain Killer consists of 90 percent homemade cherry brandy and 10 percent tap-water,
with a few grains of laudanum. The contents of Cyrus's
products and the quantity of his sales are eventually of interest to a number of state and federal government agencies,
but at the time he takes the photograph of the honey-
mooners, Cyrus lives off the fat of the land and the lean-
ness of Bible Belt morality.

He is in Hot Springs, Arkansas, to discuss preparing a
new all-round wonder tonic to be marketed exclusively by
a drugstore chain in Arkansas and Texas. He doesn't much
like the terms he is offered, but consoles himself with the
blonde manicurist who works in the hotel barbershop.

Yvonne has ambitions, and is only waiting for the right break to take herself and her reedy soprano voice to Hollywood, where she will try out for a part in the movies. Cy is impressed by her plump breasts with their hard nipples, by her hair—cut and dyed to match Harlow's—, and by the wistful look in her eyes as she sings "Ava Maria," her hands clutched tightly before her as she wanders through the upper registers. They are on a picnic at Lookout Point, and Cy has just lit up a fifty-cent Havana. The shadows on the distant mountains are mauve, and the air is crisply sweet. Perhaps this combination of scenic panorama, hard nipples, and a good Havana has something to do with Cy's reception of the song, for tears come to his eyes as he hears it. Despite his gallant concern for whorehouse madams and his own mother, Cy is no sentimentalist, so that this moment on the mountaintop has the flush of revelation on it. Yvonne, poor kid, deserves a break, what with all that talent and all them curves. He thinks he may do a bit of managing for her, sort of coach her a little in her career. He starts by suggesting that "Indian Love Call" would be a better audition number than "Ave Maria," and first thing next morning goes to the sheet music department at Woolworth's and buys a copy in the soprano range.

He is stunned to learn later that day that Yvonne has made other plans, and has in fact already left, bag and baggage, for Hollywood, with a trucker on his way West with a load of spare motorcycle parts. It is a bitter moment for a man who has just begun to see a person where before he has always seen a dame. He consoles himself with a visit to Ruby's—not sleeping with one of the girls, but just sitting in the parlor with Big Ruby, bolstered by fat damask pillows on a spindle-legged sofa in her front parlor, sipping rum toddies most of the night. It bucks him up— but not for long, because life is like a crap game, and when the dice start running against you, they don't stop that damned quick. The owner of the drugstore chain, in what should have been the last session of bargaining, announces with outrage his suspicion that Nature's Own Wonder Elixir contains alcohol. He is an honorary deacon of the First Baptist Church, and how dare a damned Yankee try to trick him into selling the Devil's brew? Too weary to argue, Cyrus walks out of the deacon's room with a suggestion of where the sample bottle could be placed. It is the first time he has blown an important business deal, and it only goes to show what happens if you take dames too seriously. He stops in the lobby to buy two Havanas, and browses through the movie magazines at the newsstand until they remind him of Yvonne. Then he wanders out to the circular drive in front of the hotel, his hands in his pockets, whistling "We're In the Money," enjoying the picture of himself as the prosperous, happy-go-lucky businessman. Dames are, after all, a dime a dozen. It is now that the man asks him to take the photograph.

The day is bright and hot, and the sun is at a perfect angle for the man and his wife to stand before the balustrade that runs round three sides of the hotel veranda. The man has already taken a photograph of his wife, and has carefully instructed her where to place her hands and where not to place them, and how to hold the camera while looking through the small opening at the top, in order to take a picture of him that is certain to be perfect in terms of exposure—neither too light nor too dark. He even marks a small spot for her with an X in the loose white gravel of the driveway. The wife, anxious not to anger her husband by making an error, very carefully and daintily places first one foot and then the other against the X, so that she looks rather pigeon-toed and precariously off-balance as she raises the camera. She squints through the opening her husband has indicated, making it all seem as sweetly, femininely awkward as if she has never before

128   held a camera in her hands. In fact, she is a good photographer, though somewhat random in her choice of subjects, and with a tendency to misjudge distances—often to very pretty artistic effect. She looks up from the view finder to say, "Now smile, Jimmy," and squints again at the miniature of her husband she finds in the glass. With the feathery lightness of her Southern voice she begs him, "Now, smile!" She clicks the camera and is about to wind the film, when her husband strides forward to take the camera from her, preferring to wind it himself rather than risk its being wound too far—or, worse, not far enough. Making a helpless flutter with her hands, the wife surrenders the camera. They comment on the light, which is perfect for photographs; so it wasn't so bad to have waited until the last day, and the palms would look perfect as background, and then one of them remarks that they really should have a picture made of them together. But there is, by now, a good deal of coming and going across the veranda of the hotel as young black boys in starched white jackets begin to raise bright orange umbrellas against the noonday sun. The man gathers up the luggage and walks to the corner where he will, in any event, have to bring the car to be loaded. The wife follows him, carrying her purse, a wooden box, and the camera in its dangling leather case. The man rounds the corner and places the luggage in a careful right angle to the sidewalk near the service entrance to the hotel.

Just as the couple have turned to walk away from the verandah, Cy MacDonald comes strolling out of the hotel lobby, his hands in his pockets, whistling "We're in the Money." He pauses at the top of the steps that lead down from the veranda to the palm garden, and as his glance sweeps the view, it takes in the couple walking toward the corner of the hotel. The girl is a looker all right—dressed so simple-but-classy that she could have been a model. His glance sweeps on, but out of the corner of his eye he seems to see the girl turn and nod to him over her shoulder. He looks again, and again she seems to beckon before she turns the corner of the building.

Having nothing better to do, Cy saunters across the garden, his hands thrust into his pockets and making a melody of the coins there. Sure enough, just round the corner the man and woman have paused, with their luggage stacked near the curb. The woman glances up at her husband, who now holds the camera, in a way that says "there he is," and beckons shyly to the stranger. When Cy seems not to notice, the man advances a few paces, introduces himself, and asks Cy if he would be willing to take a photograph of the two of them. Cy is, of course, more than happy to oblige. And so the husband marks an imaginary line where the photographer should stand, explaining that the camera has been set for distance and for light, and that all Cy has to do is to look through this little hole here and push the button. Cy waits for the man and woman to take their places beside their luggage, aligns his toes carefully against the invisible mark, looks through the view finder, and clicks the shutter. It is just that simple. Neither the man nor the woman ever sees Cy again. They, of course, know nothing about his friendship with Yvonne, even though she has manicured the wife's nails only two days before, and Cy knows nothing whatever about the man's angry courtship of the woman, or about the infant child and the others unborn for whom the photograph is secretly made. Cy does find himself wondering, a few hours later, if the wife's eyes were brown or blue, but by then the husband and wife are already in their car driving back to Memphis.

The moment in which a photograph is taken can have various dimensions of significance. It can be very important

130 for both the photographer and for his subject. It can, on the other hand, be of the utmost importance for the photographer and of no importance whatever to the subject; landscape photography invariably falls into this category. The taking of a photograph can be perfectly routine for the photographer but of immense importance to the subject—as when a young man dressed in a conspicuously new, conspicuously mass-produced military uniform sits to have a photograph made for his mother or his sweetheart. The taking of a photograph can, at another extreme, be a matter of mild indifference to both photographer and sitter. With snapshots, to be sure, the subject may not even know that he or she is being photographed, and there are innumerable combinations, gradations, and permutations of these attitudes. Cy might be described as rather indifferent when he takes this photograph, even though he could not unreasonably be expected to have some special feeling or awareness, inasmuch as this is the first and only time in his life that he makes a photograph. Only once does he press the button to open the shutter to record an image, and in doing so becomes a collaborator with this man and woman in the name of future generations. So it should have been for Cyrus Lawrence MacDonald a memorable moment, but he is distracted by thoughts of Yvonne and the torpedoed elixir sales, and reminding himself not to forget to buy his mother a pound of salt-water taffy in assorted flavors. This is all not so very surprising if we take into account Cy's personality, his general interests, and his recent history. For the husband and wife, the taking of the photograph is more significant, since it records the last moments of their second honeymoon, and they place considerable stress on the keeping of records, even if neither one could say that this interlude in Hot Springs was all they had wanted or hoped it would be. Perhaps a neat, crisp photograph, something suitable to be mounted in an album, could order the days

and give them significance, if only as a record to be ap-   **131**
preciated in decades to come. Such sentiments might well
be more appropriately attributed to the wife than to the
husband, but all this we will see more clearly when we look
at the photograph itself.

We meanwhile neglect the photographer. It is surely a
favorable comment on his worldliness that, when asked to
take this photograph, he does not delay with gestures of
false modesty or pleas of incompetence, but proceeds with
directness, speed, and efficiency, to perform the appointed
task. He does not trouble himself over the conspiratorial
nature of what he does, with the voyeuristic role he takes
toward the young couple, or the relationship he thus assumes toward their inheritors. There is something manly
and pragmatic in the way he flicks away his cigar, seizes
the camera in his fat, freckled hands, and goes about his
work. The eye that squints through the tiny glass aperture
is clear-sighted and bold, but that, after all, is his personal
style, and one that largely serves him to his own satisfaction
throughout the remainder of his life. Not without remorse,
but without a tear, he selects the country nursing home
where his mother will spend the remainder of her life.
When narcotics legislation hinders his purchase of codeine,
and war mentality erodes the old strictures against alcohol,
he makes a good enough career for himself selling real
estate, eventually prospering modestly during the postwar
housing shortage. He never marries, but clearly doesn't
remain single out of any particular feelings about the loss of
Yvonne, since he even forgets her name, remembering her
vaguely as "some blonde dame" he once knew in Hot
Springs. Just to keep this account accurate and complete,
let us note that he dies of coronary thrombosis on September 2, 1950, while playing golf with a customer interested
in buying one of the prefabricated duplexes he has just had
built. All of this is remote and irrelevant to the fact that

on a given day in 1939, he took a photograph of a young couple in Hot Springs, Arkansas, but all the same, it has a bearing on our understanding of the photograph that follows.

THE PHOTOGRAPH

The clothing and the luggage would be sufficient to establish the period of the photograph, but it is confirmed by the legend on both the right and the left borders: *1939 January 1939*. Furthermore, in the upper left and lower right corners appear the words *Copyright 1938, General Photos, Inc.* The print is so fine that the words become an abstract part of the photograph's ornamental border, balanced in the upper right and lower left corners with the words *Genuine EVERLASTONE*. The abstract Art Deco design of elongated arrows, printed round the white frame of the photograph, together with the dates, the clothing, and the luggage, places this image firmly in the 1930s, but the month of January is puzzling.

Both the man and the woman in the photograph are dressed in white—the crisp, elegant, prewar white of oceanside summer resorts. Their luggage is stacked by the curb for departure—or so it would seem, for few travelers would look so crisply turned out, would pose beside such neatly stacked luggage to commemorate their arrival. We can reasonably speculate that this is the conclusion of a midwinter holiday whose reality they have sought to preserve through the alchemy of *EVERLASTONE*. They may have departed Chicago shortly after Christmas, spending New Year's in New York and traveling on to Miami Beach for a two-week holiday. Or they may have arrived from Richmond less than twenty-four hours after their wedding in the First Methodist Church there. The idea of honeymoon is hinted at in the festive look of their clothing, the unimpeachable newness of their luggage.

But though there are a score of possible stories to account for a January visit to semi-tropical locales, and a score of variations on each of those stories (including a small legacy from Aunt Louise, a Saturday night poker windfall, a busi-

134 ness trip to check the books of the new Hoover franchise in Tampa), something in the photograph itself contradicts the simple explanation of a midwinter tropic interlude.

Perhaps the most disturbing note is the mean, red-brick drabness of the facade before which the couple stands. Surely, if commemorating some carefree, midwinter visit to St. Augustine, Tampa, Gulfport, or Biloxi, they would have sought a more characteristic background for this ceremonial record of departure—some sea vista or hint of palm garden, veranda, or umbrella-crowned tables. Instead, the building before which they are posed is of coarse red brick, and the entrance, which they partially obscure, has been covered over with a shedlike wooden structure obviously intended to offer protection in inclement weather. This crudely built addition is dark and squat, with no breath of concession to elegance or ornament, and it is in no way out of place. It seems a natural extension of the grim brick building, and it is fittingly perched over three worn concrete steps leading down to the broad sidewalk on which the couple stand. The sidewalk itself is cracked and dirty, and drops abruptly to a littered street. Everything we see of the setting has the mean-spirited, cut-rate look of a county courthouse or a cheap hotel in some small southern town. If it is a courthouse, the couple may have been married here the week before and now, dressed in their best traveling clothes, have paused for a pre-departure photograph, the building serving as mute witness to the beginning and end of their brief honeymoon. But if this is no semitropical resort, how does one account for the glare of midsummer light, the waves of heat that radiate from the sidewalk and street? Above the improvised wooden shelter covering the doorway of the building, part of a window is visible, and clearly reflected in the glass is the dense silhouette of a tree toward which the couple must be looking as the photograph is taken. From the small-leaf density of its foliage, it may well be an elm. Certainly it is no tropical **135** palm. This could be a midsummer view, then, taken in any one of a thousand American cities or small towns. The wooden shelter before the doorway would have been erected to shield visitors against chill winter winds, though it could of course be there as protection against the tropical rainy season.

Without the dates on the border, we would almost certainly see this as a summer tableau, and the suggestion of Southern California, Florida beaches, sunny little Gulf towns comes entirely from the date: *1939 January 1939*. This could, in turn, be entirely misleading. We logically suppose this legend to have some direct bearing on the image confronting us, whereas it simply designates the time at which the film was processed. Perhaps this was the first exposure on the roll—made in the summer of 1938 outside the county courthouse in Tupelo, Mississippi. Returning home to their duplex apartment in Atlanta, the couple had no other occasion for making photographs until Thanksgiving. They completed the roll on Christmas morning, and this single image of a summer holiday was returned to them with ones of winter feasting. Hence, the date is misleading.

On the other hand, there is such an air of commemoration, of statement and coda about this particular photograph that it is hard to believe it was permitted to lie dormant for half a year in the cubed darkness of the camera. Let us assume, then, that the photograph was developed within a week of the couple's return to their home in the Forest Park Apartments in Memphis, Tennessee. They had been married by a Justice of the Peace in West Memphis, Arkansas, and had driven from there to Hot Springs, where they spent a honeymoon week at The Palms Hotel. While hardly tropical, Hot Springs has a moderate winter climate and the kind of resort status that would justify white clothing even when the air has a distinct chill. But it would be simplest, no doubt, to ignore the dates entirely, since they so confuse the narration of the photograph itself.

The photograph divides neatly into three receding planes. In the first, at the bottom of the photograph, is a narrow band of asphalted street littered with small scraps of paper and cigarette butts. One half-smoked cigar is clearly visible, perhaps tossed there by the man in the photograph. The second plane consists of a broad concrete sidewalk, on which a man and woman stand with their luggage stacked beside them. In the third and most distant plane stands a simple red-brick building. The man and woman are neatly centered in the photograph, though the entire image is tilted slightly to the right. This is noticeable only because the left edge of the photograph is not parallel with the brick column that juts from the building. The tilt is slight, however, and in no way disturbing to the image as a whole.

For purposes of identification, we shall designate the man as James Henry and the woman as Dorothy, husband and wife, resident at 3252 Coleman Avenue, Memphis, Tennessee. In the photograph, the woman stands to her husband's right and slightly behind him, so that her left shoulder is covered by his right arm. She wears a white crocheted dress, with capped sleeves and a simple, rounded neck; the hemline extends to within six inches of her ankle. The straw hat she wears has a round, low crown and a narrow, flat brim. It is sloped at an extreme angle over her right ear—giving a little the effect of an askew tin doughboy helmet of the First World War. Yet the angle of the hat composes so well with the face, hair, and brows that its smartness is unmistakable. Dark blonde hair is swept sleekly back to expose the left ear, which is ornamented with a large, button-shaped earring. The brows, plucked into gossamer crescents, give the face an effect of gentle, languorous curves. The face and arms are rounded with the slightest hint of plumpness, their softly curving lines accented by

the curve of the brows, the earring, the curved crown of **137**
the hat, the gentle scoop of the neckline of the dress, the
softened epaulet effect of its slightly padded shoulders. The
total impression is one of a stylish but yielding femininity,
accented by a bow of grosgrain ribbon on the hat, and a
sash, perhaps three inches in width, tied in another bow at
the waist of the dress. Although the photograph is in black
and white, it seems probable that the hat is of a finely
woven navy-blue Panama straw; in that case, navy blue
which would also be the color of the slightly pointed kid
shoes the woman is wearing. The light that theatrically
filters through the brim of the hat intensifies the medium-
blue of Dorothy's eyes, and the sash at her waist is the
echo of the full, curved, scarlet line of her lips. In these
discreet slashes of red there is a promise of ripening sensuality, but the dominant effect is of well-tailored, virginal
white.

The woman's left arm is entirely obscured by the body
of the man beside whom she stands; the right arm hangs
loosely and with practised ease at her side. The fingers of
her right hand are slightly cupped, so that they are not visible, and it is impossible to see if she wears any jewelry
there. There is, however, a slight ridge visible a few inches
above her right wrist. Whether this is a watch, a bracelet,
or the hem of a soft white cotton glove is not clear.

Despite a disturbing stiffness in the waist and legs of the
figure (which may, of course, be an effect of the dress and
not of the body), there is a hint here of a practised model's
poise before the camera. The feet are placed close together,
the right slightly behind the left, as though to stress the
rounded elegance of the ankles, the sleek trimness of the
shoes. The face is tilted almost imperceptibly to reveal
its most flattering curves, and the eyes gaze directly into
the lens of the camera. The lips are parted in the clear
but tantalizing half-smile of shampoo and deodorant ad-

vertisements. She had always been more successful in arranging her face for the camera than in arranging her body, which never entirely lost its stiffened fear of hands. But with satiny makeup and dramatic side-lighting, it was a perfect face for modeling hats or for proclaiming the portrait photographer's skills—as, indeed, it had repeatedly done. She was never so successful at live modeling, for she was never at ease with the woman's body that had been given her too early. Her own breasts had not yet begun their first girlish swellings when the rot of cancer inhabited all the secret woman-spaces of her mother's body, filling each corner of the two-room shotgun house with the stench of death. And not long after, her younger sister's childlike body was twisted and torn beyond repair by the unwanted, over-large baby she bore.

Thus her confidence, feminity, and grace were all concentrated within her face, and with such effect that it was continually—though in non-life-altering, minor ways—being discovered by photographers, alleged Texas oilmen, promoters, cafeteria managers, and romantics. She was only sixteen when her professional career as a model began. A tremulously excited visitor to the Chicago World's Fair of 1932, she was discovered for the first time by a New York City adman responsible for arranging promotions for both dairy and morticians' conventions. Thus, within a few hours of her arrival in Chicago, she was parading along a gangway dressed in an imitation-silk shroud, its shapeless, sexless folds the perfect shield for her already ripe woman's body, and her oval, exquisitely symmetrical face, her clear blue eyes, her half-parted, full mouth provoking shouts of unqualified approval from the discreetly drunken undertakers of Wichita, Dubuque and Sioux Falls. Advance orders for the new rayon shrouds were appropriately brisk.

None of this, of course, is visible in the photograph.

What one sees is a stylish young woman, her face hovering
on the indistinct line between girlish prettiness and wom-
anly handsomeness, composed and smartly dressed and
standing slightly behind and to the right of a man who
appears to be between ten and fifteen years her senior.
They might, at first glance, be brother and sister, returned
home for a summer visit and ready to depart now for
Cincinnati; there he will change trains for Cleveland and
she will travel on to New York, where she works as a
secretary in a large Manhattan law firm. Their parents have
just celebrated their fiftieth wedding anniversary, and three
other children were at home as well, but since those three all
live within a few miles of the parents, there was no occasion for a departure photograph including all five of them.
Dorothy, at twenty-four, is the youngest child, and her
father's clear favorite; James Henry, the middle son, has
just celebrated his thirty-sixth birthday. With twelve years
difference in their ages, this brother and sister had never
been particularly close, but now they feel a kind of confederacy, both having chosen paths that led them away
from Paducah, where they were born and grew up in the
clapboard caricature of an Edwardian mansion just outside
the town center. They correspond regularly now, though
they had scarcely spoken as children; neither, indeed, had
seemed vaguely aware of the other's existence, but then she
had had a brother nearer her own age and interests and he
a sister nearer to his.

A closer look makes it clear that they are not brother
and sister. Even had she taken after a dainty, invalid Irish
mother and he after a burly, stevedoring Sicilian father, and
each so much as to seem to have been cloned from the one
parent, there would be at least some ghostly shadow of a
family resemblance. Here there is none. The woman is
all softened curves, while the man's features are rigidly

squared. His elongated head is almost rectangular in shape, his brows straight and heavy, and the one hand visible in the photograph is chunky and broad. His mouth, though brushed here by a self-conscious smile, is a straight, rigid line. His nose is large and seems to rob his upper lip of any fullness. Such details would normally suggest a brutish, Neanderthal quality, but the figure he presents is not without a certain masculine grace. Despite a thickening at the waist, his body suggests strength and confidence. The slight forward thrust of his hips marks a casual self-awareness with respect to his own body, which the woman lacks entirely. The man's feet are planted rather widely apart, in spotless white shoes. With such a stance he could deliver or receive a swift right to the jaw without losing his balance. Though he wears the regulation white of a resort holiday—white shirt, white tie, white flannel trousers and white shoes—there is nothing dandified or fashionable about him. He clearly treats the clothes as a uniform, differing only in color and cut from the one he wears as a motorcycle policeman. Indeed, any hint at mere modishness is cancelled by his shirt collar; it is smartly cut, but the top button of the shirt has been undone, so that the collar does not trimly meet the line of his carefully knotted tie. Furthermore, the belt he wears—with its faintly visible slots designed to hold revolver bullets—belongs to quite another uniform. His Gatsby-like summer elegance is a grudging concession to the woman who stands beside him now, and who will always seek to eliminate the traces of his raw, aggressive masculinity.

James Henry is clearly less accustomed than his wife, Dorothy, to having his photograph made. There is grim resignation in his forced smile, as there is in the grudging slope of his shoulders. His left arm is held awkwardly behind his back—perhaps in graceless imitation of casualness,

though there is another possible explanation as well. Since **141**
the woman's left arm is not visible in the photograph, it is
possible that her left hand grasps the man's extended hand
behind his back in a pledge of mutual trust and support.
Perhaps he fears such declarations as reflecting on his masculinity and hence can only make them in secret; indeed,
his rare public gestures of affection will at first baffle and
later enrage him. She, on the other hand, may regret or
distrust her commitment to a man of sometimes brutish
masculinity, so that her own feminine yieldings will come
to seem more and more the betrayals of an unwanted
woman's body. At any rate, if their hands are clasped, they
are not visible to the camera.

Narratively, both hands and eyes can be particularly
rich in suggestion. It is unfortunate that neither of the
woman's hands is visible, and that although her eyes strike
us with a straightforward prettiness, they are half-shadowed
by the brim of her hat, so that we can read no nuance of
feeling or hope there. Even in shadow, they suggest a faint
puffiness, as though she has been crying, but this may be
caused by the brightness of the sun. The fact that the pair
casts no shadow on the sidewalk may indicate that the
photograph was taken at noon, with the hot sun directly
overhead, and the woman's blue eyes are, after all, highly
sensitive to the sun. The man's eyes are slightly squinted as
well, and almost entirely concealed by clown-mask shadows beneath his heavy black eyebrows. One of his hands,
however, is clearly visible in the photograph. The right
arm is draped along his side and the right hand brought
slightly forward, as though with conscious intent. It is the
side and not the back of the hand that we see—the fore-
finger and the thumb—and the position cannot be a comfortable one. Perhaps the hand is presented at this awkward
angle out of vanity. Certainly it is a large, strong, well-

formed hand, with the nails neatly trimmed. During the years of his poolhall hustling, the hands are set off effectively by the green baize of hotly lighted pool tables. They seem out of place, though no less effective, when hammering to raw meat the faces of Negro suspects.

The couple's luggage is stacked at a right angle to the curb. The man's clothing is packed into a grey leather Gladstone suitcase measuring approximately thirty inches in the length, eighteen inches in height and twelve inches in thickness. The woman's holiday wardrobe is carefully folded into a small metal trunk with brass corners and leather handles, whose volume is approximately 50 percent greater than that of the Gladstone. On the trunk lies an oblong clutch purse and a boxlike object. This latter object might well be a makeup case, or even a jewelry box, and it appears to be made of wood. It could, on the other hand, be some locally-crafted souvenir, or a tightly wrapped box of salt-water taffy bought for the neighbor who has cared for the couple's infant son during their absence. It would be useful to know the contents of this box, as it would to know the particular combination of dressing gowns, halter-top dresses, swim-wear, sanitary pads, matched sets of underwear, sandals and tailored linen dresses in the woman's trunk. Whether or not there is a revolver in the man's Gladstone suitcase, along with his white cotton boxer shorts and undershirts, an extra necktie, colorful sport shirts, packages of three-to-a-pack Trojans, handkerchiefs, socks, and rust-colored linen trousers, would also be interesting. The man's suitcase is tightly packed, without the faintest crease that would designate an unfilled corner in its soft leather sides. The total effect of these carefully aligned pieces of luggage is of efficiency and practicality. Without being extravagant, the pieces are in good taste, and their newness suggests they were recently purchased for this particular

holiday—or that they have scarcely been used since they **143**
were bought for the couple's honeymoon trip in 1936.

The contents of this luggage, of the purse, of the mysterious wooden box, would clearly tell us much of this
couple's hopes and fears. So, too, would their hands and
eyes. If, for example, we could only know whether their
left hands are clasped behind the man's back, we might
qualify our sense that, despite their physical proximity,
there is a marked separation between the two. Whether
intentionally or not, there is much here that is hidden from
our perception. Even the date on the photograph, stamped
across the borders with sans-serif certainty, is of question-
able value. What we are left with is a black-and-white
photograph of a vacationing, arriving, or departing man
and woman. The background is formed by an ordinary red
building, and the couple stand on the broad stretch of
concrete sidewalk that fronts it. The photographer, then,
must be standing in the street, approximately four feet
from the curb. The man, dressed in white, seems considerably taller than his wife, who is also dressed in white, but
the effect is somewhat exaggerated by the fact that he
stands slightly forward, nearer to the photographer. To the
woman's right and slightly blocking our view of her right
foot, two pieces of luggage are carefully aligned at a right
angle to the curb. Since there are no tags on the luggage,
we can suppose that the couple have just arrived, or are
about to depart, by automobile. The festive look of their
clothing may indicate a honeymoon journey, or attendance
at some ceremonial family affair—the wedding anniversary
of the wife's parents, or the ordination of the husband's
younger brother into the Methodist ministry. The two
stand poised for the act of commemoration. "Smile, Jimmy,"
says the wife, and she clutches the hand he extends to her
behind his back. It has not been a great success, this second-

144 anniversary second honeymoon, but she feels strangely comforted by the decisive grasp of his strong, well-formed hand and she carefully, with practised, well-tutored grace, tilts her head to the right to show her face and her new, navy-blue Panama hat to their best advantage.

FIVE

...at any given moment the accepted report of an event is of far greater importance than the event, for what we think about and act upon is the symbolic report and not the event itself.

William M. Ivins, *Prints and Visual Communication*

ℰ   ℰ

You press the button and we do the rest!

Eastman Kodak

THE CAMERA

SIZE: *2 x 4½ x 9½ inches, folded.*

LENS: *Kodak Anastigmat.*

FOCAL LENGTH: *170 mm. Variable stops (f/6.3 to f/45), iris diaphragm. Range finder coupled, rack-and-pinion focussing.*

SHUTTER: *No. 3A Kodamatic, between lens elements; T, B and instantaneous, variable speeds (½ to ¹⁄₁₅₀ sec.); cocking and release levers on shutter.*

FINDER: *Waist-level, brilliant reflector, on front camera standard; pivots for horizontal or vertical format.*

BODY: *Wood and aluminium, covered with Persian morocco leather; split-image view finder located at the base of front standard; rising front.*

LIST PRICE: *$70.00.*

The 3A Autographic Kodak Special is a later model of the popular postcard-size Kodak, manufactured by the Eastman Kodak Company of Rochester, New York. A folding-bellows camera for six to ten exposures, 3¼ x 5½ inches on A-122 roll film, its autographic feature was invented by Henry J. Gaisman, New York, New York (U.S. Patent No. 1,184,941, May 30, 1916). The range finder was invented by Joseph Becker, Washington, D.C. (U.S. Patent No. 1,178,474, April 14, 1916).

The autographic principle was first introduced by Eastman Kodak Company in 1914. It required a special camera back and a special film. The back of the camera was modified near the top end by the attachment of a small hinged trap door held down by a spring. On the back of the door was a stylus, carried in a long, shallow indentation. The trap door and stylus were held in place by a sliding bar, which could be moved to open the door and remove the stylus. The film was regular photographic film but backed with red paper, thinner than the usual backing, with black carbon tissue interleaved. Once the film was in position, the user would open the trap door, and with the stylus or any sharp object, write a date or a few identifying words in the opening. This was exposed to daylight, not direct sunlight, for from one to five seconds, which registered the writing on the film. When the negative film was developed, the writing appeared in black next to the margin of the picture. Henry J. Gaisman, the inventor, approached the Eastman Kodak Company with his idea, and George Eastman paid Gaisman $300,000 for full rights to the patent.

The autographic feature was employed in all 3A Folding Pocket Kodak cameras, as on many other sizes from 1915 on, and the name was changed to Autographic Kodak Camera. The hundreds of thousands of Kodak cameras of standard sizes introduced prior to that time could be converted to the autographic system by replacing the old back with an autographic back, sold separately in various sizes ($2.50 to $4.50). The autographic system was employed on certain folding Brownie cameras and roll-film Graflexes, but it was quite carefully controlled, and no other manufacturer used it.

The other novel feature of this camera is its range finder. The use of a range finder coupled to the focussing mechanism on the Autographic Kodak Special cameras represents the first arrangement of this type on any production model camera. The range finder is of the split-image type, its base line lying across the camera beneath the lens. The operator, on looking into the left end of the range finder, sees two images of the object he wishes to photograph. These images become coincident when the object is in sharp focus. How- ever, it was not until the 1920s that range finders became really popular in small cameras.

The Autographic Kodak Special was introduced in 1914. In 1916 the range finder was added. It was produced, with various lens and shutter combinations, through the year 1934. Some time before 1920, the hinged autographic panel was modified, the sliding bar being discontinued and the stylus carried in loops at the edge of the panel.

THE PHOTOGRAPHER

Juanita Rose Lowndes, Caucasian female,
born January 2, 1910, in Nashville, Tennessee,
to Rose Marie (née Crowder) and Robert Henry Lowndes;
died December 24, 1975, in Cairo, Illinois.

Even as an infant she was dark. Indeed, she was born with
thick, coarse black hair and a tawny skin that later, with
the slightest exposure to the sun, assumed rich mahogany
tones. Even as a child she had a gypsy-like sense of color,
preferring bright, tropical hues that made her skin seem yet
more dusky, her eyes more startingly black, so that she
was sometimes mistaken for Mexican or Indian. Whatever
tropical blood bequeathed her this exotic patina came from
her mother, for Robert Lowndes was a slight, pale, asth-
matic man, who must often have wondered if such a dark-
tinted flower as this could indeed have sprung from his
own seed. But he wondered for other reasons as well, and
never solved the riddle of his first and only blind infatua-
tion. Rose Marie was an orphaned bareback rider with
The Babcock Brothers Three-Ring Circus when he first
met and fell in love with her. She was sixteen then, and had
grown up not at all unhappily with the score of well-
meaning acrobats and clowns and trapeze artists who had
taken her into their collective charge after the Flying
Crowders took a fatal plunge from the high wire in Tampa,
Florida. Balanced with feathery ease on the bare back of
a white stallion, Rose Marie seemed to Robert the incarna-
tion of all fairytale princesses. In flesh-colored tights and

spangled ballerina skirt, she pirouetted in liquid circles that
seemed to draw silken threads taut about his heart. When
he tried to find her later in the densely improvised village
of tents and painted wooden carriages, a pair of clowns
barred his way. They taunted him, spun him about so that
he lost his way among the labyrinth of dusty paths, and
collided with him round sudden turnings, knocking him
rudely to the ground, and then, with elaborate apologies,
white-gloved-flickings of dirt, violent smoothings of wrinkles, set him onto his feet again.

He never found her that day in Humboldt, Tennessee,
but he followed the circus to Jackson and found her without even trying, pouring milk for her new kitten into a
warped pie-tin. She was crouched over with her bare feet
in the powdery dust, murmuring encouragement to her
tortoise-shell kitten. Out of some unexpected storehouse,
Robert plucked courage to speak to her, and in a clumsy
rush of words lost the elegant phrasings he had so carefully
prepared as he told of seeking her in Humboldt, and then
walking for two days to Jackson to find her. She glanced
up at him but once. Otherwise, her eyes were fixed on the
kitten that stood, with trembling legs, thrusting its face
into the pan of milk. Yet when she answered him, it was
with all the practised charm of a prima donna receiving
an ardently admiring young nobleman. The scene would
have made a superb photograph. The carriage behind them
has window boxes blooming with scarlet geraniums, and
shutters with heart-shapes jigsawed into them. A photographer would have had to be briskly efficient in his movements, however, for the clowns were soon upon them,
bowling Robert over in a small cyclone of dust from which
he emerged unhurt, but with his shoelaces intricately
knotted together, his jacket reversed and buttoned down
the back, his straw boater deprived of its brim. And when
his dust-stung eyes cleared, she was gone, together with

152 the cat and the pie-tin of milk. He challenged the clowns, tearing away his jacket and raising both arms in fierce imitation of John L. Sullivan. The clowns disappeared beneath a flap of canvas, and he followed them into a pitch darkness that seemed cavernously vast. He stood still, listening for the sound of their breathing, for the shuffle of feet or a whispered message. From far away came band music, the roar of a tiger, a medley of voices shouting across space, but within the tent there was no sound. He advanced slowly, arms stretched before him, fists clenched in readiness. Nothing. The hands slowly opened as he groped before him to touch the canvas, to find some brace or support to guide him. There was nothing. Panic stirred within him as he sought some faintest shaft of light that would carry him back to the flap through which he had entered. Suddenly he encountered the warm, coarse canvas of the tent wall, and began to follow it, to move along with forward-sweeping arcs of his arm, searching each crease and seam. But the wall seemed unbroken, as impenetrable as stone, and the air felt suddenly dense and heavy. Dust filled his lungs, and they ached for fresh air. In desperation he flung himself to the ground, and slowly wormed his way under the tightly pegged bottom of the tent. Halfway through, pinned flat to the ground, he heard the raucous laughter of the clowns, and rolled his head just far enough to the side to see them lift and tilt the huge oaken bucket of dirty wash water.

He had always been easily discouraged. When, at the age of nine, he was asked to read a sentence aloud in school and with lips trembling brought forth the syllables of "mosquito" as "moss-cue-whit-oo," the humiliating laughter of his classmates so intimidated him that for two years he entered the schoolyard as an amputee would have approached the battlefield where he had once stepped onto a land mine. His persistence in the pursuit of Rose Marie

seems yet the more heroic for thus being so improbable, so
against his essential character. Yet he did pursue her, though
in Bells, Tennessee, his only glimpse of her was proud and
spangled on the back of the white stallion, and in German-
town he had to content himself with a vision of her head
(the hair tied in knots of rag to curl it) thrust briefly out
the window of what he now knew to be her trailer. In
Little Rock he almost gave up the chase, for he was
perilously near his last dollar, and couldn't risk buying a
ticket to enter the big tent. So he stood a hundred yards
away from the clustered, makeshift village, far enough to
protect his flanks from surprise attacks by the clowns, yet
near enough to see her when she left her trailer. He stood
patiently, in blistering morning sun and through a slow but
drenching afternoon rain, and in the early evening, when the
rain had stopped, she came out to him. Without explanation,
without apology for his bruised shins and soaking clothing,
she came and took his hand and wandered a while with him,
as effortlessly and casually as if they had been childhood
sweethearts. She led him to a concrete viaduct beside the
highway, and they sat watching the last of the sunset. She
held his left hand between her own cool, smooth ones, and
stroked it as he had seen her stroking the cat. Tears of
gratitude and weariness filled his eyes, and he wanted to
tell her how it bored him to work in his father's hardware
store, how he had chipped his front tooth on the handlebars
of his bicycle, how he had pursued her, that he wanted to
marry her, that he could never go to church again after
dropping the collection plate with bellclanging, jingling
music on the stone floor before the altar, that he secretly
hated it when his mother called him Robbie. But he could
say nothing, only sit and taste the salt stream of his tears
and wonder at the coolness of her hands. Suddenly she
stood, placed those same hands on his shoulders, and with
the slightest caressing pressure told him he was not to fol-

low. "I'll open the door at midnight," she said, and he realized it was the first time he had heard her voice. Its low melody so surprised him that he scarcely heard the words, and only after she had disappeared in the dusk did he really weigh their meaning. He trembled, both with excitement and from the dampness of his clothes, and felt his groin begin to tingle. But then fear seized him: what if it were a trap? The clowns would kidnap him, bind him, and throw him out of one of the carriages into a river or deserted patch of woods where only small, scavenging animals would find him.

He rose finally and walked into town, where he ate a plate of baked beans with frankfurters and then wandered the summer streets without seeing them. He was only vaguely aware of the murmur of voices and the clinking of thick glasses behind screen doors, of a platoon of patent medicines lined in brisk rows in a shop window, of the brittle sound of horses' hooves against the pavement and the occasional erratic splutter of a gasoline engine. At eleven o'clock, he walked slowly back to the circus, to stand where he had stood all morning and all afternoon, until she had come to him. At twelve he approached the darkly huddled caravans, trying to make as little noise as possible. A twig crackled under his foot, and somewhere a hound began to howl loudly, piteously. The steps leading up to her trailer seemed perilously unsteady, so fragile they might splinter under his feet, but he reached the top and extended his hand to search for a knob or catch. The door swept inward, and her cool hand caught his to guide him to the cot beside which a single candle was burning in a sardine can. And so she continued to guide him for another twelve months. The following morning, she led him briskly down the trailer steps to where the clowns and hucksters and animal trainers and trapeze artists awaited them. The clowns made him brisk, businesslike bows, and as they

straightened up, suddenly jerked backwards and tumbled
to the ground as though he had replied with hard jabs to the chin. Everyone laughed, and the laughter and singing and joking continued to set up a hum about him as he and Rose Marie were hoisted up into a carriage and driven off to the nearest Justice of the Peace. His new bride bought their railway tickets that afternoon, and the same tumbling, merry-making crowd was there at the small junction station to wave them good-bye.

Since Rose Marie is only the mother of the photographer who took the following picture, it perhaps seems extravagant to devote so much time to her courtship. But since these weeks of romantic pursuit do so much to color the father's later attitude toward his daughter, and, indeed, her attitudes as a young woman, they are hardly irrelevant to the photograph she makes in 1942. Neither of Robert's parents entirely recovered from the shock that attended the acquisition of a dusky, bareback-riding daughter-in-law, but both prayed that the union might somehow find favor in the eyes of a merciful God. Rose Marie was briskly efficient in the kitchen, immaculately thorough in her toilette, and dutifully attendant to her new husband. Such qualities of course recommended her even to pious Methodists, as did her acrobatically straight-backed carriage during the last months of her pregnancy. Though seven-month babies were often sickly, Juanita Rose seemed a wonderfully sturdy baby, and delightfully even-tempered. Robert marveled silently at his wife's madonna-like gentleness, her store of melodic lullabyes, her patient motherliness, for she was, after all, scarcely seventeen. She nursed her dark daughter, weaned her at five months of age, and one night tucked her carefully into her wicker crib, tiptoed out of the bedroom, and (according to the station master) left town on the midnight train. From that night on, she never attempted to communicate by so much as a bill of divorce. Twenty years later, to be sure, Robert felt some distant seismic flutter of recognition when he saw a poster advertising the naughty Parisian delights of a fan-dancer named Marie La Rose, but the poster was so discolored by sun and rain that he could not be certain.

Inevitably, Juanita was much more than simply a treasured only child, a delicately, adroitly feminine companion. She was also the souvenir of her father's sole romantic misadventure, of the single minute irregularity in the otherwise blandly regular, serviceable blue-serge fabric of his youth. Though the grandparents more regularly ministered to the real needs of the infant, while the father only stood helplessly, wonderingly by, Juanita soon made it clear that her throatiest laugh and the wildest sparkle of her black eyes were reserved exclusively for him. The child was only eight years old when a Rock Island freight train sliced neatly in half the new Model A Ford in which her grandparents were taking a Sunday drive. The wreck became a local legend, and for months afterward small crowds clustered beside the barbed wire fence of Hank's Wrecking and Scrap Yard to stare at what remained of it—the rear half of the car only, so clearly sliced away it might have been severed by a blow torch rather than by a steam-belching locomotive. When the train halted, nearly fifty miles away, the steering wheel was found neatly notched into the cow-catcher. Meanwhile, Juanita sat on the back seat, dressed in summery pink ruffles, like some grande dame taking the air from her open brougham. She waited, simply, for her father to come for her. A series of anonymous, shuffling black women cared for her over the next five years, each in turn compelled to leave despite their affection for the child by the steady accumulation of unpaid wages. Robert understood little of the hardware business save the drawling, gossiping, counter-propped hours he idled away with former schoolmates who stopped in for

a nickel's worth of carpet tacks or a roll of chicken wire.
He was quick to order unmanageably complex patented
mousetraps, and slow to renew the basic stock of hammers
and saws and wood-screws. Plowshares arrived after the
harvest was over, and there was certain to be a plentiful
quantity of weather-stripping on the Fourth of July, but
no window-screening. Still, he limped along, with the aid
of his father's more faithful customers and the combined
notoriety of Rose Marie and the Rock Island Railroad.
Perhaps, after all, he would have made a modest, incom-
petent success, given the generosity of the small Southern
town, had he not so regally indulged his only daughter.
Her dresses must be of the richest fabrics, her petticoats
the fullest, most lavishly lace-trimmed, and her shoes the
daintiest that the shops in Nashville could provide for her
small feet. Her bedroom was a wonderland of extravagantly
costumed dolls, gilt mirrors, satin pillows and delicate por-
celain boxes that held heart-shaped rings, cameo lockets,
fragile strands of seed pearls, and her initials spelled out in
garnet.

When his parents' modest insurance money melted away
(there was never compensation from the Rock Island, as
Mr. Lowndes had driven past a flashing signal visible for
nearly a half-mile), Robert began to supply himself from
the cash drawer with whatever funds he needed. There
was no question of extortion, for obviously the money was
his, and the sums he took were always promptly noted
down as petty cash. Slowly the amounts escalated, from
one or two dollars (enough for a visit to the local ice-cream
parlor and a heart-shaped box of chocolates or brightly-
colored picture book) to five and ten dollars (dainty new
underclothes for Juanita, sent C.O.D. from Goldsmith's
in Memphis), twenty dollars (a new fur muff for Christmas), fifty dollars (for a mortgage payment on the house).
And as the petty-cash column snaked its way down one

page of the violet-lined ledger, inched its way across another, and steadily waxed, so did the cigar box full of unpaid bills piled high to overflowing. Robert bound it up carefully with string, took it home, and hid it at the back of his clothes closet. He did the same with the second, then a third. Finally, he borrowed a small leather satchel from old Dr. Adams next door, explaining that it might be necessary for him to take a small business trip. Into it he carefully packed the neatly bound cigar boxes, locked the case, and left on the afternoon train for Nashville. There he checked it at the luggage counter, tore up the ticket, and took the next train back to Humboldt. Perhaps he hoped somehow to revive the fairytale magic of his youthful courtship of Rose Marie. But his persistent creditors failed to be entranced by his gesture, and Dr. Adams in time demanded the return of his leather satchel. When the bankruptcy notice was pasted above the padlocked door of Lowndes Hardware Company, he suggested to Dr. Adams that the case might somehow have been checked at the Nashville Railway Station. After a complex exchange of letters, it was sent to Humboldt with four dollars and fifty cents of back storage fees payable for its redemption.

Juanita was fifteen at the time of the disappearing satchel episode. Though she had been elaborately indulged, she was neither spoiled nor affected. She asked for nothing, since it had never been necessary to ask, and nothing had ever led her to wonder at the source of the flow of treasures that encircled her life. Devoted to her father, always eager to please him, she accepted the loss of house and home and business and ornately carved Victorian love seats with surprising indifference. When her father returned to their small furnished rooms with his hair and eyebrows deeply dusted from a day's labor at the local furniture factory, she always contrived to have some eye-pleasing supper laid for him. Her cooking, to be sure, was more imaginative than

edible, but he accepted it, wearily and somewhat be- **159**
wilderedly, as a gesture of devotion. And so it was meant.
But work in the furniture factory was irregular, and for
months at a time Robert might be laid off, as the last-hired
and as someone with ability to handle, after all, only the
most routine jobs of sawing and planing and smoothing.
During one of these periods, when his face assumed the
final ghostly hollowness of defeat, Juanita quit school. She
was seventeen, and she found her first job behind the short-
order counter of the Midtown Cafe. From that point until
the moment the following photograph was made, her life
curved up and occasionally down the scale of waitressing
jobs. She fried eggs to plastic brittleness on rancid grills,
guided oceans of water into the mouths of Pyrex coffee
pots, learned the music of thick crockery and thin silver-
ware, topped up salt cellars with swift-wristed efficiency,
found at last the arch-support shoes that fitted her best,
hammocked her raven hair in yet darker hairnets, and slid
a pencil behind her ear as gracefully as she would have
tucked a gardenia there. Father and daughter still made
their promenades round the courthouse square, but only on
Juanita's free evening.

Considering her pampered childhood and the gypsy
legacy of her mother, she might have been expected to
chafe against such a fate, to secretly await the Prince
Charming who would appear to her, trapped within the
witch's spell of stale cooking fat, and transform her life
with a kiss. But she accepted her destiny as lightly and
casually as she had once accepted satin-skirted flamenco-
dancer dolls or a coral brooch. She wept as for a gentle
lover tragically fallen in battle when Robert died, on duty
at the furniture factory, in the summer of 1929. But she
quickly collected her wits, the eighty dollars in her savings
account, her few tropic-colored best dresses, and departed
for Nashville. For a time, she worked at a hamburger

stand across from the Grand Old Opry, and her presence (as the manager realized when he so quickly raised her pay) was a steady lure to would-be singing stars, hayseed farmers, and the occasional downtown businessman. She worked there for six months, then left for the brighter prospects of the Stonewall Hotel dining room. Tips were good, the clientele the best she had known, and her station quickly became the most popular one. It would be interesting to know how she so successfully fended off her ardent suitors during this period, for fend them off she did, and they can only have been persistent, for her stunningly dark beauty, her sensuously rhythmic movements must always have stood out from the chorus line of slatternly, peroxided, sloped-shouldered comrades with whom she so often worked. It had, of course, something to do with her gently bantering speech, which gave generously of her most feminine sympathies, yet never promised more. Certainly there were no clowns in baggy pants to defend her against persistent courtiers, but she was her own keeper, and the older waitresses with whom she worked seemed to feel some deep, maternal urging in her presence, smoothing the way for her in new jobs, astonishingly lacking in jealousy of her success. Above all, there was a quality of patient waiting about her, which seemed fulfilled in the autumn of 1930, when a young lawyer from Memphis began to pay her just such doggedly ardent suit as Robert had once paid Rose Marie, though his style was far more urbane and subtle. He was spending a month in Nashville, arguing cases before the State Supreme Court, and was thus a long-term guest at the Stonewall. Perhaps because he did not press his suit so obviously or so aggressively as some of the other guests, Juanita found herself opening up to him. In brief phrases, over the pouring of a cup of coffee, she learned the difficulties he expected to encounter in court that day, heard tales of the stratagems of reluctant witnesses

and the secret vices of judges, and whether or not he
intended to return to Memphis for the weekend. In the
evening, placing a gravy boat before him, filling his water
glass, taking his order for dessert, she received a capsule
summary of the day's progress. He began to linger, casually
smoking, uninsistent, outside the service entrance of the
hotel, to nod to her as she left for the small room she
rented in a nearby but much less fashionable hotel. Occasionally he strolled along beside her to the first intersec-
tion, then said good-night and returned to the Stonewall.
Or he might simply nod a faint smile of greeting as she
passed. One night as she was leaving, drawing a brightly
embroidered shawl around her shoulders, he said, "Tomorrow is your day off, isn't it?" "Yes," she answered.
"I've got good seats for us at the Opry. I'll pick you up
for dinner first. Around six-thirty." Without waiting for
her reply, he turned and walked back to the brightly
lighted entrance of the hotel. He never made requests, and
he never made promises. He simply told her what they
would do, and she always voicelessly agreed. She was comforted by his unique mixture of strength and assertiveness
with an almost feminine gentleness. He took her to the
horse races, he took her boating, he brought her, from
Memphis, a necklace of black jet, and he finally took her
to a house just outside town, owned by a vacationing frater-
nity brother from Vanderbilt University, and made love to
her—urgently, rather too quickly, but all the while murmuring a gentle music of love. These events took place in
November of 1930. Charles Lee Longstreet came to Nashville less often in December, though he sent Juanita a
handsome pearl bracelet for Christmas. He returned in the
New Year, when the Supreme Court was in session again,
and announced, simply, that he had found her a better job
at the Peabody Hotel in Memphis. She knew, of course,
that it was a yet better, more storied, more fashionable

hotel than the Stonewall (it was said that the Mississippi Delta, with its rich plantations, began in the lobby of the Peabody Hotel), and she nodded ready assent.

It was not so much that she was surprised to learn, shortly after her arrival in Memphis, that Charles was married, for he had never pretended to be an eligible bachelor, though he had also never made formal declaration of a Southern belle wife and two healthy male heirs. And while she had never allowed herself to think ahead to the extent of imagining afternoon teas for other lawyers' wives, Cotton Carnival balls, breakfast table tête-à-têtes, or shopping for china at Broadnax, she still felt vaguely betrayed—not by him but by her own body. She had hardly nurtured Hollywood-inspired visions of saving herself for a particular man or a particular bridal hour, though she was a fanatical moviegoer. Rather, she felt betrayed because there seemed so little pleasure for herself in the intimacies she allowed Charles. There was feminine satisfaction, to be sure, in the intensity of his lovemaking, as there was in the weeping, schoolboyish gratitude with which he caressed her afterward, but it seemed slight when compared to the numbed sense of violation that followed. And deep within her mind, so securely locked away that she had never lent it the shaping mold of words, was the fear that if a child flowered within her, its birth would betray the blackest of African ancestors. The fear sprang from meaningless playground taunts by two little girls jealous of her extravagant dresses with their yards of foamy white petticoats. "Nigger-girl, nigger-girl!" they had shouted, and a flush of rage and fear had risen beneath her dusky skin. She never thought of the taunt as a childishly, naively intuited truth, for it was too absurd to be thought about. Yet it lodged in her mind, filed away in a dim recess together with the legends of her mother's exotic appearance and her sudden, mysterious departure, to emerge only as

a secret fear that she might produce a child of her own **163**
whose skin would be glittering ebony. Meanwhile, she
accepted Charles's adoring passion as her due, for even
with a child's prescience she had known that she possessed a
particular power to please men. She cultivated the art with
a score of other men as well, yet she was never sufficiently
hard to exploit it. There was altogether something too
yielding, too passively accepting about her character. Although she grew to distrust men, to pick out with unerring
feminine radar their shuffling duplicities, their clumsy,
single-minded insistence, their failure to detect the tides of
hope and fear, pity and need that rose and fell in her own
body, she nonetheless yielded to their importunings, for it
seemed so clearly her role.

Juanita never bore children and married but once; she
was over forty at the time. Her husband, an ex-prize fighter,
ran (predictably enough) a diner in Cairo, Illinois. Despite
the fierce look of his broken face with the puffed, welted
stripes of scar tissue round the eyes, he was a gentle man
and an adoring husband. When he died in 1960, Juanita
tried to run the diner alone, but despite the generous use
of Ace bandages and supporthose, the fourteen-hour days
were too much for her swollen ankles and bunioned feet,
and she sold out at a tidy profit to a Burger King franchise.
With the proceeds she bought a small plot of land on a
nearby lake, a new Oldsmobile, and a house-trailer. She
imagined grand adventures, explorations of the Grand
Canyon, a junket to Niagara Falls, a visit to Kay in Memphis. But the trailer remained parked on the small plot of
land, jacked up onto concrete blocks, and a fading awning
over an attached, concrete-block verandah soon proclaimed
its immobile destiny. The money went quickly—a good
deal of it to the county sheriff, who used to call in to be
certain she was not being troubled by the teenage gang
that roamed the area in the winter, breaking into shuttered,

sheeted summer houses. His slight stoop and bronchitic rasp perhaps reminded her of her own father. She bought him a new outboard motor for his fishing boat and a pair of ruby cuff links, and always had on hand for his visits a generous supply of Jack Daniels Black Label. When he failed to win re-election the year after they met, he decided to move to California, where a cousin owned a few orange groves. Juanita was nearly sixty when she resumed her maiden, waitressing name and started to work on the Delta Queen. The work was easy, the customers readily entertained, the hours short, and the river life a new, unexpected adventure for her. In five prudent years she accumulated more than $10,000 in savings, and returned to the rusting trailer on the lake, where she died of kidney failure (never once having seen a doctor or a dentist in her life) in 1975. In the single photograph I have of her, she appears a stunningly beautiful woman, with the sultry, exotic good looks of certain Hollywood stars of the 1930s, those who always played devious or doomed (or devious *and* doomed) women of passion. Certainly she was not the fair, delicate heroine who waltzed off with Dick Powell or Fred Astaire in the last reel. Perhaps for that reason she was drawn to Kay, sealing with her a bond of friendship that was to endure long silences and absences. The telegram she sent when she learned of Kay's death read: "A part of me has died as well. The better part." The two women had not seen each other for more than fifteen years.

But all of that denouement comes after the following photograph is made. Juanita had met Kay as a fellow table-waiting recruit at the Peabody Hotel. They shared complaints and gossip, and they were soon sharing a room, beauty secrets, giggling midnight discussions of their ham-handed dates, and their best hats and handbags; they would have shared best dresses as well, if Juanita had not been four inches taller. From the beginning, Juanita was sus-

picious of Jimmy's courtship of Kay. Whether she un-
selfishly feared for her friend's future, or selfishly feared
being left, once more, alone, she could not have said, and
it would not have mattered. Let it be clearly stated: she
treasured Kay's delicate blonde beauty and felt (though
they were virtually the same age) a huddling, mothering
impulse to protect her. It was Juanita who vigorously
encouraged the photo-modeling career, persuaded Kay
to give up waitressing to devote herself full-time to it, saw
her through with small loans between assignments, helped
fix her hair for special engagements, and often intervened
to arrange better fees. By now Charles Lee Longstreet,
anxious about his public image in what was, after all, an
overgrown small town, had disappeared from her life, and
Kay had taken his place as comrade, yet without the quality
of threat he had posed. So she feared Jimmy's presence,
perhaps even hated him. She reminded Kay that a motorcycle policeman had no real future. What would he do
when he got older—sell Eskimo pies from the side-car?
And there were the stories of his brutality, his pride in
putting mothballs into all the motorcycle gasoline tanks as
they sat idling at the mouth of the tunnel in which a Negro
parade was assembling. Meanwhile, Kay should remember
the rich Texan who sent her such devoted letters, the
New Orleans businessman who telephoned her once a
week, and all the fascinating, eligible men she would meet
in the course of her career. Yet despite her arguments,
Jimmy's attraction seemed to grow stronger, and Juanita
became mother-confessor to the roller coaster course of
their courtship. Kay found him too wild, too undisciplined,
too rough. He would give up drinking entirely, dress with
almost somber self-restraint, and court Kay with gracious
attention. Then, when she would even tentatively agree to
marry him, he would go on a two-day drunk to celebrate
and arrive at her door in the middle of the night, raving

with happiness, unshaven, unwashed, uncombed, and wearing his most pungent fishing clothes. The engagement was promptly cancelled. Even had he moderated these extremes somewhat, Juanita would have found that his insistence on keeping crocodiles and boa constrictors as pets put him far beyond the pale. Nonetheless, when Kay and Jimmy were married by a Justice of the Peace in West Memphis, Arkansas, in 1936, Juanita was one of their two witnesses (the other the tobacco-chewing, aproned, flour-knuckled wife of the old man who married them). No member of Kay's family was there—not because they disapproved of such a match, for that would be too rigorous a reaction for a family with so little claim to social standing of any measurable sort, but because they feared this often violent man with his checkered past of broken marriages, poolhall hustling, and promiscuity, as well as his reputation for brutality to petty criminals, wayward blacks, and the small shopkeepers from whom he extorted chocolates, spare tires, paint thinner, salami, Havana cigars, corsages for a string of girlfriends, and neckties for his poker-playing cronies.

Juanita was to stand witness to other family occasions as well. She was there as godmother when Kay's first son was christened, and it was she who packed them both onto a midnight train for Indianapolis when Kay went there to live and await her divorce. During those months she was also a testy but finally unsuccessful foil to Jimmy's efforts to learn his wife's address (which he finally found through a file clerk at City Hall who simply ran a standard check on Kay's social security number and produced the name of the laundry at which she was employed). Juanita's godson is five years old at the time the following photograph is taken, and his parents have not yet become a divorce court statistic. She has come for Sunday lunch, as she often does, and her affection for Kay has only become

deeper, for she has intimately witnessed her friend's un-
complaining descent into the brackish waters of a punish-
ingly ordinary marriage. Yet she shares Kay's joy in the
pale, precocious child of that marriage, and has spent hours
of agonized, mothering fear beside his bedside, as he fever-
ishly wrestled with murderous viruses. Juanita has by now
advanced to chief hostess at the Peabody Hotel dining
room. She lives alone, but at the moment is being rather
persistently courted by the owner of a feed and grain
store in Byhalia, Mississippi. He has given her a new camera,
bought at Lowenstein's the last time he was in town, and it
is with this same camera that she takes the following picture of Jimmy and his son. Nothing in the photograph
anticipates Kay's death by surgery-violated, multiple can-
cers, or Juanita's by kidney failure, and little enough is
visible of the destiny of the child who stands before a
brick-edged flower-bed with his father. Perhaps because
she so rarely sees Jimmy wearing a suit, or perhaps simply
because she has the new camera with her, Juanita calls to
them before entering the car, and asks them to pose for
a picture. With a single delicate pressure of her index
finger, she records father and son standing awkwardly
together in bright summer sunlight. Then she turns to wave
good-bye to Kay, who remains within the shaded recess
of the sprawling front porch, and enters the car. Jimmy
drives her to the nearest trolley stop, where she catches a
number three that stops directly in front of the Peabody.
She is thus easily in time to begin her duties for the dinner
shift. As she arranges flower-like clusters of sundae glasses
on a wooden tray, she remembers with disgust that Jimmy
had pared his nails at the dinner table, and thinks sadly
of all the lost chances in Kay's life missed. Two weeks
later, when she again comes to Sunday lunch, she brings
her friend the following photograph.

THE PHOTOGRAPH

To the left stands a child who appears to be five or six years of age. He wears long trousers, a plaid jacket, and a cap with a brim in the front just sufficient in size to shade his forehead from the sun. The jacket, though smartly cut and with generous, ornamental lapels, fits him rather baggily, as though it is a hand-me-down from an older brother or cousin. Or perhaps it has only been purchased with a thrifty eye to young boys' sudden spurts of growth. (The elegantly tailored suits and top-coats with meticulously hand-stitched lapels with which he was once so splendidly outfitted were, after all, often outgrown before there was a sartorially appropriate occasion to wear them.) The jacket thus represents a tentative compromise between fashion and economy. Its windowpane checks are smart, but the shoulders sag over thin, delicate shoulders, and the sleeves rasp against the backs of his hands. In a later photograph, the same jacket looks tight as sausage-casing across these same shoulders, and skinny wrists protrude scarecrow-like for an inch or more after the let-down sleeves have resigned. Still, the total effect of the photograph before us now is of a smartly-dressed and well-groomed little boy of five or six. He seems at ease in his prematurely mannish outfit, with none of the stiffness of children posing in their Sunday best. His flannel trousers are smartly cuffed, but their knees betray the running, jumping, squatting, tree-climbing activities common to children of his age. He wears a pale, open-collared shirt, carefully folded back across the collar of his jacket, and it, like his jacket, is trimly closed with dark buttons. The cap would appear to match the paler background of the jacket, whereas the trousers are coordinated with the darker lines that form its large-checked pattern. The cap is a trifle small for his head, and perhaps once was partnered by a double-breasted camel's

hair overcoat purchased by the now bankrupt, handbag- **169**
manufacturing godfather. With his hair cropped so short,
razored round the ears and up the back, and the cap
snugged onto the top of his head, it is difficult to determine
the color of his hair. It could be light brown, but if his
faint brows are any indication, it is probably pale blond
like his mother's. Though the hair has always been bluntly
straight, the mother once "dressed" it in waves and curls,
its golden silkiness her joy, and some consolation for the
arrival of a male infant.

Even without the shadow that partially obscures the
child's face, it would be difficult to read much into its full
anonymous curves. The sun is directly overhead, so that
the cap's slight brim shadows most of his face. Only the
eyebrows, cheeks, and nose catch the sun directly, making
them appear touched with the dead white of clown's paint.
This, in turn, may lead us to see more sadness in the eyes
than is really there, as though they have been baffled witnesses to some violent tableau. The chin is tucked downward so that the eyes must glance up to greet the camera,
and this lack of directness, gives to the entire figure a quality
of uncertainty, of barely contained fear. Even the timorous,
lip-trembling half-smile contributes to this effect. But
perhaps he is only uncomfortable. The folds in his jacket
and trousers suggest they are made of wool, and the closely-
fitting cap is certainly of camel's hair. Yet the full-leafed
trees and shrubbery visible in the photograph suggest midsummer, and with the sun overhead, the wincing look on
the child's round face may be the result of coarse wool
chafing his skin. At any rate, he seems uncomfortable and
shy, with feet pigeon-toed awkwardly together. The single
detail that argues against this impression is that he has
hooked his thumbs into the pockets of his jacket, and his
surprisingly long, lean fingers lend the gesture a note of
adult confidence, even of swagger. These hands, which

will later be much admired, are thus unconsciously arranged in a posture that will become habitual. There is another photograph, taken a quarter-century later, in which the hands are identically arranged, with the thumbs hooked into the pockets of a midnight-blue tuxedo jacket. And yet, taken in its entirety, there is little enough visible here to provoke narration. Indeed, the cap, the chubby, boyish face, the sagging jacket, the wrinkled trousers are assembled into an almost anonymous image of a well-fed, modestly well-dressed little boy. Those who knew his son at the same age would have seen an astonishing similarity to the child who poses here, but the son is not born until nearly two decades after this photograph is made.

"Stand just there, by your father," Juanita says. He moves stiffly to the left, never taking his eyes from the camera in her hands. "Closer, now." He inches his left foot out, and brings his right up to join it. Then he ducks his head to avoid the stabbing midsummer rays of the sun, but still keeps his eyes firmly fixed on the camera, as though it is the only presence here besides himself, its twinkling eye his trusty guardian. Suddenly his slight body stiffens, as a large hand is placed firmly between his shoulders. It feels immense, and he thinks it could crush his back as easily as it crumples an empty package of Lucky Strikes. And now his own hands, which had hung loosely at his sides, feel weak and threatened. They will never possess the strength of the densely muscled, tightly tendoned hand that rests sinisterly on his back. He fears that as he grows, they will remain weak and small, never capable of seizing with carefully aligned thumbs the leather-wrapped handle of a golf club, of grasping the butts of revolvers, the ivory steering wheel of an automobile, the wooden T of lawn-mower handles. Yet he cannot be ashamed of them, for they are sturdy enough, capable of holding open the pages of a book, of guiding pencils and crayons into recognizable approximations of houses and horses and dump-trucks, of making Kool-Aid popsicles in icecube trays, and of elaborate nose-picking. Unsure though he is of their ultimate abilities, the child nonetheless takes premature joy in the work of hands, and cannot be ashamed of his own. Therefore, he brings them slightly forward, hooking his thumbs into his jacket pocket, and lightly curling his fingers down against the windowpane plaid of the fabric. The trembling that began in them when the man's large hand was placed between his shoulders is stilled now.

The boy's pale cap and shirt, the bright splashes of sunlight on his face, suggest the lengthening suns of boyhood summers. In contrast, the figure of the man beside him is one of darkness. His suit, with its tightly-buttoned waistcoat, is of some dark color—grey or brown, or perhaps navy blue. He wears a high-crowned, broadly brimmed felt hat, with the brim tilted downward so that his face is entirely shadowed. Indeed, the shadow of the hat brim is so large that it forms a generous collar, covering the visible V of his white shirt and dark tie, and the upper portion of the notched collar of his suit coat. Despite the somberness of the total effect, there is an occasional touch of ornamentation here. Just visible in the upper left-hand pocket of the man's coat is a tuck of gleaming white handkerchief, like a footnote to his starched white shirt. Draped across the front of his waistcoat, furthermore, is a plaited gold key chain, which gravity shapes into a sharp V by the weight of a gold key or charm which hangs from it. Indeed, there seem an astonishing number of these arrowed shapes about the figure. The crown of his hat is creased inward near the crown to form an upside-down V. The starched halves of his collar add another pair, followed by a single large V that forms the top of his waistcoat, and that is flanked in turn by the notches in the lapels of his jacket. The waistcoat itself ends in two V-shaped points. Thus, the watch chain is a kind of signature, a golden, hieroglyphic summary of the total figure. It is, of course, tempting to see this casual convergence of V's as some intricate symbol system. Is the father's name Vincent? Is he a victor or only a victim? Perhaps, as the conservative cut of his clothing suggests, he is a successful politician who has recently stood for the office of Sheriff of Shelby County and won with a two-to-one margin. Or perhaps he is one of the smooth-tongued but policy-rough negotiators who talked hill farmers into making way for the brimming waters of the Tennessee Valley Authority dam. He may also be a former motorcycle policeman who now directs shipments in and out of the Army depot in West Memphis, Arkansas. Such a position would hardly seem victorious unless we think of it as a patriotic part of the total war effort, and the most he could do (other than a V-for-Victory garden patch), when even after trimming two presumably critical years from his age, he was denied admission into the Navy in 1941. Of course, these V's are mere sartorial coincidence, and yet they seem so firmly notched into the surface of the photograph as to be momentarily quite arresting. If they were a visual shorthand for his name (Victor, Vernon, Vance, or Vincent), we might think his identity to have forced some chemical mutation in the surface of the photograph. But his name, in fact, is Jimmy—or so, at least, he is known at this point by his wife, his closest friends, and his immediate superiors at the Army depot; and the name of the son who stands beside him is David.

Jimmy's left arm hangs at his side, holding a lighted cigarette. The right arm, placed between his son's shoulders, is of course not visible in the portrait. There seems a clumsiness in the angle of the right arm, as though the hand rests neither easily nor with any accustomed sense of con-

tact on the boy's back. Indeed, the angle of the arm might
almost suggest that he is about to push the boy forward;
whether with the idea of advancing or introducing him, or
of flinging him to the ground is not clear. What is clear,
in the stance of the father and the face of the son, is that
such contact is awkward to them both. The awkwardness
is hardly surprising, for David was scarcely a month old
when the father was sent to prison for embezzlement, and
the child was raised by the two women—by his mother,
who sold sheet music at Woolworth's, and her friend
Juanita, who worked nights in the steaminess of a shirt
laundry. The father is thus a stranger to the child, who
knows better the face of the milkman and the roughly
loving touch of his Uncle Frank than he does the face and
hands of his own father. Their few days together have not
mended the gap of five years. Indeed, it will widen with
the passage of time, and only once will it promise to close.
As this single moment concerns the father's hands, and
hands are, altogether, the hallmark of this particular picture, it may be well to consider that moment in detail.
Unfortunately, no photograph exists of this rare meeting of
the father and his adult son, let alone of the few fragile
seconds in which the gap nearly closed. If such a photograph did exist, it would show the father stretched forward
with the upper half of his body hovering above the cool
baize of a pool table. His left hand rests on the table, and
the right gently nudges and aligns the pool cue between
his left fingers. There is a rare intensity of concentration on
his face, and a surprising grace about his entire figure.
Despite his grey-fringed bald head, his plastically white
teeth, the unmuscled sag of his stomach, the old man seems
lithe and supple, poised with total, sensuous presence over
the table. He aligns the shot carefully, as his son watches
him. It is the very shot that formerly won him beers,
quarters, and barroom blondes in Kansas City, St. Louis,

and Little Rock. In this highly photographable moment, a lifetime's coarseness seems cleansed from him, and he is bathed in the transforming splendor of a seventy-five-watt Sylvania lightbulb that dangles from a spartan, much-taped lamp cord above the table. Carefully the right hand draws the pool cue back, tests it with tentative half-strokes, and taps with quick force against the ball. It drives forward, then loops to the left as though drawn by an invisible string, nudging one ball, rebounding off another, scattering the group of three clustered in the center of the table. The balls spin in a dizzying ballet of color, and come to rest. None of them have dropped into the webbed mouths that await them. "Shit!" says the old man, and snaps the pool cue neatly in half across his bent knee. This unphotographed event occurred in the summer of 1972. Whether David would have visited his father again before his diabetic death if the shot had been successful is, of course, entirely a matter of speculation.

Until this moment, the son had thought of his father's hands as peculiarly lifeless despite their strength, like plaster art school models frozen in perpetual grip round plaster rods. And he remembered to the most minute detail the blunt fingernails, irreproachably clean and never varying in length. Now, of course, the son realizes they must have been fetishistically cared for, though he had always thought his father free of all physical vanities. He remembered only his mother's repugnance at after-dinner finger-trimmings and the quick, silverfish parings that collected on the dining-room table. He failed, however, to see the shared ritual that was proffered here. From his trouser pocket, the father draws a tiny, pearl-handled penknife. Where the two brass brads clamp the slices of mother-of-pearl together, the surface has discolored with faint brown stains. This very knife had been left behind by the father's father when he used his Rock Island Railroad pass for the last

time, to depart for a destination unknown. Whether the
father carries it with him at all times as some kind of talisman or merely as a handy device for cutting string, opening
letters, and paring his nails is not known. He had first carried it as the sole constant in an ever-changing collection
of bottlecaps, screws, cigar bands, cigarette papers and
Indian head pennies. Later, it was attached to the end of a
braided gold watch chain, together with a sturdy gold-
plated railroader's watch bought in a Kansas City pawn
shop. Barely an hour before the present photograph was
made, it was in the right-hand pocket of a pair of grey-and-
white-striped seersucker trousers, together with a dollar's
worth of small change and an automobile ignition key. The
father pushes his emptied plate a few inches away from the
table edge, draws the knife out of his pocket, and begins to
trim delicate shards from his nails. "Oh, Jimmy!" says his
wife—half in reproach, half in still fond, mocking intimacy.
She casts apologetic eyes at Juanita, who nods silent concur-
rence to the brutishness of men, and reaffirms the pact that
will preserve the child from such waywardness. (Indeed,
so successful were these protectoresses that the child in
later years would no more perform table-side manicures
than he would pick his nose, belch meatily, or fart com-
fortably at a black-tie dinner in his honor.) The child
scarcely sees the hands, but sees instead the translucent C's
and S's and U's that spill onto the damask tablecloth and
the gravy-filmed edge of his father's plate. Freely and without thought of recompense, the father shares with them these
shards of his own body. The women should gather them
carefully, lifting each with non-bruising gentleness, and
together with the strands of fallen hair they have plucked
from his pillow, burn them with drops of musk oil on the
red tiles of the hearth. Then each should take one of his
hands to her bosom, caress it, wash it with her tears, and
pat it carefully dry with the loosened tresses of her hair.

Instead, they rise as though on secret signal, and begin with brisk, noisy efficiency to clear the table.

In the photograph, it is impossible to see that the nails are so carefully pared, though there is something in the very angle of the hand that suggests vanity. The left arm is brought slightly forward, so that almost the entire hand is visible, and a cigarette is balanced with graceful nonchalance between the first two fingers. This detail, together with the heavy gold watch chain and the only slightly visible wisp of white handkerchief in the father's pocket, brings considerable relief to the somber conformity of the total figure, in its conservative business suit and heavy fedora hat. The slender but strong length of hand is echoed in miniature in the boy's hands as the sole point of resemblance between these two males. There is thus the abundant logic of poetry in the fact that a quarter of a century later the son will be so moved by the sight of his father's hands manipulating with erotic refinement the wand-like, tapering length of a pool cue. In that instant, an earlier image of the hands locked in a death grip is forever cancelled. The balls pirouette in rainbow circles, part, rebound, spin with dizzy brilliance, and come to rest again in the even meadow of green baize. If even one had been sucked noiselessly into the waiting nets, David might well have visited his father again.

The background of the photograph suggests nothing but a comfortable middle-American prosperity. Directly behind the two figures is a brick-bordered flower bed, the bricks angled into the earth and snugged against each other to form a saw-toothed edge, and they, like the stone bench partially visible to the right of the picture, are freshly, brightly whitewashed. The bed is planted with rosebushes, none of which at this time are in bloom. Jimmy and his son would thus seem to be standing on the lawn of a front or back garden which adjoins others much like itself. We can see portions of two houses quite distinctly, with thick, house-hugging, multi-angled 1920s roofs, and the chimney of a third house, at some distance away, appears beside the father's arm. Trees and shrubbery grow thickly and generously here, even before the porch of the nearest house, and so we rightly conclude that the houses have not been newly built. Most of them were completed in 1921, and now, twenty-one years later, have clearly entered the period of their majority. The rawness of youth, the brashness of concrete foundations, are well concealed by layers of thick oil paint, by the lush silhouettes of azalea bushes, evergreens, wisteria, and morning glories. Not visible in the photographs are the metal gliders on most of the neighborhood porches, each with brightly-striped canvas cushions. Their rhythmic grating can be heard most summer evenings (though never later than 10 P.M.), together with a steady chorus of cricket song and the occasional crunch of tires on graveled driveways. There is such a glider, together with a pair of dark green wicker chairs, on the porch of the house before which the boy and his father stand. The fat, brow-like overhang of the roof shades the porch on even the brightest summer days. On hot summer nights, the family often sits here, with a pitcher of iced tea, to listen to "Amos and Andy," "Fibber McGee and Molly," and "Your Hit Parade." During the week, the father is often away at night as well as by day, for the quantity of shipments from the Army depot has increased beyond all expectations, and it is often necessary to work round the clock, plotting the movements of trucks and goods across the mosaic face of outsized graph paper. On such summer evenings, the boy sits alone with his mother, unless her friend Juanita is there. He claws with secret pleasure at the welts of mosquito bites and trembles as the Green Hornet zooms off to another scene of villainy. Both summer and winter evenings somehow entwine themselves with the idea that there is war. The six o'clock news is studded with foreign-sounding names, of cities and towns ever further away than Chicago and Knoxville and New Orleans, and which one bafflingly can't reach by train. David's older half brother is on a faraway island, killing small yellow Japs that swarm out of the jungle like ants at a picnic, and Uncle Frank is praying with homesick soldiers at an army camp in Georgia. Somehow, the father's absences are connected with these activities, as is the fact that the boy saves nickels and dimes for the stamp lady who comes to the kindergarten each week. Pasted into the War Bonds book, these make the flimsy pages wonderfully thick. There are other pleasures, too, which mysteriously contribute to defeating the enemy. One of them is to break open the circle of saffron-colored powder and stir it into the creamy white of the margarine. It makes great circles of color, loops of orange and sunshine yellow that stand out in neon relief against the white background and then slowly fade into a uniform, pale-yellow glow. At night, after dinner, he carefully cuts the bottoms from the day's tin cans, tucks top and bottom inside the tin cylinder, and holding to the kitchen table for balance, rides them into oblong flatness beneath his feet. He also delicately peels away the tinfoil from cigarette wrappers, and packs it hard against the large, dull silver ball he has collected. Threading all these activities together is a cabalistically secret significance, which he does not understand, but which therefore seems only the more wonderful.

Two women stand within the dusky shade of the porch, looking out toward the front yard. Though one is fair and the other not only dark but considerably taller, something about them suggests that they are sisters. This has, perhaps, something to do with the summery freshness of their dresses, with the general air of thrifty but intensely cultivated fashionableness. The smart, mannish stiffness of padded shoulders is annulled by pleated softness, an edge of ruffling, the flower-petal drape of the skirts. Leaning together, each with her arms about the other's waist, they talk in the pale, liquid voices that certain Southern women use when exchanging secret female wisdom. From the yard, the voices are an indistinct duet; the intertwining syllables belong to the secret rites of an ancient vestal community. They can speak of hemlines, of the best techniques for preserving peaches, or the tedium of P.T.A. meetings, while with sibilant stresses and communing pauses they are in fact reviewing the dark tides of woman's blood, the vulgarity of men, and the sanctity of children. They pause only briefly on the shadowed porch before the darker woman descends the steps to join the man and boy, and yet in these short moments they reaffirm, even in the trivial talk of promised telephone calls and possible shopping expeditions, the emotional sorority that has bound them together for nearly a decade. Juanita comes less often now. Since her promotion to hostess at the Peabody Hotel grill room, she has both lunch and dinner duty, and her day in fact begins at 9:30, when she assays the orderliness of tumblers, the whiteness of aprons, the hand-ready bounty of forks and knives and spoons, ketchup and Worcestershire sauce. On her single day off, a Thursday, she is busy cleaning her small apartment, shopping, skimming the *Reader's Digest* beneath the feathery whisper of the hair dryer. Of course, the two women occasionally meet for lunch on Thursdays, especially if there is an interesting sale or rumor of genuine silk stockings in some overlooked backstreet shop. And once a month, relieved from her lunch duty at the Peabody, Juanita comes to join the family for an invariable Sunday menu of roast, potatoes and vegetables, cake or pie. But Juanita must return to the hotel no later than three o'clock, and it is now nearly two. Jimmy will drive her the three blocks to the streetcar stop, then return home, pick up his wife and son, and take them to West Memphis, where he will be presented with an imitation-parchment scroll in recognition of his efficiency as chief traffic controller at the Army depot. Hence, the son and his father are so sprucely dressed. The mother is not quite ready to leave, having postponed putting on her best black dress until just before departure, to minimize wrinkles. Juanita has placed her camera on the small wicker table beside the glider, and after giving Kay a light peck on the cheek, she picks it up and walks down the steps to where the father and son await her.

"You look so fine I've just got to take your picture." The voice floats before her across the lawn. The father, about to open the door of the Model A Ford, scowls in a way that does not so much say no as demand to be persuaded. Women always seem to think a camera is a toy. He knows better, understanding that it is a precise, mathematical instrument. While he made the lowest mark in the photography class he was compelled to take as a rookie policeman, he was the one who was asked to photograph everyone else's babies. Most women couldn't even get the focus right.

"Now come on, Jimmy, we want a record of your big day."

She pronounces the word "your" with two distinct syllables and the hint of others patiently lurking in the wings. With the melody of her voice, she lures him into grudging consent; such tactics have assumed, with her, the high refinements of an art. Thus, father and son stand together before the brick-edged flower bed, but with more than three feet separating them, like improbable co-participants in a police line-up. Juanita lifts the camera, sights through it, and is unhappy with the results. "I can't get you both in," she protests. (The word "in" has three active syllables, to stress her dependence on their masculine ingenuity.) Jimmy shifts slightly to the right, his head

cocked toward her at an angle that seems to wish to impale
her female incompetence and mount it like a laboratory
specimen. "And now you move, honey," she says to the
boy. "Stand there, by your father." The boy, always eager
to please women, yet anxious to maintain some separation
from his father, moves stiffly to the left, never taking his
eyes from the camera in the woman's hands. "Closer now."
He inches his left leg out, then draws his right one up to
join it, tucking his head down slightly to avoid the glare
of the early afternoon sun, so that his entire face is cast
into shadow by the slight brim of his cap. "Smile, honey,"
his mother calls from the porch. He tries to oblige her, but
the half-smile is frozen on his face when he feels the large
hand placed on his back. "That's better," Juanita says, and
briskly clicks the steel lever that triggers the lens.

The photograph shows a small boy, of perhaps five years
of age, standing beside a man wearing a conservative three-
piece suit. The man would appear to be in his late thirties
or, conceivably, in his early forties. The man is tall, his
body well-formed and, so far as we can see, strong and
healthy. There is a slight thickening about his waist that
betrays the onset of middle age, but it is chiefly by his
face that we can appraise his age. Even though the face is
too darkened by the shadow of the hat brim to make out
particular details with very great assurance, the impression
is of a man to whom a good deal of life has happened,
without his either inviting or entirely comprehending it.
He is capable of immense concentration in mathematics,
golf, automobile-driving, and lovemaking, but the concentration is entirely physical. Even when his mind is
engaged, it functions, simply but effectively, as a binomial
computer. The remainder is under stout lock and key—
the yearning, dreaming, non-mathematical functions of self
which might be bruised or, worse, ignored if exposed to
public view. Yet the strain of such tireless custodianship

shows clearly in the face, in its downward-sagging lines, as it does in the slope of the shoulders.

The child who stands to the man's right may well be his son, though the two bear scarcely a trace of family resemblance—unless it can be read in the graceful curve of a hand. The son, for example, is fair, whereas the father is dark, and he stands with his feet close together (almost pigeon-toed), while the father's are spaced wide apart and point outward. In noting this, we also note that the shoes of both, though brightly polished, appear badly worn, a fact rather easier to comprehend in the case of a roller-skating, tree-climbing boy of five or six than in a man who is otherwise so carefully attired for an award ceremony. This rather decrepit condition of the shoes could be a signal of the family's real poverty, otherwise disguised by bargain-basement, ready-to-wear finery. But the father's gold watch chain, the trimly bordered bed of roses, the general well-nourished air of the two would scarcely suggest poverty. Thus, we can account for the condition of the shoes only if we remember that they are scarce in war-time, that the father in any case wears a size twelve AA which is difficult to find and outrageously expensive. There is no poverty implied here, but there is a cultivated, self-conscious thrift which edges toward meanness. For the next ten years of his life, the child will wear Boy Scout shoes, recommended for their toughness and practicality, and will grow to despise them as a symbol of drably unimaginative common sense. There will be frequent quarrels between the father and son over just such shoes. The father's bafflement at his son's lack of gratitude for these $5.95, then $7.95, and $10.95, and $12.95 shoes will easily convert to rage when the shoes are not regularly polished and buffed. But that, of course, is still in the future. For now, he cherishes this heir, so unlike the first son, born twenty years before and now fighting somewhere in the

Pacific. Perhaps the first one (also named James Henry,
like his father, and eventually to have a son of his own with
the same name) was too much like his father, too aptly
named. That first son had flouted all convention, left home
at sixteen to hop boxcars and shuttle back and forth across
the country, and was quick to join a fist fight, if slow to
provoke one. Yet father and son had both become in time
the enamored servants of respectability, as though they
sought in its somber robes to conceal all their lust and
courage and imagination. Each James would have professed
to love the other but, if pressed, would confess to seeing
his life as uninteresting; yet each was a mirror of the other,
as though they were twins born by biological caprice
sixteen years apart.

Although the father could never have said why he felt
this, David was different. He was the son who would
bring laurel to weave a crown for his old age. He would
please. He would excel. He would be well-groomed as
mother wished, but manly; intelligent and educated but
without pretension; handsome without a trace of prettiness;
gallant to his mother and companionable to his father. He
would be, above all, everything that his father and his
older half brother had had no chance to be, and for that
blessing he would offer up the chalice of his gratitude. And
yet, as David becomes everything the father wants him to
be, the child seems to draw away from him into the secret
confederacy of women. Thus, the father is jealous of
Juanita, not merely because he senses her secret ties to his
wife, but also because her own floridly sensual female
presence seems more prompted by the child than by himself. And so he finds her perfume cheap and heavy, sees the
lace handkerchief twisted and pinned into orchid folds at
the waist of her dress as a worthless ornament. He com-
plains of her promiscuity and wonders aloud to his tearful
wife if she is the best influence for the child.

184   He places his hand in the center of the boy's back. It is in large part a gesture of pride, to form the link of flesh to this miraculous child, this precocious devourer of books, charmer of ladies, this delicately beautiful son. Yet the gesture also lays claim to the child in a manner that would draw him back into a man's world, that would perhaps be more secretly joyed if the son became a neighborhood bully, an eye-gouging footballer, a comradely roughhousing guzzler of beer, a wencher without conscience. Still, there is something conflictingly suspended and tentative in the gesture with which the man places his hand on his son's back. Perhaps, after all, the sense we have that he is about to push him forward is the conscious decision to relinquish him, to surrender him to the camp of the enemy women in which he will be simultaneously shaped to the father's dream and lost to him forever. The boy winces as the hand touches him, lays its hard width against him, its span covering his shoulders. The hand might crush him in a single gesture. And so he flinches, but contains his fear, hooking his thumbs into the pockets of his jacket to still the trembling that begins in his own hands. His eyes seem to see only the camera that his mother's friend holds before her. His mother calls from the shaded porch, "Smile, honey." And though she calls his father honey too, sometimes, he knows that her words are for him. He would oblige her, but the weight of his father's hand clips his mouth into a frozen half-smile. He is, furthermore, always somewhat awkward before the camera, though never unwilling to pose. Still, any occasion for being photographed seems to demand a seriousness of expression, and so he always rearranges his face into an image he imagines to be appropriate, and hence rarely looks like himself in photographs. As he grows older, the tendency becomes more pronounced, whereas in the pictures taken of him as a baby there is, of course, no such conscious posing. A number of these very photographs once graced local photographers' windows, and more than one has appeared on the cover of a national magazine. He is only five years old at the time his mother's friend Juanita takes this particular photograph, but the sense of special occasion awkwardness is already there on his face, though the slight squint of his eyes is, of course, a consequence of the bright summer sun. The photograph in which he and his father appear was made in August of 1942, three months after the boy's fifth birthday, and two months after his father's thirty-seventh. It is black and white, measures three-by-five inches, and is, from any objective standpoint, a perfectly ordinary, aesthetically undistinguished example of the "snapshot."

SIX

This book is an exercise in historical actuality, but it has only as much to do with history as the heat and spectrum of the light that makes it visible, or the retina and optical nerve of your eye. It is as much an exercise in history as it is an experiment of alchemy. Its primary intention is to make you experience the pages now before you as a flexible mirror that if turned one way can reflect the odor of the air that surrounded me as I wrote this; if turned another, can project your anticipations of next Monday; if turned again, can transmit the sound of breathing in the deep winter air of a room of eighty years ago, and if turned once again, this time backward on itself, can fuse all three images, and so can focus who I was, what you might yet be, and what may have happened, all upon a single point of your imagination, and transform them like light focused by a lens on paper, from a lower form of energy to a higher.

Michael Lesy, *Wisconsin Death Trip*

THE CAMERA

SIZE: $1\%_{32}$ x $1\frac{1}{16}$ x $3\frac{1}{8}$ *inches.*
LENS: *"Minostigmat."*
FOCAL LENGTH: *15mm. Fixed stop (f/3.5).*
SHUTTER: *Guillotine, in front of lens; T, B and instantaneous, variable speeds ($\frac{1}{2}$ to $\frac{1}{1000}$ sec.); shutter cocking coupled to film advance with opening and closing camera, release button on right side of camera.*
FINDER: *Eye level, optical.*
BODY: *Stainless steel; two-part; cover opens for use; exposure indicator and other controls on right side; built-in filter.*
LIST PRICE: *$79.00.*

This rigid-body, semi-miniature Minox camera was manufactured by Valsts Electro-Techniska Fabrika in Riga, Latvia. It has a capacity of 50 exposures, 8 x 11mm., on 9.5mm. unperforated film in specially loaded double cassettes (British Patent No. 495,149, December 22, 1936).

The Minox is the epitome of the sub-miniature "spy camera." Combining effectively small size, precision construction, and sophisticated controls, it has probably figured prominently in many cases of military and industrial espionage, and has had a starring role in numerous spy movies. In addition, it was and is exceedingly popular with the reasonably affluent traveller, who prefers not to be encumbered with the customary bulk of a camera, and who will settle, in general, for wallet-size prints.

The Minox was first commercially produced in 1937

by VEF (Valsts Electro-Techniska Fabrika) in Riga, Latvia. It was a marvel of precision, and word of its existence spread rapidly. The camera used a fixed-aperture f/3.5 lens, which had a focusing adjustment from eight inches to infinity. The very short focal length of only 15mm. yielded adequate depth of field even at full aperture, and a depth-of-field scale was provided. Exposure was controlled by varying the shutter speed, which ranged from ½ to 1/1000 second, in addition to Time and Bulb settings. A yellow filter, having an exposure factor of 2X, was built into the camera and could be slid into place. By closing and opening the camera, one automatically cocked the shutter, advanced the film, and advanced the exposure counter.

The first such camera was originally called the Minox, and its subsequent designation, Minox I, was applied only retroactively, following the introduction of additional models. Approximately 20,000 of the original model were manufactured until production was discontinued in the early 1940s because of World War II. Following the war, the camera was produced by Minox GmbH., Giessen, West Germany. The model introduced after the Second World War (around 1949) was designated the Minox II and differed in certain respects from its predecessor. Its body was of much lighter aluminium. A four-element lens was incorporated to replace the original triplet. The shutter and view finder were improved, and built-in orange and green filters were provided. Subsequent models of the Minox have kept pace with current trends in camera technology, and such features as parallax correction, flash synchronization, electronic flash, and built-in exposure control have appeared on successive models.

Although the Minox was introduced in 1937, word of it apparently did not reach the United States until 1938. Surprisingly, the camera was to be exhibited for the first time in the United States at the Chicago conventions of the N.P.D.A. and the P.A.A., two years after its production was announced. It was first imported in July of 1940 by Photo Utilities, New York, and around fifty cameras from the initial shipment were pilfered from the shipping cases on the docks.

THE PHOTOGRAPHER

David Bonner Dyer, Caucasian male,
born May 5, 1937, in Memphis, Tennessee,
to Dorothy Kathlyn (née Jarvis) and James Henry Dyer.

Despite the fact that he possesses only the most tenuous, lyrically abstract apprehension of the chemical-mechanical secrets of photography, David sets greater store than most photographers on the value of the photograph itself. He sees in it an act of commemoration, celebration, narration, authentication, and a ritual exorcism of the demons of mortality. Hence, he will frequently be seized by near-erotic spasms of picture-taking, in which passion tends to dim the eye. The results might typically include a dozen shots of decapitated sunbathers, fragments of famous paintings, blurred landscapes, or a fatly thumb-covered lens. But his indiscriminate passion sometimes results in a well-focussed, harmonic, collectable study like the one before us now. This picture of four middle-aged picnickers—two men and two women—is crammed with broken narrations, irretrievable flashbacks, and blurred histories, but such complications are scarcely visible in its well-composed, well-focussed surface.

David is the first of two sons of an ideally mismatched couple. Any misalliance possessed of such sweep and scope must inevitably absolve either partner of feelings of responsibility for his or her own shortcomings. Furthermore, it can serve as a wonderfully handy capsule explanation for disasters private and public, for bodily grievances, Republi-

can presidential victories, cosmic irregularities, seismic caprices, and terrorist uprisings in distant banana republics.
Like lotus-eating, a bad marriage can have its own splendidly heady, narcotic moments. But at the time their first
son is born, the parents imagine that if some single overlooked ingredient is supplied, the alchemy of a happy
marriage will swiftly transform them and their world.
Without speaking of it, they both ardently believe that a
child will accomplish this transformation, and though the
mother secretly desires a daughter, druidic urgings whisper
that a son will ultimately tame her coarse husband and draw
him to her. So she gladly presents him with a sturdy male
heir, and when alchemy withers she whispers new incanta-
tions as she hems flowered curtains for the breakfast nook,
enamels the kitchen table in apple-green, cultivates a jungle
of ever-blooming African violets, allows her hair to grow
long, and invites her husband's withered mother to spend
a holiday in the smile-wreathed presence of a new grandson. Meanwhile, the husband lights his own incense. He
carefully sharpens the lawnmower blades with a rasp and
a pumice stone, tunes up the wife's decrepit Ford until it
croons, provides her with a miniature Black Forest cottage
from which Hansel and Gretel emerge to announce good
weather and a wrinkled witch to predict ill winds, conducts
his after-dinner fingernail-carvings with a new, self-
conscious elegance, and ritually changes his socks twice
rather than once a week. Neither knows how fiercely the
other works at completing the incantation begun with the
uttered words "I do." The child ties them without binding.
A second honeymoon gives them their first real debts,
aggravated soon by the child's complicated, prolonged illnesses. Only before the columned, fluted, scrolled, and
chambered massiveness of the new R.C.A. radio do their
thoughts truly mingle, but chiefly in the bodiless presence
of "Amos and Andy." The Second World War helps, of

course, to give them a sense of mutual purpose, as they cultivate a victory garden, count their vitamin intakes (EAT FOR PEACE!), murmur over Japanese atrocity stories, trade gasoline rationing stamps for sugar stamps, and buy black-market meats. When the war threatens to end, it seems for a moment as though they must face their mutual failure. Indeed, amid ominous whisperings of peace in Europe and following a quarrel over whether the dining-room wood-work should be done high or semi-gloss, the husband begins to strangle his wife—not violently and with angry splut-terings, but with the same systematic coolness he would have used in setting up a difficult pool shot. Whether or not he would have completed the maneuver remains a moot point, for his attention is deflected by the screams of the frightened child who observes them. By now both parents are too addicted to their mistakes to live without them; even the ensuing divorce seems to bring them into denser mis-alliance, which they seal with a Christmas remarriage in 1945 and another son in the summer of 1946. This sepa-ration in their ages, as well as the fact that each was, literally, the child of a different marriage, resulted in each of the sons, David and Michael, being raised as an only child.

Despite a series of childhood illnesses that saddled his parents with debt until he was twelve years old, David survives both the rigors and the joys of being an only Southern son. A generous Jewish godfather, one of the score of older men who, in her youth, had worshipped his mother's dramatically photogenic face, takes charge of his wardrobe, accompanying the child twice a year to Chi-cago to be exactingly measured by his own tailor and outfitted in hunting tweeds, Chesterfield overcoats, and ele-gantly outmoded grey flannel knickerbockers. Of all those semi-annual sartorial crusades that ended abruptly with the bankruptcy of the godfather's handbag factory, only one remains etched in David's memory. Dressed in the smartest

camel's hair trousers and a matching double-breasted over- **195**
coat and cap, the small boy saunters down the marble
steps of the Palmer House with a richly theatrical sense of
the expensive figure he cuts, only to lose his footing on the
time-rounded edge of a step and come to rest in a pool of
vomit freshly spewed by a drunken resident.

Otherwise, and excluding the brief, confused witnessing
of attempted murder, his childhood is relatively free of
trauma. Summers are spent on the cotton plantation of a
wealthy uncle, a Margaret Mitchell world of black mam-
mies and the dense perfume of the sorghum mill and black
pots of wash boiling over open fires and vast cotton fields
arrested only by the ruler-edge of the horizon. There, of
course, he enjoys the wit and wisdom of the court jester,
the old black uncle who like a cliché come true teaches
him to fish, builds him a miniature cabin in the woods, and
leads him tirelessly round the plantation on a swaybacked
plow horse. If there is a note of trauma in the summer idylls,
it is when—in thanks for the gift of some now-forgotten
but clearly extraordinary treasure or skill—the boy throws
his arms round his ancient friend and gives him a grateful
kiss. As he does so, he notices for the first time his peculiar
smell, not thinking it undesirable, but only remarkably different from the smell of his own father, who gives him
neither treasure nor skill, and later the smell becomes mixed
with his mother's stern, tight-lipped rebuke: one doesn't
kiss darkies. "Why not?" he wonders, but never aloud, and
some cord within him seems to draw taut, and then snap.
Perhaps the trauma is still there twenty years later, together
with assorted myths of black sexuality, when he sleeps with
scores of black men—singly, in pairs, in trios, in great
rutting, hard-cocked packs.

But the social lapses of his childhood are rare: he has a
talent for pleasing elders, and artfully cultivates the image
they wish to find. He thinks nothing of having taught him-

self to read at the age of four, until he discovers with genuine surprise that the adults around him set considerable store by such a skill, and so he becomes "bookish," compiling great lists of the slender and then the fatter volumes he more inhales with the eye than reads, and his comic book periods are brief, anemic spells, for there is such a paucity of words in there. Such details mislead, however. It is, of course, not all precocity, Delta plantations, and trim Chesterfields with velvet collars. The Chesterfields vanish with the ill-fated handbag factory, and the lyric plantation life with the death of his uncle, and precocity seems to fade when one's playmates all learn to read (if only in halting syllable-soundings) and set, in any case, more store by the skills of baseball or football. Like most children, he survives more despite his surroundings, parents, and education than because of these things. The neighborhood in which most of his growing up takes place has its obligatory haunted house, together with a certified witch-fortuneteller, a bramble-grown marble swimming pool which is all that remains of a millionaire's great estate, and a pathetic clump of "woods" that will do for Robinhooding and stoning snakes. As though on pubescent cue, a vacant house snares a youthful Italian couple, both of whom work long hours at their small grocery, and hence leave largely to her own devices a slender, delicately beautiful daughter of eleven or twelve who lures the willing boy into the dusky shadows behind a blue plush sofa and lets him stroke the hairs that have begun to sprout between her legs. Never permitting him to remove his trousers (even had he been bold or imaginative enough to make such an effort), she nonetheless inserts an insistently helping hand past the waistband of pants and boxer shorts, and jerks him off with a few skillful strokes. When he comes for the first time, months after this daily play has begun, he fears that he has become pregnant, or perhaps that she is pregnant; it all has something vaguely to do with her being Catholic. For variety of sexual play, there are always sleep-outs with fellow Cub Scouts in leaky tents, or the neighborhood bully, who becomes friendly only when bent bare-assed over a log in the woods and begging to be "corn-hoed." It is perhaps no more and no less erotic than the average childhood.

Saturdays there is the "Nickel Uproar," when for only five cents the boy can spend a time-suspended afternoon in the noisy cavern of the Normal Theater, watching Roy Rogers and Gene Autry and the Lone Ranger and Captain Marvel master every most menacing evil. And there are the hypnotic rhythms of school, of paste-heavy collages produced in vacation Bible school, of riding tin cans into rectangular flatness for the war effort, of collecting newspapers for scrap and delivering others for news, of lengthening lists of books read and passing obsessions with Tarzan and the Hardy Boys (both perhaps too abruptly ended by the premature discovery of *David Copperfield*). And through it all there continues to burn the fattening flame of desire to please, together with a fascination with the mother's storied past of sailboats and disappearing millionaires and tennis parties and Hattie Carnegie hats. The father's life, filled with wonderfully disreputable adventures, sexual peccadilloes that long predate the birth of his first legitimate son when he was sixteen, and assorted roughhouse careers, is all taboo—forbidden more rigidly by the father, who of course wants something better for his son, than by the elegant and beautiful mother who increasingly becomes the boy's model.

David receives his first camera on his tenth birthday—a crude, brittle plastic box with chunky, Coke bottlethick lens that produces blurred photographs two by two inches. He photographs all his playmates mounted on bicycles and scooters, but at an artfully panoramic distance of twenty to thirty feet. In the few photographs from this period that survive, the actual subjects seem merely to have wandered by chance into studies of the anonymous suburban land-scape. This first camera soon becomes fissured with minute cracks, until its plastic surface resembles a road map, and is interred in the back of a closet together with other broken and outgrown but perhaps someday usable toys. At seventeen David receives a Kodak Brownie camera, a good deal more sturdy than his first, and with it he photographs scenes from his award-wreathed high school graduation, the family's annual reunions, his freshman year at Harvard, and a hitchhiking summer in Idaho, Nevada, and California. Its shell fatally warped by a desert sun, this camera, too, is in time abandoned. The scenes it documents are no doubt valuable in establishing certain physical movements on the part of its owner, and many of them reveal his continuing desire to please. Certain photographs not taken might, how-ever, tell us rather more. There is, for example, no photo-graph of the aging but expert mistress of the Harvard years. Her mannishly handsome features are already being blurred by fat, but it cannot disguise the cat-like, sexual sleekness of her movements. In one of the photographs not taken, she sits at the piano, her shoulders held squarely erect and her beautifully tapered fingers tautly spread, as she attacks one of the more challenging passages of Gershwin's first sonata. Such a photograph would no doubt reveal much about the young man's education. So, too, would the stiff and painfully smiling picture taken on the day this woman welcomes David's mother to tea. Unfortunately, these do not exist. And there is but a single, badly focussed one of the graceful Cajun boy with whom David enjoys his first totally uninhibited sexual experiences. This one shows the boy in an Army uniform. It strikes us at first as a clumsy pose, until we realize that only the clothes are clumsy, stiff, inelegant, made to seem the more awkward and ill-fitting by the languid sensuality of their wearer. Though techni-

cally imperfect, this particular photograph is highly in-
structive.

And there are other photographs that might help us achieve insight into the photographer. Since, however, this is not his story, but merely an account of the major events that led up to his photographing four middle-aged picnickers, it will suffice to take a quick glance at some of the other photographs that document his arrival at this historic moment. Taken more or less at random from a small, brass-bound blue trunk, but arranged in roughly chronological order, they include a wedding portrait from the *New York Times* of David and a willowy, half-pretty Southern belle, taken outside the small Christopher Wren church where they are married; David in cap and gown, looking prematurely middle-aged and somewhat bewildered as he receives his first graduate degree; the coal freighter Mülheim Ruhr about to sail from Norfolk to Emden, Germany; the horse stall at the back of a walled garden in Brighton; David's small son, his head wreathed in blond curls that glisten in the sunlight, sitting on the rim of a fountain in Cadiz; David and his wife on a beach near Aosta, his thinning hair combed forward over a forehead that like his face seems absurdly young for his body, and his wife squinting painfully into the sun, her face and body already eroded by alcoholism; and, finally, the photograph of a darkly, almost sinisterly handsome Englishman, dressed in tight trousers and a cashmere sweater, stretched out invitingly on a tufted velvet sofa.

It would be interesting to study each of these photographs in more detail, for both singly and as a group they have such obvious narrative potential. But our focus is on a black-and-white photograph of two men and two women, taken no doubt in midsummer, in what appears to be a public park. The camera with which David makes this photograph is not his own but his mother's—the old Minox

I sub-miniature his father bought for her in New York two decades before. David in fact has a later model of the same camera, given him the preceding Christmas by his mother, but it is in one of the two suitcases that he has not unpacked. Only a few hours before he makes this photograph, he stands before a urinal at O'Hare Airport in Chicago to take his first American leak in five years. He does so to the brassily echoing tones of a portable radio, turned up full volume by the shoeshine boy-toilet attendant who hovers morosely round each toilet visitor. And as David mingles his water once more with that of his mother country, the ubiquitous American huckster voice cries from the radio, "COME OUT HERE TO FOREST ACRES AND SEE THESE HOUSES, FOLKS. YOU WON'T BELIEVE IT! WE'VE RUN THE BULLDOZERS RIGHT ROUND THE TREES." Holding his limp, dripping cock in his hand, David begins to weep. Later, of course, it is better, though the picknicking crowd with whom he mingles knows all too well the increased property values implicit in running the bulldozers round the trees. But for a time it doesn't matter. His son is there, to amuse them with his faintly Cockney accent, and indeed he plays nearby at the edge of a lake, with a meticulously rigged toy sailboat, a lap-carried souvenir of Germany, while the following photograph is being made.

The quartet of two men and two women pose with such easy assurance that this is clearly not the first time they have been photographed together. Indeed, on this very day they have already stood before a United Nations of cameras—Waldo's Nikkon, Jimmy's Polaroid, Bernetta's Agfamatic and Ginger's Hasselblad (Ginger is the cousin who married the rich neurologist). And yet it is no simple matter to gather them together, though they are willing enough, for each is easily distracted by the cries of a knee-scuffed child, by subtle variations in the preparation of potato salad, by legends of the dead and gossip about the absent. Charles and Thelma Ritter are not present, for she has been in the Methodist Hospital for more than a month, so totally encased in plaster she resembles a bizarre surrealist sculpture. She had got out of the car to open the garage doors when Charles's hand accidentally slipped the shift from neutral to drive, and pinned her legs bonebreakingly against them. A shocking accident, of course, but Charles had never been very mechanical. It was, however, difficult to explain how he could have backed the car away, then once more somehow slurred the gears into drive rather than park, to shatter Thelma's arms, collar bones, and ribs. A few hinted, with sage reserve and lengthy, lashfluttering silences, that the incident was not unconnected with Charles's weekly visits to the waitress in Byhalia. And so each member of the quartet was easily deflected, though ready enough to stand for his portrait, and particularly willing to form part of the chosen group of four.

Though one of the women is critically ill and should never have ventured out in such heat, she is the first to take her place, standing in patient expectation that the others will complete the group, for she would have been too shy to pose alone. A man joins her, supporting her firmly but unobtrusively with an arm draped round her waist. These two figures appear to the left of the photograph. The second woman arrives and takes her place to the invalid woman's left. Nearby, the absent member of the quartet is nearing the end of an elaborate joke he has been telling his nephews, and he wheezes so with laughter that he can scarcely formulate the punchline. The three who stand ready begin to scold him, but their insistence seems only to prolong the arrival of a series of obliquely sexual puns. And when he has rounded off the joke with a gush of laughter, and left the nephews puzzling over what they have obviously missed, he approaches the other three with self-conscious dignity, unhurried and precise in his movements. He takes his place to their left (that is, on the right of the photograph we are studying), and they seem at last to be ready. But then the last man to enter seems to reflect, and with gentle pressure on her arm, suggests he change places with the woman to his right. Thus they compose together: man, woman, man, woman. It takes a further moment for the four to consider this sequence and nod approval. However, arranged in this way, the left arm and shoulder of the woman on the right and the right arm and shoulder of the man on the left extend beyond the range of the camera. David notices this, though he is more typically oblivious to such niceties of framing. He suggests they move closer together, and therefore the smaller woman in the left half of the photograph has taken a step forward so that the two men can shift toward one another. This arrangement lends them, with respect to her frail person, a protective air. The woman on the right shifts her body so that her right shoulder covers the right arm of the man beside her. Thus composed together, they stand for the day's last act of commemoration. It is also the last of an uncountable series of photographs that have been made of them over half a century. If this were the final photograph of some royal family before the merciless tide of revolution struck, or of a theatrical team before its final performance in a theater that was to collapse thunderously during the curtain calls, it would be endowed with no greater dimension of tragic foreboding.

THE PHOTOGRAPH

Group photographs such as this one of course present special problems. There is, first, the matter of deciding whether the persons in the group have some natural and significant relationship to each other, or whether they have clustered before the camera for casual reasons. Two lovers, for example, might seek to have their union extended beyond the swift holiday weeks by standing before the lens together, but at the last minute one or the other calls out to a casual acquaintance nearby, "You come be in it with us!" And so the reality of the moment is anchored by the face of a near-stranger—a woman in a sun-halter and long skirt, or a man in a cocoa-palm hat encrusted with pink seashells. Such casual clusters infinitely multiply the possibilities of story-telling; they also muddy and confuse it by intruding too many broken narratives.

There seems, however, no casual clustering in the picture before us now, for the two men and two women appear particularly comfortable together. There is no forced merrymaking and no shyly overcome reluctance about them—only a genial self-confidence that such a picture should be made, that it is their right. On the far left of the photograph stands a man who would seem to be in his mid-fifties, and beside him a woman who might be ten or fifteen years his junior. To her left stands the second man, clearly the senior member of the group, and on the far right-hand side of the photograph a pretty but rather worn-looking blond woman. In the distance, in the right half of the photograph, stands a large pagoda-like structure, with a Volkswagen parked nearby. The pagoda, the dense cluster of trees visible in the distance, and the open field separating the two men and two women from the pagoda would suggest that this is a kind of park. Perhaps, then, these are picnickers—two middle-aged couples who meet here almost every summer Sunday to eat cold fried chicken and Waldorf salad and discuss the achievements of their at-last-grown children. The men were roommates together at Ole Miss and the two women have known each other since they were children and lived and played on the same block on North Coleman. The men first met on Iwo Jima the day after the landing, and each in turn was best man at his comrade's wedding. As the women came to know each other later, they became fast friends, and friendship grew as they compared information on diaper rashes and exchanged recipes for pies and preserves, while the two men shared only their memories of the war, which bored them even more than their wives, but gave the well-rehearsed comfort of the familiar. And so, each summer Sunday, one or the other would say, "Hey, do you remember when those Japs came up out of that gully while you was takin' a crap?"

Any of this would be possible, but all of it assumes we are correct in seeing the four as couples. It is equally possible that the man and the woman on the far right are married, but that the other two are the wife's brother and sister; or that they are the husband's brother and sister. That they are the wife's brother and sister seems more likely, since there is a faint resemblance between the two women, something in the tilt of their heads, in their wistful half-smiles. One thing is certain: they know each other well. There is nothing casual or hurried about their poses. Each has taken his place carefully and consciously, and there is a sense of their composing together as though they share a conviction of their collective worth. The arrangement of man/woman/man/woman suggests this. They stand in close proximity, united as though in a common front, though none of them appear to touch in any direct way. Each poses independently, but lends the strength of that independence to the collective impression. The woman on the left stands slightly forward, so that the men seem to protect her. This is only right, for she is the youngest of the group and the smallest. She is also dying of leukemia.

There are numerous different photographs of this same cluster of four people, with a pagoda showing in the background. There are Kodak snapshots in rather glaring midsummer color, and there are quite professional slides made with the Minolta that Hugh Boyce bought at the PX when he was a soldier in Germany, and there is one made with Jim's press camera. This one is in black and white, but I can hand-color it where color seems useful. Reading from left to right the four people are Hugh Boyce Jarvis, born August 3, 1910, in New Albany, Mississippi, died November 25, 1969, in Cleveland, Mississippi; Margaret Eileen Jarvis Barrilleaux, born May 2, 1922, in New Albany, Mississippi, died December 1, 1969, in Memphis, Tennessee; David Franklin Jarvis, born February 14, 1908, in New Albany, Mississippi, died July 3, 1975, in Humboldt, Tennessee; and Dorothy Kathlyn Jarvis Dyer, born August 4, 1914, died February 15, 1972. These are the four legitimate children of Charles Bonner Jarvis and his first wife, Alma Cox Jarvis. They were not actually born in New Albany itself, but in a narrow sharecropper cabin beyond the edge of the town where their paternal uncle owned a broom factory. In 1927 they at last moved away from the hard, parched earth that teases with an annual half-crop of cotton. The smell of decay in the mother's bowels follows them into the stuffy train carriage that takes them to Memphis, where she dies and the father finds a new wife and a stepson. The stepson does not appear in this photograph.

But we understand now the faint air of self-importance that links the four people. They have survived, to begin their ultimate apprenticeship as the "elders." Outside the range of the photograph, Aunt Minnie curls in a deck chair, her head bent onto her breast, her white hair a delicate, silken halo that shimmers in the faintest breeze. She knows every name and every birthday of every member of the family for five generations, but does not always remember to ask one of her strong grandsons to carry her to the toilet. Everyone ignores the small pool that forms under her canvas chair. Her dress, made to the same pattern she has used for fifty years, has lace trim on the bodice, and she wears black, high-top P.F. Flyers on her feet. Each year the frightened little ones are thrust under her eyes to receive her grunts of approval. Beforehand, they are told that they must be good, for this is the last time anyone will see old Aunt Minnie, but no one is surprised to see her again the following year. Indeed, some of those once thrust under her stooped face for approval have grandchildren of their own. Aunt Minnie's grandson Luther, now in his fifties, takes her entire four-poster bed down every year and rebuilds it in the back of his pickup truck. Then he covers the top with canvas to keep off sun and rain and drives at thirty miles an hour all the way from Tupelo, just to have her here by noon. But Aunt Minnie won't come to many more of these reunions. Both her sons are now dead of old age. Her nephew, Uncle John, long the patriarch of the tribe, has had two strokes, and everyone agrees that the Lord could take him at any moment. His brothers and sisters, his first wife and his own eldest son are already dead.

So these four who stand posed together with such eager grace have had their honorary futures bestowed on them. There are many who are older, but none who present so solid a front to time, welcoming middle-age with such stoic dignity. They have learned their family catechism well, and can safeguard it for the new generations. There is no discussion of this role, no election—only a quiet, general consent that these will be the new elders of the tribe. They will be tomorrow's old ones, and they are ready to accept their roles—with modesty, pride, and self-effacing dignity.

They have survived together, survived ringworm and pellagra and the death of parents, summer sun and appendectomies and sick children and the Great Depression, two World Wars, Korea, mounting taxation, automobile exhaust fumes, Republican presidents, the N.A.A.C.P., and mortgage payments. They have reverenced the old, treasured the very young, and been largely baffled by everything in between. Thus they have earned this moment of glory, and though no one would dare to voice the idea with Aunt Minnie sucking on her lace bodice nearby, this photograph is the proof of their ordination. But perhaps elevation has come too soon, has angered some unappeased god, for as soon as this image is struck into the paper, the mark of doom is on all four of them. No newborn heir will be held up for their blessing.

Hugh Boyce Jarvis dies first, sitting in his Barca-lounger watching *Bonanza*. Doctors at the University of Tennessee Medical School had been proud of the delicate parings and splicings of enlarged heart muscle that they said gave him another twenty years of life. He had learned to breathe again, fighting the deep, constricting pain that lined the deep incision across his chest where flesh had been severed and bone sawed apart. Yes, with the aid of a pretty little red-haired medical technician from Bells, Tennessee, he had learned to breathe again and then gone home to his family, and was even talking of going back to the lumber mill where he supervised the charcoal fires that cured and aged the great slabs of hardwood. Everyone knew he was out of danger now, and he had always been the strongest one of them all, and when he died they could scarcely believe it. His wife sat beside him, the peas she was shelling dropping with metallic melody into a tin bucket. She asked a question and got no answer, and when she looked over she could somehow tell at once that he wasn't asleep but that he had died, sitting there in the Barca-lounger the kids had given him as an early Christmas present, in front of the new color TV that everyone at the mill had chipped in to have waiting for him when he came home from the hospital in Memphis. He had never missed so much as a day of work before the operation.

The sisters and the surviving brother were there for the funeral of course, and the older brother prayed, and the sisters twined together for support and wept as though tears had become their way of life. Everyone wondered later where Margaret had got the strength to stand through so much of the funeral service, and to stand later by the side of the raw grave. The leukemia cells, still for two years, had already begun the last mad dance through her body, reeling, bowing, gracefully pirouetting, and she was to die herself in less than a week. Did she think with envy, as she watched the glazed walnut box lowered into the earth, that her brother had at least had a life for himself? They were astonishingly without jealousy of each other, these brothers and sisters, but might she not have thought for a single unkind moment that he had had all the luck? Slow, easy to please, he had married a gentle, simple, cow-like woman, who bore him many healthy children, most of them sluggish and simple like herself, but all deeply devoted with a steady, clinging, consuming devotion to their father and mother. And Margaret, always fiercely craving love, had found its shadow first when she was thirteen. Her mother dead, her father married now to another woman, she had allowed the handsome blond sailor to find whatever pleasure he could in her thin, undeveloped body, and then he went away, leaving her with a stomach swelling with child. She saw the baby once, or so she claimed, as it was carried away from her in the delivery room, though she did not even say that much about it until twenty-one years later, when she knew that somewhere her lost son had become a man. A series of infections set in after the de-

livery, and so the doctors had carved out her womb, dou-
bling the emptiness she already knew. She married at fifteen
and divorced at sixteen, ran away with a traveling salesman
the year after, and then settled down to become a fat and
frowsy waitress at a greasy corner cafe in Greenwood,
Mississippi. There she met Hal Boyce, and beneath the
compulsive fat he saw the shy, frightened girl greedy for
love. He loved her and comforted her, and in the heat of
his devotion the fat melted away. At twenty she became
the wife of the richest cotton planter in the Mississippi
Delta—a man thirty years her senior, a bachelor who doted
on her with the combined, pent-up emotions of father,
brother, lover, and friend. They adopted a son, and two
months after he arrived in the farmhouse, to be ceremoni-
ally installed in the room decorated with pastel-colored
jigsaw silhouette drawings of lambs and squirrels, Hal died,
clutching her so hard in the grip of a heart attack that he
broke three of her ribs. It was hours before she could
struggle out of his grasp to go ring the great plantation
bell for help, and he had long been dead by then. After
that there were husbands who wanted only her money, an
adopted son who stayed long enough to hate her for not
being his natural mother, then to claim his inheritance and
sullenly vanish. And she knew in abundance the bitter joys
given her by a growing clan of nephews and nieces. So
she may have envied her brother—may even have envied
the quilted-plastic Barca-lounger of which she could have
bought dozens for herself; may have envied her gentle
brother, the son who finally settled down and got his own
bread delivery route, with free uniforms and two-weeks
paid vacation a year.

The two sisters clung together at the edge of the grave,
and perhaps saw their own faces mirrored back from the
shiny walnut coffin lid. Canvas straps slid the coffin noiselessly into place and then snaked away. Reverend Wood

pronounced the final prayer, Frank concluded with his own soft "Amen" in the name of the family, and dirt was fanned out onto the coffin lid, tarnishing its gleam. In less than a week, Margaret was dead, and only Dorothy and Frank, the two oldest children, were there to represent the patriarchs. Uncle John and Aunt Minnie were too old to travel in winter, and the others who survived were too distantly related, or too deeply shocked by the treachery of this second dying. The four of them had seemed only that summer to hover on the brink of immortality together, to stand united as guardians for the new generations, and so they had posed together for this photograph. How bewildered the survivors must have been now, their ranks reduced by half, and how conscious of their own mortality. Like a tightly budded flower, the tumor already grew in Dorothy's brain, slowly turning its petals outward, and the walls of artery leading into the right side of Frank's heart must have already begun to give way, like the garden hose that tells its age in flaccid bulges and swellings.

But for this one moment, as they stand together in Overton Park, self-conscious but proud of their senior roles, they are the new old ones. And our foreknowledge of what is to come should not distract us from the drama of the photograph itself. There are four persons shown here, all dressed in the kind of casual attire appropriate to a summer outing. From the thickness of foliage on the trees in the background, the time might well be midsummer. It is, in fact, late August, 1969. There is no peculiarity of dress, no particular object visible that would date the photograph to that year, however. It might well have been made at any time between 1955 and 1975. There is nothing distinctive about the two men and two women who pose here—that is, nothing that would reveal their professions, their matrimonial states, their dreams or fears. All seem middle-aged, and the women perhaps appear rather younger than the men, but this could be a trick of cosmetics, hair style, and general manner. They might, at a glance, be graduates of South Side High School, class of 1937, gathered here for a reunion picnic. They might be two couples on a summer outing, with their grandchildren playing just outside the range of the camera. One of these grandchildren, a three-year-old girl named Martha, has eyes of such intense blue that strangers frequently stop on the streets to admire her when she goes for walks with her mother, the kindergarten teacher. Another, a boy, has a harelip, but it has already been much corrected by surgery, and another operation on the soft palette is scheduled for September.

All of these things could be true. The four persons could also be brothers and sisters, standing here with the dignity of age just beginning to brush their handsome features. In height, coloring, and general physical appearance, there are striking differences among the four, and they are perhaps not related at all. On the other hand, they share a common jaw-line—full, strong, generous and sensitively modeled. Their noses are straight and faintly aquiline. If they lived to be old, these noses would seem more prominent, even too large, as the flesh sank away on either side, as the jaws hollowed out and the cheeks sagged. At this moment, though, they are the kinds of noses termed "handsome." Their Chickasaw Indian grandmother has thus left her mark on their faces. We would see that ancestry in their feet as well—long, straight, strong, and with no tendency to point either outward or inward. They are, all in all, four strong, healthy-looking Caucasian adults, and the family resemblance is quite striking. A closer look shows why this was not at first so apparent. The man on the left, Hugh Boyce Jarvis, had broken his nose as a youth, and it was improperly set, or perhaps not set at all. At any rate, it is crooked, and so we lose at first glance that proud, straight Indian line. The woman beside him has the family nose,

212   but it curls slightly downward at the tip, so that the line is unexpectedly softened. All four, however, have high cheekbones. As the flesh bares the bone structures of these faces in old age, they will be singularly striking; indeed, they will be precisely the faces of patriarchs and matriarchs, serenely beautiful, even when the symmetry is disturbed by a broken nose. Infants will be presented for their blessings, glossy new installment-plan automobiles for their approval, and they will be consulted on baking techniques, insurance policies, marriages and divorces, careers, hemlines, and the relative merits of floor waxes. Unlike Bedu sheiks, they will not physically dispense justice, and they will demand no tribute in dates or camels, but they will nonetheless be supreme arbiters and authorities, and reverence will be rendered unto them as their due.

For such duties and privileges, they stand posed in this photograph, offering their handsome faces as beacons of comfort and wisdom to the new generations. They compose well together—a healthy phalanx that represents nearly two centuries of accumulated experience (if not, consistently, of wisdom), buffer against the terrors of an unknown future. Their deaths betray that future, loot the unborn of their patrimony, beggar the art of tomorrow's Sunday photographer. The man on the left is the first to die. He is shown here wearing a striped cotton shirt (no doubt with some mixture of synthetic fiber) of the sort available at J.C. Penney's for $2.98. His dark trousers, like those of his brother, almost certainly have a matching jacket hanging in some darkened closet, for these are not men to buy trousers idly. They would of course not wear the trousers of a new suit to such an outing in the park, but the trousers of the second-best suit plus an open-necked, short-sleeved sport shirt makes a nice compromise. Both brothers wear glasses of two-toned plastic, and a squinting look about the eyes suggests the women may have left theirs aside only out of vanity. The brother on the left has a slightly sunken look about the mouth, as though he wears false teeth of less than perfect fit, but his mouth and jaws are still strong and assertive. His hair is cropped short, but even so seems to defy the comb. It lends an unkempt line to his face, as does his lopsided nose, broken when a mule kicked him in the face as a boy of thirteen. The man's hands are behind his back, but if we could see them we would see ropes of muscle and tendon, knottings of veins, layers of calluses, blunt-cut fingernails, scarred knuckles that make the hands resemble reconnaissance maps of rocky, uncultivated terrain. Carved into these hands are the histories of splintering plow handles and hoes, saws and hammers, broken lawnmowers, slipped bicycle chains, cords of firewood, axes, broken beer bottles, women's breasts, dirty diapers, knives, .22 calibre rifles, rabbit traps, barbed wire, and lengths of fine Tennessee and Mississippi hardwood. If the face suggests a certain bewilderment that so much life has happened to it, the hands seem more sure, controlling and correcting and easing life. But they are not visible here. What is most visible is the shirt, ironed with a firm mastery that would become the finest damask, the most regal embroideries. Its muted stripes in red, white, and blue seem to stand at attention, joined by three buttons that announce closing, fastening, holding, and deny all pretense at ornamentation. His wife has chosen the shirt, and it is a perfect fit. He approves her choices in shirts, if not always in neckties, and is proud of the good sense that leads her to shop at Sears or Penney's, where you still get something for your money. They had all read the Sears catalogue when they were children, and they called it their wish book. But he was perhaps more fascinated by the pictures of plowshares and corsets and kerosene lamps than any of the others. He would sit in the toilet for hours, carefully reading each line of print on the page before tearing it out and wiping himself with it. Even on the coldest days, he sat reading both sides before he tore the page out, and he knew that Frank and Margaret and Dorothy didn't always do that, because they sometimes went at night, when there was no light to read by. And now here he was with a Penney's shirt and a Sears belt, and the pants to a Sears suit, and Sears shoes and socks and underwear. A person really could get on in the world. Behind his back, his hands cradled together like sleeping children. When they finished this picture-taking he'd play a little softball with the kids.

The woman standing slightly in front and just to the left of this man seems scarcely more than five feet tall. Her hair has been arranged to give her added height, and her shoulders seem drawn up unnaturally straight, so she may actually appear taller than she is. We can only see the blouse that she wears—a loose cotton affair with a plain, straight neckline, and sleeves ending in ruffles at the elbow. The blouse is white, and printed all over with small red flowers. The perfectly arranged hair, the trim and jaunty blouse don't entirely disguise the fact that she is unwell. There is a puffiness round her eyes, and flesh drapes limply on her neck. Yet we cannot see that the violation that has been her life continues now in her blood. There is something delicately childlike and vulnerable about her, which seems to ask for protection—not to beg or implore it, but to whisper timidly for it. As a child of five, she had dragged a cotton sack behind her through parched harvest fields; and she had ridden her own bay mare through acres of the richest cotton land in the Delta, stretching unbroken to the horizon, and had paused to enjoy the dark, pungent smells of the sorghum mill, or to watch black women boiling clothes in great iron pots. She had begged men to fill her barren body with seed, and she had blushed in genuine dismay when an off-color joke was told in her presence. She sold everything from the plantation house where her husband died but the dark cherry bedroom set he had given her for a wedding present, and she could never sleep in the bed again. She enjoyed buying expensive gifts for her sister, her brothers, her nephews and nieces, but was always afraid that they only pretended to love her, because she gave them expensive gifts. And while her last husband, a sexy Cajun, spent long weekends hunting deer and carhop waitresses, she sat among growing accumulations of pills and ointments and tonics whose names she could not pronounce, following elaborate charts that told her when to smear, swallow, dissolve, and chew them, and watching soap operas on the largest color television set made by Westinghouse. Her hands, not visible in the photograph, hang limply at her sides. They are twisted by arthritis, and scarcely seem strong enough to sustain their freight of diamonds and emeralds.

To the left of this woman stands Frank, who even for a summer outing can't put aside his work as a college registrar and a circuit preacher. He wears a short-sleeved white shirt, open at the neck, but it is the kind of shirt with which he could wear a necktie, the badge of his professional status. In his left-hand shirt pocket is an unmatched pair of ball-point pens, arranged in fail-safe order, each ready to back up its brother to the final flow. A plastic liner is also there, to protect the shirt from indelible leakages and seepages, but there is nonetheless a bright, telltale stain at the bottom of the pocket. Somehow all this seems to guarantee his wisdom and good judgment, for this is the oldest of the four brothers and sisters, the family historian, preacher, college professor, intellectual. There is something rather elegant, perhaps even a borderline decadence, about the long, iron-grey hair combed smoothly back from his face—something definitely not foreign to reason, research, modest little college libraries in small southern towns, a knowledge of minor Civil War skirmishes, and a winning way with choir mistresses. Less obvious, perhaps, is his skill as a cook, displayed with most lavish ceremonial on Thanksgiving, when he rises before dawn to bake bread, biscuits, cakes, and pies, before roasting a turkey and ham and simmering great pots of potatoes, yams, green beans, lima beans, black-eyed peas, crowder peas, and giblet gravy. In memory of the dissertation he almost wrote (he bought the paper, and the children used it to color on), he teaches an occasional class in American history, staking a claim to the family's frail intellectual tradition of preachers and school-teachers. He likes nourishing minds, as he likes nourishing bodies with the overwhelming plenty of his table, and most of all he likes nourishing souls in the series of tiny country churches that he visits in turn each Sunday. He was a student at the Methodist Seminary when the telegram came from Memphis that his mother was dying. He had last seen her stretched on the noisy corn-shuck mattress of the old iron bed in which he had been born, but with the move to Memphis he had imagined her cured, lying on crisp, faintly perfumed sheets in a fine mahogany bed. He found her instead in the public ward of St. Joseph's Hospital, her face a death mask and her breathing scarcely audible. He was proud to think that they shared the same blood type, that he could perhaps give her back some measure of the life that had flowed into his body from hers. An hour later they lay on adjoining tables, and her eyes opened to stare at him across the maze of rubber tubing and bright metal clamps. He reached for her hand, and her eyes seemed to ask the thousand mother questions that her body was too weakened to utter. A clamp opened, his blood flowed to her, and he saw her body convulse in the long, horrible shudder with which she died. It was a time when blood was not cross-matched before transfusions. Her dying from his blood had shaken his faith, though he held out long enough to be ordained before he entered night school to train himself to be a hospital dietician. He married a widow who always pointed to her own healthy son as proof that their failure to have children was his fault, not hers. He seemed to have no gift for life, and without a gift for life he was uncomfortable even with family baptisms and weddings or the occasional Sundays as a guest preacher. But he chose to go to war as a chaplain, not because he was afraid of the battle lines, but because he wanted the chance to pray the wounded back to life. While he was in Japan in 1945, he learned that his wife had divorced him, and he rejected the ministry. But later, remarried to a pretty, lazy Delta belle, he learned that his first wife had deceived him, for he begat a daughter a year for seven years, and finally the son he craved. Knowing, then, that he had the gift of life after all, he could return to the ministry, traveling his little country circuit to preach to the grateful, upturned faces of simple farm people, who had come as much as twenty miles to hear him. He had an inexhaustible stock of corny jokes, family anecdotes, recipes, and good will, and Civil War stories gathered during research for his unwritten dissertation. He, above all, had the makings of the patriarch. I often wonder, though, if he ever forgot the look in his mother's eyes as the metal clamp opened, the rubber tube expanded, and his blood raced to mingle its poison with hers. The imperfections of science once more draw us into the dark caverns of our own mythic past. Had he not more than once wished her dead, as the smell of rotting flesh clogged the lifeless air trapped within the dark barrels of that weathered, decaying shotgun house? Of course, he had wished it for her sake, not for his own, but did he always remember that as he tried to force death's perfume from his own nostrils? He had escaped it by joining the army, and now in penance he brought her the gift of his own blood, that she might be cleansed and healed, that the sweet attar of his own youth might wash away her blight. And so he was joined to her with the candy-pink umbilicals of rubber tubing, the tiny clamps glittering like bright wrappings for Valentine candies. The clamps opened, and his blood rushed to embrace her with the rapture of a returning lover, and embraced only her already rotting corpse. Did he ever forget the blankness that froze in her eyes like the turning of a switch—brown liquid Indian eyes that turned to him over the lianas of tubing and greeted, embraced, thanked him before their final focus on oblivion? Did he ever see them in the faces of young girls who floated honey voices toward him to wonder if the Battle of Shiloh was really *nayussusairy?* Perhaps he glimpsed them in the eroded face of an old farm woman who always raised her cracked but triumphant song from the front row, focusing her eyes so totally on the pulpit that one might have thought the others were there only on her sufferance.

Nothing in the photograph before us reveals the answers to such questions. There should be some clue—something, perhaps, in the three deep furrows that crease the man's forehead as surely and regularly as a sharpened plowshare creases moist spring earth. (There might even be some hint in the brace of ballpoint pens protruding from his pocket, one white with a red tip, one black.) As his own body sags toward death, to be stilled by the gravity of years, it must surely reveal its secrets, as the spirit's signature becomes more firmly inscribed upon the flesh. But the distinguished stripes of black and silver hair form no verse, and the mouth that seems poised between laughter and a cry of pain utters no secrets. A finger points to the photograph: this was your Uncle Frank, cousin Billy, playmate, father, savior, mentor, uncle; but there is only a shadow here, a chemical shadow of a false election. We can stare at it until the brain replays its silhouettes as negative images against the night cave of our closed eyes, and this will not be revealed to us. There is no answer in the filigreed mass of the trees in the background of the photograph, and none in the slightly lopsided pagoda. The pagoda was designed by Henry Green, a young architect who took a honeymoon trip to China and returned with this germ of inspiration. Actually, the shape more closely echoes the wood-and-reed structures of a particular tribe of farmers in northern Tanzania, but Mr. Green, son of the Parks Commissioner, could not have known this. The four would-be elders in this photograph have a cousin, Wallace McBryde, who arrives at the park each year at 6:00 A.M. to "reserve" this pagoda for the rest of his tribe. By common agreement, it will serve nicely in case of rain, though it has never rained in the more than thirty years that these annual reunions have taken place. No one—least of all Wallace McBryde—knows how he was appointed to this task, but it is taken for granted that he will always be there to greet the tribe, sitting in a canvas deck chair in the center of the pavilion, in the early morning chill of its shaded interior, while the ground outside glistens in the bright new yellow sun. Even knowing this much, we cannot penetrate the secrets of the photograph. Everything we seek to know is here, but we fail to unriddle a shadow, to decipher a straying lock of hair, to decode a fold of fabric or a sunscorched patch of grass.

We have, however, neglected the fourth figure, the woman to the extreme right in the photograph. Although all four stand with ease before the camera, she is the only one who stands with a practiced grace as well, as though she is perhaps more accustomed then the others to being photographed. Indeed, as we have already learned, she was often photographed in the past. The face is of the kind usually termed "handsome," but a closer look reveals that beneath the flesh that has begun to shift with age and worry, there is the structure and even some of the freshness of a young woman who could only have been termed beautiful. A light seems to glow about this face that does not irradiate the others, even though the pattern of shadows would suggest they are all facing directly into the sun. This may, of course, result from some imperfection in the lens of the camera or from a greasy finger-smudge on the glass. It may also be the effect of some skillfully practised cosmetic art. We should be wary of confusing Revlon with revelation. Yet even with generous allowance for artifice or error, and for the slight but welcoming tilt of the head learned from a score of expert photographers, there does seem some quality of pleasure or pride in this face, some inner radiance that the others lack. Perhaps she, more than the rest, takes pride in their survival, and hence in this moment of their ordination. At ten years of age, and even before, she had cooked and sewn and cleaned for them all. Her blunt child's fingers took long irregular stitches in coveralls and flour-sack smocks, but the seams held. In a sled-like wooden box, she dragged the noon meal to her brothers and father in the fields—Knox fruit jars of water, stony biscuits made in clumsy but earnest imitation of her mother's quick-fingered skill, a pot of tepid turnip greens. She had nourished and cherished them, her bright love and shy smile their only shield against the slow, relentless curve of the mother's decay. She had nurtured them, and together they had survived. Perhaps some of the glow we see comes from the fact that her eyes are fixed on the two sons she has strengthened and sweetened and smothered with her devotion, or they may be fixed on her first and only grandson, who sits out of camera range, trying to puzzle the intricacies of a toy sailboat's rigging. The eyes, though they take in the photographer, are not fixed exclusively on him. They look out and over his left shoulder, to include a person or persons behind him. A photograph of what she sees there would, of course, add an interesting dimension to the one before us now. It is, however, more than some vague play of light about the face that sets this figure apart; the eyes have a quality of greeting about them, in contrast to the two men, whose eyes are almost invisible behind their glasses, or the other woman, whose lids are so puffed and heavy that her eyes are scarcely visible. These eyes, in contrast, are bright and clear, seeming to welcome life as though it may yet make their owner a visit. They speak of some undefined expectation, as though with strained cheerfulness they still await their reward for the clumsy mendings of frayed fabrics, the miles of corrugated earth across which rattling boxes of food were dragged by a chafing hemp rope, the dutiful weekly submission to a sweating, insistent male body.

Although I can, of course, see these qualities in the eyes, I must continually return to the photograph for confirmation. As I remember them most vividly and not always in nightmares, the right eye was rolled upward to the ceiling, while the left wandered drunkenly, as though seeking the hidden path its lost partner had taken. As accompaniment to this grotesque ballet there was only the obscene, rasping sound of the liquid being sucked up out of her lungs and sloughed off behind a chrome panel in the wall. The music grew louder as she drowned in the fluids that washed her lungs, and shortly before she died—by what magnificent, tortuous upheaval of agonized nerves and violated will, no one can know—the eyes focused for an endless space of seconds to beam a final message of total love or total despair. Its intensity was too great to be read.

But why must this simple, sunny photograph become a chronicle of death? Outside the range of the photograph, tables wait, heaped with the bourgeois bounty of a prosperous and numerous tribe. There are fried chickens and roasted chickens, potato salad with and without onions, jars of homemade sweet pickles and bread-and-butter pickles and dill pickles. There is Waldorf salad, fruit salad, caramel pudding, cold bread pudding, chocolate cake, double chocolate cake, and German chocolate cake. Paper plates are heaped with thick, satiny pink slices of ham, with blood-red tomatoes, strips of carrots and garden-fresh cucumbers. There are oatmeal cookies with raisins, and oatmeal cookies made by Aunt Clemmie's recipe with raisins and nuts, as well as chocolate chip cookies, glittering packages of Oreos, graham crackers, and fig newtons. Aunt Jennie has made angel food cake, Wallace's wife, two pineapple upside-down cakes, and there are even two Sarah Lee pound cakes, smooth and predictable as paving stones. The heaped plates and platters, pie-tins, cake pans and Tupperware bowls stand among the bright flashes of bottles of catsup, mustard, pickle relish and steak sauce. There are brimming pitchers of iced tea and lemonade, and a washtub nearby holds dozens of cans of Budweiser and bottles of Coca-Cola, Orange Crush, Grapette and Dr. Pepper in a glittering Arctic of crushed ice. The tribe has already begun to feed, and they will continue for hours—eating, gorging, nibbling, sampling, tasting, commenting, criticizing, and complimenting. By mutual consent, one mound of potato salad is declared this year's champion. Jean-Marie's fried chicken is judged too salty, but no one voices that conclusion aloud because she is so young, and her new husband still feels awkward here. J.W.'s tomatoes are universally praised, and everyone asks what he uses for fertilizer, as they do each year. Buddy breaks his glasses and Hughie's one-year-old shits noisily and wetly in her pants. Babies cry, and Fat Frances eats an entire Sarah Lee pound cake, but no one minds, since he is only going through a phase. Everything goes in phases, and everything will "straighten itself out" by and by. Feasting on this optimism as well as on the labors of wives, mothers, daugh-

ters, and sweethearts, the tribe renews itself. Chickens, pies,
apples, Baby Ruths, grilled hamburgers, and frankfurters
are consumed, that the cells may replace themselves, that
muscles may grow, that blood may pump, that cocks may
stand hard and high to spurt new life into the tribe. It is
a feast of love, of life, of blind faith; it is a celebration of
the new elders.

But the elders will betray the sacred host of Aunt Clemmie's oatmeal cookies and Aunt Jennie's double chocolate
cake with fluffy-marshmallow frosting. They will betray
it by dying, leaving vacant the gaily striped canvas chairs
in which they should have sat, with silvered hair and bunioned feet and tremulous bowels, to bless the newborn.
Even the pagoda in the background—whimsical souvenir
of a honeymoon in China—becomes a charnel house. We
should lay them out here—the man in the striped J.C.
Penney shirt, the woman with her mock-peasant blouse in
cheery red and white, the distinguished gentleman with
his neat brace of leaking ballpoint pens, the former model
with her bright, life-embracing face. Or in garishly-painted
Indian canoes, laden with potato salad and fried chicken,
and garlanded with fireproof Christmas tinsel, we could
launch them out into the Mississippi, to float with the
stream to whatever half-breed happy hunting ground awaits
them at its tidal mouth. But it is a sunny midsummer day,
and the sound of children whooping the victories and de-
feats of a game of tag punctuates the glittering air. The
slightly tilted roof of the pagoda hovers above them like
a crown. Forsaking its shade, they feast, love, gossip, pry,
and rejoice in the bright southern sun of a lengthening
summer afternoon. Later, they will pack half-empty bowls,
folding chairs, thumb-sucking infants and chocolate-faced
children into Mavericks and Mustangs and pickups and a
lone, incongruous Volkswagen to return to Tupelo, West

224 Memphis, Jackson, Holly Springs, Grenada and Little Rock. But not before they have made images of their new elders and celebrated them in feasting.

Why, then, must this sunny day become a chronicle of death? Why must the photograph become a straw swept up in the tide of dying? For a moment, it preserves the illusion that capillaries are not erupting like tiny slow-motion fireworks displays, that feet are not growing horny callouses, that muscles are not losing their suppleness and strength, that the cellular catechism is not warping toward heresy. But ultimately photographs are morbid objects, and the making of photograph albums is the assembling of books of the dead. Tip all the photographs in carefully with prim little black corners, or invisibly with double-faced tape. Align them with wonderful symmetry and in flawless chronology—perhaps with date and place written in a fine, neat hand beneath each one. There may be an outrageous one of Aunt Kitty in bloomers on a bicycle, and of your Ned with his new speedboat, and of Louise looking coltish and not at all as she looks now in her poodle skirt with its acres of brittlely starched petticoats. Tuck the book carefully away, well-screened by mothballs, and slowly it becomes a litany of death. Hank's first wife died in an automobile accident near Athens, Ohio, and Fred's second boy of bone cancer, and Mildred married three times and spent the lonely last ten years of her life in an old folks' home in Minneapolis. Books of the dead. Litanies of the dead. But for a moment the living was preserved, laid down in a swift chemical flash onto the film, and so it is the life we want to know about, not death. We search these faces, the silvery shadows, the garish Kodachrome surfaces, the yellow-streaked early Polaroids, the elegant studio portraits, the high school class photograph squeezing grandfather into oblivion between a monstrously fat Italian girl and the steak-knife thinness of the old maid Latin teacher. Our eyes

sing them back out of death, giving these flat surfaces life,
flesh, memories, histories, complexes, destinies, purpose.
Dialogue begins, is born fresh out of our own deep, dread
yearning. Somewhere in that dialogue is hidden the clue
to who I am, if I could but understand the language in
which it is written. Your history is here too—written in fat
faces and lean faces, happy and sad; written in rejection
and acceptance, mother love, victory, defeat, lust or honest
passion; and in the cutting edge of a crisp new celluloid
collar. It would be interesting to have a photograph of
everyone who is now alive and who will ever be born, for
then we might read the future, rather than being washed
back into the past. The drugstore, with its dainty vials of
insulin, its contraceptives and ice cream and diapers and, at
its center, the twenty-four-hour developing service, could
become our soothsayer rather than our historian. But from
the history, perhaps, we can at last pull the plum of a
story—the story of a young newspaper boy with his dog,
of a vacationing couple dressed in summery white, of two
girls trembling with near-sexual pleasure as they sit in a
lacquered goat-cart, of four middle-class, middle-aged picnickers in a summery park. But pieces of the story grow
brittle; they shatter as we seek to hold them and sift, in our
hands, to dust.